DESTINY

"I do not like that word 'hostage,' or 'captive,'" High Hawk said. "It is not my habit to take either. And I do not see you as my captive. You are with me for a specific reason. The moon's glow showed me to you. Destiny made it so."

"A specific reason?" Joylynn gasped out. "Destiny? The moon showed me to you? What sort of nonsense is all of that? You heard my horse and came for it, to steal it, and then could not pass up the opportunity to take a woman to your lodge with you to do...to...do whatever you plan to do with me."

"Plan to do with you?" High Hawk said softly. He reached a hand out for her, to touch her face, only to have her slap it away. "In time you will understand why I had to find you and bring you to be among my people."

"I will never understand why you abducted me," Joylynn cried. "It is wrong. All of what you have done tonight is wrong."

Other *Leisure* and *Love Spell* books by Cassie Edwards:
TOUCH THE WILD WIND
ROSES AFTER RAIN
WHEN PASSION CALLS
EDEN'S PROMISE
ISLAND RAPTURE
SECRETS OF MY HEART

The *Savage* Series:
SAVAGE BELOVED
SAVAGE ARROW
SAVAGE VISION
SAVAGE COURAGE
SAVAGE HOPE
SAVAGE TRUST
SAVAGE HERO
SAVAGE DESTINY
SAVAGE LOVE
SAVAGE MOON
SAVAGE HONOR
SAVAGE THUNDER
SAVAGE DEVOTION
SAVAGE GRACE
SAVAGE FIRES
SAVAGE JOY
SAVAGE WONDER
SAVAGE HEAT
SAVAGE DANCE
SAVAGE TEARS
SAVAGE LONGINGS
SAVAGE DREAM
SAVAGE BLISS
SAVAGE WHISPERS
SAVAGE SHADOWS
SAVAGE SPLENDOR
SAVAGE EDEN
SAVAGE SURRENDER
SAVAGE PASSIONS
SAVAGE SECRETS
SAVAGE PRIDE
SAVAGE SPIRIT
SAVAGE EMBERS
SAVAGE ILLUSION
SAVAGE SUNRISE
SAVAGE MISTS
SAVAGE PROMISE
SAVAGE PERSUASION

CASSIE EDWARDS

SAVAGE TEMPEST

LEISURE BOOKS NEW YORK CITY

A LEISURE BOOK®

Published by

Dorchester Publishing Co., Inc.
200 Madison Avenue
New York, NY 10016

ISBN-13: 978-0-7394-7372-6

I lovingly dedicate Savage Tempest
*to a darling friend, Joylynn Pratt, who is no longer
with us, but who will be remembered forever in this book,
whose heroine is named after Joylynn. Before God took her
away, Joylynn was aware of her name being used in*
Savage Tempest, *and that the book would be,
in part, dedicated to her.*

*I also include some other special people in this dedication:
Bob and Kay Ostermiller of Colorado, and also Sandy
Harkcom, who was Joylynn's loving caretaker.*

My soul whispers softly,
A heart cries out loud.
Do you hear it?
Is it not loud enough?
A spirit abandoned,
A soul betrayed.
My soul whispers softly,
Our past but blood in the earth.
The only drums, my heart pounding
in my chest.
The only pride, that which is hidden
deep beneath my breast.
My heritage, I will never lay to rest.

—Mordestia York,
poet, fan, and friend

CHAPTER ONE

Nebraska Territory—August 1861

Westward, the horizon swallowed the sun, belching red skyward, turning everything in its path a lovely violet color. A village of one hundred tepees sat in a horseshoe shape beside a winding river, everything peaceful at this early evening hour. The children ran and played, sending laughter into the air. The elderly men of this Wolf band of Pawnee sat around a huge outdoor fire, smoking their long, feathered pipes. The women were cleaning up after the evening meal, some taking their baskets of wooden dishes to the river, some washing their dinnerware in small wooden basins in the privacy of their lodges.

High Hawk, a young warrior of twenty-six winters and son of the band's chief, Rising Moon, sat with his father. Beside the lodge of his *ahte* were thick, rich pelts where they could rest comfortably. They

1

were talking of serious matters, man to man, while High Hawk's *ina*, his mother, was at the river with the other women.

Although it was August, the evenings had a coolness to them, and a soft wind stirred the entrance flap behind High Hawk.

"High Hawk, again I remind you that you are the last of the bloodline of our family who can be chief, until you yourself have a son," Chief Rising Moon said. He rested the bowl of his pipe on his bare knee, smoke spiraling in tiny wisps from it. "Your brother, Sleeping Wolf, who is three winters older than you, can never be chief. He is crippled and cannot even fire an arrow from a bowstring."

Rising Moon placed the stem of the pipe between his teeth and, sucking on it, brought the rich aroma of the tobacco into his mouth and down his throat, gazing with proud admiration at his younger son.

While Rising Moon wore beaded moccasins and a warm buffalo robe decorated with colorful quills, his son, who could bear the changing temperatures better, wore only a brief breechclout and moccasins.

Rising Moon wore a lone eagle feather secured in a loop of his raven-black hair that hung down at the right side, as did his son.

When Rising Moon too was stripped down to only a breechclout, it was scarcely evident that the older man had once been as muscled as his young son. Now his chest caved in, and the skin was wrinkled across it.

It was not only the muscles of his son's young body that attracted women to High Hawk, but also the sculpted features of his face. He was admired as a noted hunter and warrior, an energetic young man who would one day work as tirelessly for the good of the Wolf band as his chieftain father.

Thus far High Hawk had ignored such attention from women, for he had not yet found a maiden who made his heart pound inside his chest, as Rising Moon's had when he had first laid eyes on his wife of thirty winters, Blanket Woman.

It was Rising Moon's deep desire that this son would find a woman soon, for as old age now claimed Rising Moon, he was afraid he might never see his grandchildren. He longed for a grandson whom he could teach—how to shoot an arrow, how to ride a pony. When a son was born to his second-born, Rising Moon did not plan to be chief any longer. He would pass that responsibility on to High Hawk. The new chief's duties would take him from his son, leaving the boy in the care of his grandfather to learn things only a man could teach him, as it had been when Rising Moon had first had a son.

Rising Moon's *ahte* had tried hard to teach Rising Moon's first-born, Sleeping Wolf, the skills of a young brave, but to his sorrow he learned that Sleeping Wolf would never be able to do anything that normal young braves did. He had been born with his affliction.

High Hawk, on the other hand, had been born with a straight back and was a quick learner. Rising Moon had been determined that his second son would be everything his first son was not.

And, ah, how High Hawk had brought pride into the heart of his chieftain father.

But Rising Moon loved his first-born no less, for it was not Sleeping Wolf's fault that he came from his mother's womb with a twisted back.

Even now, as Sleeping Wolf walked in the moccasins of an adult, he could not ride a horse or even hold a bow straight, much less fire an arrow from its string.

But even so, this son was loved as much as the second-born, and was shown that love in every way that a father and mother could demonstrate it.

"*Ahte*, your mind seems to have drifted from what you were saying about my being the last of our family's bloodline," High Hawk said. He studied his father's expression as it changed quickly from contemplative to serious.

"*Ho*, yes, my mind wandered, as it is prone to do too often of late," Rising Moon said. "That is proof, in itself, why your attentiveness to what I say this evening is important."

"What do you want of me that brings such seriousness into our conversation?" High Hawk asked, searching his father's eyes. Those midnight-black eyes had faded as his age progressed, something that seemed to be happening much too quickly of late.

It sorely pained High Hawk to think of the topics they were discussing, yet he understood why they must be broached. Because of his father's age and inability to think as clearly as before, it was time for such talks.

And it was also time for High Hawk to get serious about finding a woman for himself. He would be chief one day soon, and the chief of the Wolf band should have a wife and son to share the honor with him.

Thus far, High Hawk had paid little heed to the maidens of the nearby villages. They had given him special notice with flirting smiles and presents of beautifully beaded moccasins, and other things women made as they sat beside their lodge fires. Perhaps some even dreamed of being the one chosen to be the wife of the young and virile Pawnee chief.

These women, who came with their parents from other bands of Pawnee to have council, would make good wives for him. It was not the custom to marry someone of his own Wolf band.

Yet he had yet to see any woman who fit his idea of an ideal wife.

But he must stop being so particular.

"My son, since your duties as chief await you when I choose to step down, you do not have much time left to prove to the people of our Wolf band that you are worthy of being chief," Rising Moon said solemnly. "*Ho*, although I am almost certain that everyone already sees you as our next chief, it is up to you to give them more reasons to want you as leader."

"And what do you ask of me that will please our people?" High Hawk asked, his spine stiff. "What more can I do beyond what I have already proudly achieved?"

"You *have* proven yourself, time and again. You are worthy of being our people's leader," Rising Moon said. "But I would feel more confident about the matter if you were to prove it one more time by taking on the challenges I ask of you now. I would prefer that there is no doubt whatsoever in our people's minds and hearts about you when the time comes for you to step into my moccasins as chief."

Rising Moon leaned closer to High Hawk and gazed into his eyes. "My son, there are two things I ask of you tonight," he said solemnly.

"And what are these two things?" High Hawk asked. "What would you have me do?"

"Go. Steal horses. Steal enough to impress our people, and . . ." Rising Moon paused.

"And?" High Hawk prompted, lifting an eyebrow at his father's suggestion that he steal more horses. High Hawk already had more than enough from his many raids on their enemy, the Sioux. "What else, *Ahte*, would you have me do?"

His father's gaze wavered, and he took several puffs from his pipe, then rested the bowl again on his knee.

Yet still he seemed uncomfortable about what he wanted to say.

High Hawk scarcely breathed as he continued to wait. If his *ahte* was so hesitant to name this new challenge, then surely it would be something that would make High Hawk even more uncomfortable in the doing.

"My son, the pride of my life, this thing I ask of you is very important," Rising Moon said, his voice tight. "Although it will be something I know you will not want to do, it must be done."

He leaned even closer to High Hawk and looked more intently into his eyes. "Do you understand?" he asked.

"*Ahte*, please just say it," High Hawk replied, trying to hide his mounting frustration from his father. "Then I can make my own decision about the importance of what you want of me."

"You must abduct a white woman," Rising Moon said all at once, causing High Hawk to flinch as though he had been shot.

Rising Moon eased slowly away from High Hawk, yet his eyes remained fixed on his son's.

"Abduct . . . a . . . white . . . woman?" High Hawk gasped, the words sounding unreal as they came from his mouth. Never had white captives been brought into this village of Pawnee.

7

That his *ahte* could even ask such a thing of High Hawk was shocking; he could not envision himself ever carrying out this command.

"*Ho*, a white woman," Rising Moon said. He laid his pipe on the piece of soft white doeskin that he used as a wrapping for it. "There are two reasons for the abduction. It is not only to show our people that you are capable of meeting any challenge you might face as chief, but also so that this white woman cannot bear sons who will only grow up to kill red men and women. And I remind you, my son, that many of our own women have been abducted by whites. Stealing a white woman will be an act of vengeance against those who do not think twice about the cruelties they visit upon people of red skin."

Still stunned by what his father asked of him, High Hawk was not sure what to say. He had always obeyed his father's wishes.

But . . . this?

No. It seemed neither right nor logical.

"*Ahte*, horse stealing is a simple enough challenge, for I am well known for my skills and cunning," High Hawk said. "I agree to add more horses to my corral. But . . . I . . . cannot agree to abduct a woman. It does not seem an honorable thing to do. A mere woman taken by such a strong man as I? What challenge is there in that?"

Rising Moon's eyes narrowed angrily. He leaned closer again to High Hawk and again gazed into his eyes. "Is this son of mine challenging his *ahte*, and worse, challenging his chief?" he growled out. "Would you truly rather choose to disobey your chief than abduct the woman?

High Hawk had rarely seen his father so angry with him. For a moment, he was again at a loss for words. But to show that he would stand up for what he believed, High Hawk held his chin high as he challenged his father with his eyes.

"And after she is abducted?" he asked, not allowing his father to win this battle.

"What do you mean?" Rising Moon demanded. He leaned slowly away from his son. He was taken aback that he had actually shown anger toward High Hawk for the first time in their lives.

This, too, proved that it was time for Rising Moon to step down as chief, for it was not normal for him to get angry at High Hawk for any reason. They had always talked through any disagreement with civil tongues and love in their hearts.

Yet despite his dismay at the turn the discussion had taken, Rising Moon would not change his command.

"Our Pawnee women will resent a white woman's presence," High Hawk said, hating to seem disobedient to the father he had admired and loved since he was a small child. "You know that if a white woman is here, she will have to work alongside our women, for the more hands there are to plant and harvest and bring in wood and water,

9

the better it will be for all our people."

"My son, do not concern yourself about what our women might think or do," Rising Moon said tightly. "Only worry about what your chieftain asks of you tonight. Abduct a white woman and steal more horses. Then you will have passed the final test . . . you will have proven yourself worthy of being chief after your *ahte*."

Realizing that nothing he might say would change his father's mind about this particular challenge, High Hawk knew he had no choice but to abduct a white woman. If he did not, he might lose his father's respect, possibly even his love.

"And . . . where am I to find this woman?" High Hawk asked softly, relieved when he saw his father's eyes soften.

"This woman I speak of will be directly in your path on a night of the full moon. Tonight is such a night," Rising Moon said, glancing upward toward the smoke hole.

He smiled when he saw how the sky had darkened while they had been in council. His smile deepened when he saw the light of a full moon bathing his face.

He turned his eyes back to High Hawk. He reached a hand out and rested it on his son's bare shoulder. "Go, my son," he said thickly. "Seek and you will find her."

High Hawk nodded, then fell into his father's embrace when Rising Moon opened his arms.

"My son, my son," Rising Moon said, his voice breaking.

Their embrace continued for a moment, then High Hawk rose to his feet and left the tepee without another word.

Just as he emerged from the tepee, his *ina*, Blanket Woman, blocked his way.

It was obvious to him she had heard all that had transpired between father and son. And he could tell by the way she was gazing up at him with flashing black eyes, she did not approve of something that had been said, or perhaps all of it.

As he waited to hear what she had to say, he could not help admiring her. For a woman of her age, she still held beauty in her face, with only a few wrinkles crossing her copper brow.

She was named Blanket Woman because of her ability to make the prettiest blankets of all the women in their Wolf band.

She also made lovely dresses such as the one she wore tonight. By the glow of the huge outdoor fire behind them, he saw that she wore an exquisitely beaded and fringed doeskin dress and heavily beaded moccasins.

She wore her raven-black hair in one long braid down her back.

"I heard what your *ahte* asked of you," Blanket Woman said, her eyes flashing in the moonlight. "I disagree with him. It is wrong to abduct a woman, no matter what the reason. My son, stealing any

11

woman, white-skinned or not, is a dishonorable act."

She framed his face between her hands. "My son, you must stand up against your *ahte* about this," she said softly. "Refuse him. And if you do this for your *ina*, I will see that you are named chief after your father no longer holds that position."

She slid her hands away and smiled softly. "As you know, my son, your *ahte*'s weakness is your *ina*," she murmured, her eyes twinkling. "He never goes against my wishes. Go. Hunt and bring back many beautiful horses, but not a white woman."

Torn now between the differing wishes of his parents, High Hawk embraced his mother, then went around and informed his favored warriors about his plan to steal horses. He purposely did not tell them about the other challenge of the night . . . the white woman.

As they all went to their personal lodges to choose which weapons and horses would fit the night's planned activities, High Hawk entered his own tepee and chose his weapons.

He sheathed his favorite knife at the right side of his waist, grabbed a rifle and the bag that he carried with him on his horse at all times, then hurried to his personal corral at the back of his lodge. This was where he kept the most valuable of his horses.

Elsewhere, he had two other corrals, hidden from anyone who might think of stealing his powerful steeds.

He took his favorite from the corral, a roan with

a black mane and forelegs, and readied him for riding with his Indian saddle. He slid his rifle in the gunboot at one side of his horse, and secured his bag of provisions to the other, but just as he started to mount, he saw his brother, Sleeping Wolf, walking toward him.

His brother's back was so twisted, he could not help dragging one foot as he walked. Although it hurt High Hawk to see what a struggle it was for his brother to walk, High Hawk had grown used to it and never allowed his brother to see pity in his eyes.

He smiled at Sleeping Wolf as his brother stopped beside him.

"Where are you going, my brother?" Sleeping Wolf asked, noting the rifle and the sheathed knife, and the bag of provisions that his brother always carried with him. He was prepared with food and water and weapons for any eventuality.

"On a search for horses," High Hawk said. He placed a hand on his brother's shoulder, the one that was more level than the other.

"You already have so many," Sleeping Wolf said. He always took comfort from his brother's touch, even if only for a moment. He did not envy his brother his handsomeness and perfect body. He admired and loved him.

"A proud warrior cannot have too many steeds," High Hawk said, trying not to think about the other reason he was leaving his village tonight.

"I do not have any," Sleeping Wolf said, hanging

his head. "But of course I do not need any because of my inability to ride them."

High Hawk took his hand from his brother's shoulder and placed it beneath his chin. He slowly lifted it so that Sleeping Wolf's eyes met his.

"My brother, you know that my horses are also yours," High Hawk said. "Even though you cannot ride, they are yours anyhow."

Sleeping Wolf smiled. "I do ride often, my brother," he said softly. "In my dreams I am whole and able to ride. It is good to feel the wind against my face and to feel my hair blowing behind me."

"You do feel those things in your dreams?" High Hawk said, marveling that his brother could imagine such feelings that he had never felt in reality.

"When I am dreaming, I feel no pain, but I experience everything in my dreams that I cannot when I am awake," Sleeping Wolf said, nodding. "My brother, I have even flown in the sky with eagles!"

"I am glad that you can dream such dreams and experience things even I have not known," High Hawk said. "I have never dreamed of flying with eagles."

"The eagles are our brothers," Sleeping Wolf said, slowly nodding. "You will dream one night that you, too, fly with them."

"I hope so," High Hawk said, looking past his brother as his warriors rode up on their steeds, some with bows and quivers of arrows, others with firearms.

He then hugged his brother, feeling a surge of compassion when he touched sleeping Wolf's twisted back and heard him groan as he returned the hug.

"My heart is with you tonight as you ride," Sleeping Wolf said. "I wish you well, my brother. I wish you a successful hunt."

"I will bring home horses for us both," High Hawk said, his mind drifting suddenly to what else he would be hunting tonight.

A white woman.

His *ahte* had said she would be standing in the path of the full moon.

Sleeping Wolf nodded and stepped back as High Hawk mounted his steed.

High Hawk wheeled his horse around, waved at his brother, then rode off with his warriors.

High Hawk gazed heavenward. "*Tirawahut,* Great Spirit, lead me in the direction that I should go tonight," he whispered. "I cannot please both parents."

CHAPTER TWO

The moon shone down on a small cabin, nestled in the forest far from humanity. Smoke spiraled lazily from the stone chimney, making its way through the tall trees that surrounded Joylynn Anderson's home.

Nearby, a lone horse, a magnificent chestnut stallion, grazed in a small corral. Joylynn had constructed it herself after arriving at this abandoned log cabin only a few weeks ago.

Joylynn, nineteen, her long auburn hair flowing over her shoulders, had dropped off to sleep as she sat rocking before the fire in the hearth.

Dressed in a loose dress to make her more comfortable in a pregnancy that was barely showing, she slept peacefully, her hands resting in her lap.

Suddenly her hands curled into tight fists, her closed eyes twitched, and she moaned as she began to have a recurring dream that plagued her most nights now. In her dream she was reliving the

17

dreadful moment of her rape by an outlaw high-wayman. He had held her up while she was on her Pony Express run. His stench of sweat and cigars made her wince even in her dream.

It had been a beautiful spring morning and Joylynn was between towns, riding her chestnut stallion. She was one among many who made the Pony Express run traveling from town to town to deliver the mail.

She was proud to be a part of history-making, a player in what some were calling one of the most colorful episodes of American history. The 1,800-mile route required about ten days to cover, with the bags of mail changing hands up to eight times between the 157 stations.

Joylynn had even had the pleasure of meeting one of the Pony Express's most famous riders, William Cody—Buffalo Bill.

As Joylynn rode along, she knew this might be one of her last jaunts, for there had been rumors that the service might cease with the completion of the transcontinental telegraph system.

Although women riders were rare on the Pony Express, Joylynn had proved that she wasn't like most other women. Because of an abusive stepfather, who beat her mother almost daily, Joylynn had fled her family, but not before she was old enough to fend for herself.

Working on her father's farm before he died of a sudden heart attack, she had plowed alongside her father, hoed the gardens way into the night, and developed the muscles and grit of a man.

Even her stepfather had known better than to fool with her, for he realized she could very well defend herself against his blows.

When she had heard about the Pony Express, it seemed the perfect escape. She was an expert rider and owned a fast horse; the chestnut had been a gift from her real father a short time before he died. She had signed on, even though men hooted and hollered and poked fun at her, saying she was a mere woman and women couldn't stand up to the grueling work of being a Pony Express rider.

She had proven them wrong . . . until that one fateful day when she had been taken advantage of by a man who crudely reminded her that she *was* a woman. He had taken from her by force what men wanted from women, the pleasure of her body.

She had almost reached her final destination that day, proud to complete another run, when she spotted the fearful highwayman everyone was talking about. He seemed to come out of nowhere, appearing in Joylynn's path with a pistol aimed at her belly and his mouth twisted into a nasty sneer.

This was a bold, bad man, restless and roving, as lawless as a prairie wolf, a terror to friends and foe. He was easily identified by the many grotesque moles on his face, which had given him the nickname Mole.

Because he was proud of his reign of terror, Mole didn't even hide behind a mask anymore.

With thick trees and brush on both sides of the road, Joylynn had no choice but to stop. She had not seen him quickly enough.

Joylynn grabbed her rifle from the gunboot at the side of her stallion, but Mole quickly shot the firearm from her hand.

She asked what he wanted of her, but she knew that he had stolen a pack of mail only a month ago from another rider, then shot him dead before riding away.

She saw no chance of getting out of this ambush alive, so she set her jaw and awaited her fate. She was powerless without her firearm, and if she tried to make a run for it on her horse, she knew that Mole would shoot her in the back, then steal her pack of mail.

As Joylynn continued to dream, with tiny beads of sweat now on her brow, she could even smell the man as he had sidled his horse closer to hers and ordered her to follow him.

Her heart pounded as the nightmare continued. She had had no choice but to follow Mole. He led her down the road a piece, then nodded to a path that diverged into the woods. When the trees grew so thick she could go no farther, Mole told her to dismount.

Joylynn saw her life flashing before her eyes, because she believed that Mole had brought her there to kill her. But having no other choice, Joylynn dismounted.

Mole dismounted, too.

As he got closer to her, she could see even more clearly the many ugly, dark brown moles on his face, and the strangeness of his eyes. They were the palest blue she had ever seen, more white than blue . . . and bottomless.

As he removed his sweat-soaked, wide-brimmed Stetson hat, Joylynn saw that his hair was prematurely gray, for everything else about him was young. It was curly and worn long to his shirt collar. His lips formed a thin line, which seemed locked in an ugly sneer.

When he told her to undress, that he wanted to watch her, she died a slow death inside. It was at that moment she knew he was after far more than the mail. He was after her virginity, for she had never been with a man yet. He . . . was . . . going to rape her!

She stood her ground, said an adamant no.

He slapped her hard across her face, then threw her on the ground, his one hand still holding his pistol.

Suddenly Joylynn awakened with a start. Looking desperately around her, she was infinitely relieved that she was only dreaming, that she was in the security and warmth of her own home. The end of the dream was too hard to bear . . . the true memory of what had actually happened to her.

Tears filled Joylynn's eyes as she slid a hand to her belly. What grew inside her was memory enough of that day. Why did she have to constantly relive the worst time of her life in her recurring dreams?

She knew why. She could not let herself forget even one thing about that man who had raped her. Afterward, he had stood over her ravaged, naked body, one foot on her belly as he took the time to smoke a cigarillo.

Once he had finished his smoke, he had viciously strangled her, leaving her for dead. He had left the heavy bag of mail behind. All he had wanted that day was her body.

But somehow she had survived his strangling, gasping for air after he had left the forest.

Defiled, in pain, with his fingerprints marring her throat, she had finally managed to get on her horse, which Mole had carelessly left behind. Perhaps he was so satisfied with what he had achieved, her horse had slipped his mind.

Joylynn had decided not to complete her mail run. She had not wanted anyone to see her in that state . . . to know she had been raped.

Realizing someone would come to check on her if she didn't arrive at her destination in time, she managed to hang the mail bag in a tree, low enough to be seen. Whoever came searching for her would find the mailbag and see to it that the mail was delivered to its rightful destinations.

Joylynn had then gone home and bathed and made plans. She had left for parts unknown to anyone. All she wanted was to hide from the world. If she was pregnant as a result of the rape, she would have to make a decision about what to do with the baby when it was born.

She did know that she could not raise a child of rape. And she was also certain that she would find the sonofabitch who had done this to her.

Finally, she had reached a place where she could make her temporary home, far from anyone who knew her. The abandoned cabin, set deep into the forest, suited her needs perfectly.

She had been lucky. Although everything was dusty and old, the cabin was partly furnished. There was enough furniture for her to get by for the short time she planned to live there.

Even a kerosene lamp, half filled with kerosene, had been left in the cabin, and also books, yellowed, with some pages missing.

She had gone to the closest town and bought enough supplies to last many months, and a wagon with which to transport them. She had even bought seed to plant a garden. Then she had left civilization behind.

"And here I am, in Nebraska, and definitely pregnant," she whispered to herself.

She had counted herself to be twelve weeks along and was now beginning to show, but only barely. Someone who knew pregnancy well would recognize that she was with child.

But no one else could tell, not yet anyhow.

Though soon they would be able to. That was why she was staying hidden now, with enough food and supplies to last until after the child was born.

She had finally made a decision about the child. After the baby was born, she would take it to the nearest church and leave it on a pew at the front of the church so that the minister would quickly see the tiny bundle wrapped in a blanket.

She could not, would not, raise this child.

Angry that she had had the nightmare again, Joylynn went outside in the moonlight to get a breath of fresh air, and to check on her chestnut stallion, which she had named Swiftie.

She had built a small corral not far from the cabin for her beloved steed. If not for her horse, she would be all alone in the world.

Yes, they were best friends. She was glad that the evil man hadn't taken Swiftie that day, for without her stallion, she was not sure she could have survived this life of isolation and loneliness.

Tears shone in her eyes as Joylynn stroked the stallion's sleek mane. When a loon cried its eerie call somewhere close by the creek, the sound made Joylynn's loneliness twofold. In her mind's eye she saw her father, his rusty-red hair blowing in the breeze as he rode his white mare alongside Joylynn after giving her the beloved chestnut stallion.

Those days were oh, so long gone. She wondered what the future now held for her. In her eyes it looked nothing but bleak. . . .

CHAPTER THREE

The moon was high and bright in the sky as High Hawk and his warriors rode toward home, with several head of horses secured behind them.

High Hawk felt he had stolen enough horses for the night, at least enough to appease his father. Once again, he had raided the Sioux, proving his cunning at stealing horses from the enemy.

To his people, captured horses were the legitimate spoils of war. The wealth of the Pawnee was in their horses.

He smiled at how easy it had been to take the animals. At least a hundred powerful steeds had been grazing on land a short distance from the Sioux village.

It had been as easy as a falcon sweeping from the sky to capture a snake within its talons.

High Hawk had been careful, though, not to steal too many steeds. It would not do for the

Sioux to notice the theft and go on the warpath to look for the horse raiders.

Now that they were far enough away from the the Sioux village, High Hawk wanted to wash the war paint from his body before venturing toward home. Up ahead, he saw the shine of water.

"We will stop and wash up in the river," he said, bringing his horse to a stop.

The warriors dismounted, then led their steeds and the stolen horses to the stream, where they could drink while High Hawk and his warriors washed themselves clean of the paint.

When that was done, High Hawk spotted a bluff not far away. It would give him the opportunity to survey the land below. He would look as far as the eye and the moon would allow. If all still seemed well, and he saw no one following them, he and his men would continue their journey home.

"I will go and see if anyone follows us," he said, grabbing his rifle from the gunboot at the side of his horse. "You stay. Watch the horses."

His warriors nodded.

High Hawk hurried up the slight incline until he came to the bluff. It commanded a far stretch of land, as well as a forest of trees just below him.

He cupped one hand above his eyes and slowly scanned the countryside in all directions.

The moon was still bright.

The air was clear.

The breeze was soft and sweet and silent except for a lone loon making its strange call in the distance.

Suddenly the wind changed, bringing with it the clearly identifiable smell of smoke.

Stiffening, knowing that where there was fire there was man, High Hawk stepped closer to the edge of the bluff and slowly scanned the land beyond. Then he surveyed the trees below him again.

His eyes widened when he saw a slight clearing in the forest this time.

He clutched his rifle tighter when he saw a small cabin in the clearing, where smoke spiraled up from a chimney.

And then he saw movement outside the cabin. He could not tell from this distance if it was a man or a woman.

His eyebrows raised when he heard the whinny of a horse and then saw the animal in a small corral near the cabin.

The horse was too far away from him to see if it was worth stealing.

But the truth was that he could always use one more horse, especially since it was there, so close, and ready for the taking.

He tried again to spot the figure he had seen. Who was this person who had established a home so far from everyone else? Didn't this person understand the danger of being so isolated?

Too curious not to go closer, to see who this person was who lived so alone, and to get a better look at the horse, High Hawk hurried back to his warriors.

"I have seen movement down below," he said, seeing how each man placed his hand quickly on his knife or gun. "I cannot tell if it is one person or many. Nor can I see the color of their skin. But a house made of logs sits amid the trees, and only white people live in such homes."

He smiled devilishly. "I also heard a horse whinnying," he said. "If I find that it is worth taking, I will add one more steed to those we stole tonight."

"Do you wish to go alone, or do you want us all to go with you?" Three Bears asked, always eager to join his best friend on exciting jaunts. "Or do you wish for only one of us to join you?"

High Hawk placed a hand on his friend's shoulder. "All but you and I will stay behind," he said, smiling. "Come, Three Bears. Let us go and see who makes their home so far from other people."

He and Three Bears mounted their steeds and rode off while the others stayed behind, keeping an eye out for any Sioux or outlaw who might happen along.

Lately the countryside had been plagued by a particularly vicious outlaw.

His name was Mole.

He was the worst of all outlaws the Pawnee had ever heard tell of. If High Hawk, or any of his

Pawnee friends, could find that man and stop his reign of terror, everyone would rest more easily.

Having now entered the forest that he had observed from on high, High Hawk and Three Bears rode onward for a little while, with only the continued sound of the loon disturbing the silence.

When High Hawk and Three Bears got the scent of smoke, they gave each other looks and nods, then stopped and dismounted.

"We should leave our horses tethered here and go the rest of the way on foot," High Hawk said, already securing his reins to the low limb of a huge oak tree. "Three Bears, follow a short distance behind me, and stay hidden. When we arrive at the cleared piece of land, stop and keep an eye out for anyone who might come upon us. Also, if you see my life threatened, act quickly. You are a crack shot with your rifle. Shoot to disarm the one who threatens me. Kill only if it becomes absolutely necessary."

Three Bears nodded. "Go with care, my friend," he said, gripping his rifle.

High Hawk nodded, then, clutching his own rifle, he ran on ahead of Three Bears.

Noiselessly High Hawk's moccasined feet fell like the velvet paws of a cat on the thick covering of fallen, browned and rotted leaves, his glittering black eyes scanning every object that appeared within their view as he searched for anything that might be a threat to his and Three Bears's safety.

Nothing escaped his piercing glance, and before long, he could see the cabin and corral through a break in the trees ahead of him.

The person he had seen outside the cabin seemed to have gone back inside.

Lamplight glowed through the window that faced toward High Hawk. He came to a stop to observe the cabin before deciding what to do.

Being of a curious nature, he could not just turn around and return to the others.

He did not plan to accost those who lived in this cabin, but he had to at least see who made their home so far from others.

The moon again revealed to him the small corral near the cabin. In it stood one of the most beautiful horses he had ever seen.

The moonlight was bright enough for High Hawk to see that the horse was a magnificently muscled chestnut stallion, its eyes bright and alert. It seemed to sense someone was near.

Its right hoof pawed nervously at the earth beneath it. It shook its thick mane, then softly whinnied.

Seeing such a beautiful horse sent shivers of excitement down High Hawk's spine. How could he see such an animal as this and ignore it?

He could picture himself on this horse, riding into the wind, fast and free. Never had he been as intrigued by a horse as he was now.

And it was obvious to him that whoever owned

this steed cared a lot for it. The stallion was impeccably groomed, its coat shiny and sleek, its mane brushed so that surely there was not even one small knot in it.

Longing to stroke his hands down the horse's withers, and forgetting everything but the thrill of doing so, High Hawk stepped out into the clearing and slipped past one of the cabin windows. He started toward the corral, but his throat constricted when the click of a rifle being readied for firing caused him to stop in mid-step.

Joylynn stood there, her insides trembling, yet her aim accurate as she leveled the rifle directly at the red man's gut.

She had seen a shadow pass across the window a moment ago.

She had crept to the window and peered from it, fear gripping her when she saw that she was no longer alone. An Indian stood just outside, a rifle in his right hand.

Praying that there was only one Indian, she had grabbed her rifle and stepped outside.

"Throw down your rifle or I will shoot you dead," Joylynn said, fighting to keep her voice steady.

The loon's cry from somewhere close by continued as High Hawk's breathing came rapidly and shallowly. He gazed back at the woman, and then at the rifle.

She seemed to know enough about firearms to

shoot him, especially since she had been courageous enough to come outside her home with the rifle and face him, a red man, straight on.

It was humiliating for him, a man who would be chief, to have been stopped by a woman, when usually he was so careful. No man had ever cornered him in such a way.

He thought quickly about the situation.

Since there was only one horse, surely she was alone.

But would her husband arrive soon? If so, he would not hesitate to shoot High Hawk at first sight.

He wanted to look over his shoulder to see what was delaying Three Bears.

Surely he saw the rifle aimed directly at High Hawk's belly!

Then a thought came to him that made his heart sink. If Three Bears had been discovered lurking in the forest by the woman's husband, the man would have silenced Three Bears quietly, perhaps with a knife.

Suddenly a gun blast rang out, silencing the loon's cry, and causing the stallion behind High Hawk to buck with fright.

CHAPTER FOUR

Joylynn screamed, and pain rushed from her fingers up the full length of her arms at the impact of the bullet hitting her rifle. The gun had been knocked from her hands.

Her heart thudded hard in her chest as she rubbed her hands together. Her eyes never left the Indian who still stood before her . . . until another Indian stepped out from the cover of the trees, the moon's brightness showing smoke spiraling from the barrel of his rifle.

She was now at the mercy of two Indians, not one. What if there were many more lurking amid the shadows of the trees, waiting to take their turn with her?

Oh, surely her cabin was surrounded by them.

She knew now that she should have stayed inside. She would have had a better chance of surviv-

33

ing. Inside, she could have picked off the Indians one at a time.

As it was, she was at their mercy. She realized that her knees were trembling so much, she wasn't sure how much longer they would hold her up.

All of those months she had worked for the pony express, she had not had one incident with Indians.

Now, when she was trying to live a peaceful, isolated life, she was surrounded by them.

High Hawk stepped closer to Joylynn. Up this close, with the lamplight coming through the door of the cabin, and the full moon above bathing her in bright light, he saw much defiance and courage in her eyes. There was a unique beauty about this woman; her every facial feature was beautifully, perfectly sculpted.

As they stood there facing one another, challenging each other with their eyes, High Hawk remembered his *ahte*'s words: "Abduct a white woman and steal more horses. Then you will have passed the final test . . . you will have proven yourself truly worthy of being chief after your *ahte*."

High Hawk also remembered his *ahte* saying, "This woman I speak of will be directly in your path on a night of the full moon."

Surely destiny had placed her in his path tonight.

Surely destiny had brought them together for a purpose.

He grabbed Joylynn by one wrist. "Go into your

lodge," he commanded. "I will accompany you there."

Terror struck at Joylynn's heart.

Was she going to be the victim of a second rape? Could life be that cruel?

"No," Joylynn spat out, trying hard to keep her voice from trembling. She was desperately afraid of what lay ahead of her in the next moments. Stubbornly she stood her ground. "I absolutely refuse to do anything you tell me to do. I won't . . . go inside my cabin with . . . with . . . the likes of you . . . you . . . savage."

High Hawk was stung that she should call him a savage. No other word was hated as much as that word . . . savage . . . by people of red skin. It was a word too loosely thrown around by white people, a word that was ugly and despised by those who were wrongly labeled with it.

Yet he could not help being impressed by her courage as she stood up to a red man.

Ho, he admired her, but he would not allow her to realize it.

Continuing to hold her wrist tightly, he forced her inside the cabin.

Once there, High Hawk quickly scanned everything, his eyebrows rising when he saw no sign of a man's presence.

He gazed directly into her eyes again. "Do you live alone?" he asked, for he had to be certain about whether or not a man might show up at any moment.

Joylynn was afraid to speak, afraid to keep silent. While he was slowly looking around her cabin, she studied him. What she saw was someone so handsome that, had they met under different circumstances, she would have been attracted to him. He was uniquely handsome, with sculpted facial features, penetrating coal-black eyes, and long, raven-black, unbraided hair held back from his face by a beaded headband.

His hair hung down past his waist, and she could envision how it would blow in the wind when he rode across the land.

He was dressed in only a breechclout and moccasins, and she admired his muscled, bronzed body. She wondered how it might feel to be held by those muscled arms if he were not someone who had come upon her in the night, threatening her very existence.

"Answer me," High Hawk said, seeing that she seemed too frozen with fear to respond to his questions. He regretted causing that fear, for he had not come here to harm her.

He had not come here with her on his mind at all.

"Tell me," he said, his eyes gazing deeply into hers. "Do . . . you . . . live alone?"

She knew now that he would insist on an answer. Hoping that if she responded, he would leave her in peace, she cleared her throat, then blurted out, "My husband will be home anytime now. He'll kill you if you violate me."

That word "violate" disturbed him, for he was a man of honor, who would never take advantage of a woman.

But of course this woman had no way of knowing this, and he did not feel now was the time to tell her. He needed to know, first, whether or not she had a man to protect her.

"I see nothing to show that a man lives here with you," he said, still holding her wrist, yet not as tightly.

Joylynn felt trapped, for she knew that there *was* nothing in the cabin except her own possessions.

But she refused to admit the truth, so she said nothing.

"You do live alone," High Hawk said, releasing his hold on her wrist. "Why? I have never seen a white woman live without a man to provide food for her and look after her safety."

His eyes moved to a shelf that held dishes, as well as the cooking utensils that white women used to prepare food; then he gazed into her eyes again. "If you have no man who hunts for you, *who* puts food on your table?" he asked.

Joylynn still remained silent, feeling it was best not to confirm his belief that she had no husband. She must wait and see what his intentions were. She had no other choice. She was truly at this man's mercy.

High Hawk sighed heavily when the woman still would not respond to his questions.

Then he thought of someone else: his father, and his father's premonition about finding a white woman on the night of the full moon. High Hawk realized that somehow his father had known that he would find this woman tonight. Not for the first time, he was awed by the powers of his father; Rising Moon truly could see things that no one else saw.

And then High Hawk remembered his mother's words . . . that he should not take any white woman as his captive.

Considering how the events of the night had played out, the mystical way he had found the woman his father had predicted he would find, he chose without further thought to follow his father's bidding, ignoring his mother's.

And seeing how alone this woman was in a world where women amounted to only one thing to most men, seeing how vulnerable she was for any man's taking, he made his decision. He felt that he was saving her from a future that might include being raped by any man who might pass by; he felt that he was not truly taking her as his captive, but that he might actually be saving her life. It was true that no woman lived for long, alone. If he were to leave her there, her days were surely numbered.

He thought ahead, to her life in his village and realized that she was accustomed to a vastly different existence from the one the Pawnee women lived. To prove to her that what he was doing was not all bad, he would see that she would take some comforts from her home, which would make her life with him and his people more tolerable.

He searched for a travel bag, and when he saw a large leather satchel, he grabbed it and shoved it into her arms.

"You are coming with me," High Hawk said tightly. "Take what clothes and provisions you wish to bring with you and place them in this bag, for you will not be returning."

Joylynn's heart skipped a beat.

Her throat went suddenly dry.

She searched his eyes as tears threatened to spill from her own. "Please, oh, please don't make me go with you," she said, her voice trembling. "I'm no threat to you or your people. I . . . I . . . am only one small speck on this earth. Why can't you forget that you found me here and go on your way? Surely there are those who are waiting for your return home. And . . . surely they wouldn't want to see you bring a white woman among them."

"Curiosity brought me here when I saw this lone cabin from a high butte," High Hawk said. "When I decided to come and see who lived so isolated from everyone else, at first it was only to observe. But when I heard your horse whinnying, I knew I would not leave without it. It was my intention to come only for the horse. Not you."

"Then what changed your mind?" Joylynn asked, clenching and unclenching her hands as she tried to think of something she might say, or do, that would convince him what he was doing was wrong.

She was horrified to hear that he planned to take her horse! Without Swiftie, she would be alone in the world. She would no longer have a companion, nor a means to get supplies.

But none of that seemed to matter now, for she knew that this warrior was not going to change his mind about taking her.

"Pack your things," High Hawk said more determinedly, shoving the bag in Joylynn's arms. "I know it will be hard enough to live among my people without having anything with you that is yours."

Joylynn's eyes widened at his show of consideration for her. Could he be a different breed of Indian? No, not only of Indian, but of man?

Or was it just a ploy to make her begin to trust in him?

But no matter how she tried to figure this man out, the fact remained that he was taking her as his captive. Surely in his mind she now belonged to him, and he would feel free to do whatever he chose to her.

She sighed heavily, for she knew that she had no choice but to do as he said. Still, she would find a way to get free at her first opportunity. Neither this

Indian nor his friend had eyes in the back of their heads.

She doubted now that there were any others out there in the dark, or surely they would have come and joined the first two.

Fighting off her fear of what the future held for her, Joylynn hurried around the cabin, grabbing those clothes that were the most comfortable for her now that she was pregnant. She hoped the loose dresses would help hide her pregnancy for as long as possible from the Indians with whom she would be living.

She shoved these dresses in her bag along with her hairbrush and some underthings.

She gazed up at High Hawk, finding it strange that this man was being kind to her on one hand, by allowing her to take some of her things with her, yet cruel, too, since he was taking her captive.

High Hawk stood there watching her; then something caught his eye. It looked like a strange sort of weapon, but what were those two eyes on it?

He went to the table and picked up the strange apparatus, turning it from side to side as he studied it.

Joylynn saw his interest in it. "What you are holding is called binoculars," she said, hoping to get on his good side by being friendly.

"What does it do?" he asked, glancing at Joylynn, and then again studying the binoculars. "Shoot? How do you load it?"

Joylynn realized he knew absolutely nothing about binoculars. She laughed softly, hoping he would not think she was mocking him.

"It isn't a weapon," she said. "Put it to your eyes. Look through it. Look at one thing in particular. Can you see how it seems to magnify what you are looking at?"

She was relieved when he didn't seem offended by her laughter, but instead looked through the lenses as she'd suggested.

"Take it with you," she murmured. "You might find it of value one of these days."

High Hawk lowered the binoculars from his eyes.

Surprised by her generousity, especially since she was his captive, he held the binoculars in his hand a moment. Thinking she was somehow trying to trick him, he started to place the binoculars back on the table.

Then, too intrigued by them, he changed his mind and slipped the long strap they hung from around his neck.

Pleased that he had decided to take the binoculars, Joylynn lifted her bag and stepped outside with him.

When she saw her breech-loading rifle still on the ground, only a few feet from her, she thought she might have found the opportunity to escape that she'd been looking for.

She took a quick step toward it, but High Hawk quickly saw what she was trying to do and grabbed up the rifle himself.

Her heart pounded as she wondered how he would react. Joylynn gazed nervously into his eyes, where the moonlight glowed in the dark depths, then turned her head away when she heard the whinny of her horse. The other Indian led Swiftie to her, saddled and ready for traveling.

"Take your horse's reins," High Hawk commanded. He took her bag from her. "Come with me."

She glanced around to see what the other Indian was doing. But he was already lost to sight, invisible in the darkness of the forest.

They went into the forest and walked until they came upon Three Bears, who was already on his horse, holding the reins of High Hawk's mount. He held them out for High Hawk as he stepped up to him.

"Mount your steed now," High Hawk said over his shoulder to Joylynn, swinging himself upon his saddle. "Come now with me and Three Bears. The others await us."

Joylynn's heart skipped a beat at hearing that there were others. Being with two Indians was frightening enough; she had no desire to be in the company of many.

But she had no choice except to continue doing as he told her. She mounted Swiftie and rode onward with the two Indians, one of whom she now knew to be called Three Bears.

She glanced over at the other Indian, wondering what his status was among his people.

Was he someone of great importance, or just another warrior under the command of a powerful chief?

When they reached the butte, Joylynn went cold inside when she saw how many Indians were there, awaiting the arrival of the other two.

When they all raked their eyes over her, she could not help shivering.

And then she saw the number of horses that were with these Indians. It was obvious they had been on a horse raid. She wondered if these Indians were Sioux, or of the more friendly Pawnee tribe.

If these were Pawnee and they had stolen horses from the Sioux, the owners would be even now searching for their stolen steeds; she could die alongside her abductor.

Or she might be taken captive by the Sioux. She knew how the Sioux felt about white people; she had learned while riding for the Pony Express. She had been told by those in charge to be especially wary of the Sioux since they were on the warpath more often than not. She knew that there would be no kindness granted her by them.

She eyed the handsome Indian, beginning to believe that she would be better off with him than with the Sioux. His kindness toward her attested to that.

But she had to remind herself that there were many hours ahead of her during which the situation could change. This warrior might be showing her kindness now, only to fool her into letting down her guard, so that later he could have his way with her!

"Stay close beside me as we ride to my village," High Hawk said, giving Joylynn a friendly smile that made her feel somewhat less afraid. Sternly she reminded herself that she must not trust him.

One rape in a woman's life was surely all a body could take!

CHAPTER FIVE

Wishing that she was brave enough to knee her horse and try to escape from her captor, Joylynn glanced over at the handsome Indian as he rode straight-backed on his steed. She had caught him glancing oftimes at her horse, and remembered that he had said he had originally come to steal Swiftie, then added her to his plan of abduction.

She looked over her shoulder at the many warriors riding behind them, their eyes straight ahead. Fortunately, they were paying her no mind, at least not at the moment. The only one who seemed truly interested in her was the one who had grabbed her and taken her inside her cabin.

She was relieved that so far he hadn't done anything worse than abduct her. Had she been raped a second time, she would have wanted to die.

But as it was, this warrior seemed not to have rape on his mind at all, but instead, kindness toward her. Still, he wasn't kind enough to listen to reason when she pleaded to be released.

She tried not to think about what lay ahead of her, but just to take one moment at a time. Soon enough she would know what his true intentions were.

"I am High Hawk of the Wolf band of Pawnee," High Hawk suddenly said as he looked over at her. "And your name is?"

"My name is none of your business," Joylynn said bitterly. Angrily she lifted her chin, refusing to look at him. But inside she was relieved to know that she was definitely in the company of the Pawnee, not the Sioux.

She looked far to the right, where the trees grew thick and dark, knowing that anyone could be hiding in their depths . . . even the Sioux. If those were Sioux horses that had been stolen tonight, surely their owners would discover the theft and come to take revenge on the thieves.

She looked quickly at High Hawk again. "In my world, men hang for stealing horses," she blurted out, bringing his eyes quickly back to her. "I wonder if your decision to indulge yourselves in the adventure of stealing those horses will be the cause of your demise."

"Horse stealing is not all for adventure," High Hawk said defensively, his jaw tight. "It is an accepted means of acquiring respect among my people. A man's wealth is measured by his horses.

They are essential in the hunt, our means of acquiring food, clothes and shelter. Horse stealing is also necessary to offset thefts of Pawnee horses. The survival of our whole tribe depends on having enough horses so that our warriors can protect the women and children."

"Yes, you can make all sorts of excuses for what you have done tonight, but I still believe it is wrong to take another man's possessions," Joylynn argued back. "And worse yet, you stole *me* . . . a human being. What can you say to try to convince me that is right?"

"You were in the path of the moon tonight, and so it was meant for me to take you to my home," High Hawk said matter-of-factly.

"What . . . ?" Joylynn gasped. "I have never heard such hogwash as that. The moon led you to me? What else will you allow yourself to think to make what you did to me right in your eyes?"

"Hogwash?" High Hawk said, raising an eyebrow. "What is this word . . . 'hogwash'?"

Joylynn's lips parted. She gazed back at him, stunned that such a powerful man should be so innocent in some ways.

"Hogwash is a term used when one wants to say that what has been said is foolish, even . . . stupid . . ." Joylynn said, her voice not as accusing now, for the longer she was with this man, the more alluring she found him.

"That word 'stupid' is new to me, as well," High Hawk said, glancing away from her when he saw the shine of a stream to their left.

"I doubt that you would want to hear my explanation of that word, especially how it applies to you," Joylynn said, her eyes following his. She, too, saw the glimmer of the water.

"I'm thirsty," she blurted out, hoping that if he stopped and allowed her to dismount long enough to get a drink, she might find a way to distract him and flee into the dark, where she could hide.

High Hawk looked quickly at her, then over his shoulder at the horses that he and his warriors had stolen. They needed watering, as well.

He gazed at Joylynn again. "We will stop for a while," he said. "Not so much for you as for the horses. They need to be watered."

Joylynn realized that he did not want to appear to be catering to her wishes, but that didn't matter to her. All she wanted was the right moment when she could slip away, perhaps while he was focused on leading the horses to the water.

Although she knew that her chances of getting away were slim, she could not rest until she at least tried.

He stopped and shouted to his men that he wanted to water the horses. Then he went on with Joylynn until they came to the stream. "Dismount, but stay close," he ordered. "You will be foolish to think that you can get far, should you decide to run."

Realizing that he'd seen right through her ploy, she had to accept that she wasn't going anywhere tonight, except with him. She sighed and nodded.

"Come with me," High Hawk said as he suddenly lifted her from her saddle.

His hands at her waist were strong but gentle. As he took her from her horse, the closeness of their bodies, the heat of his breath on her face, awoke a feeling Joylynn had never experienced before. It was a strange sort of thrill that shook her from her head to her toes.

And when their eyes met and held as he placed her on the ground, Joylynn caught her breath. There was something in his eyes that told her she was much more than his captive. She could tell that he was as intrigued by her as she was by him.

She looked quickly away, for she knew that it was foolish to think of him with anything but loathing. This was the man who had come to her in the night and uprooted her from the refuge she had made for herself.

He had changed everything for her, and she wasn't sure now where it all would end, especially once he realized that he had abducted a pregnant woman.

She looked back at him just as he stepped away from her. He went to his horse and got something from his travel bag.

He came back to her and held it out.

"This is *wasna*," he explained. "I always take

wasna with me. It is very nourishing and easily carried. Take some. Eat. It will give you energy."

"And what makes you think I need energy?" Joylynn demanded, placing her fists on her hips in a defiant pose. "Do I look weak?"

"No, but it is the middle of the night and a time when you would be asleep normally, not traveling," High Hawk said, placing a piece of the *wasna* in her hand. "Take. Eat. Then come with me to the water for a drink."

She stood her ground and stared curiously at what looked like a piece of cake in her hand. Then she questioned him with her eyes.

"*Wasna* is made by the Pawnee women," he said, understanding her hesitance. "It is meat pounded with chokeberries and pressed like white people's cheese so that it remains nourishing and wholesome for long periods of time."

He broke off a piece and ate it, nodded at her, and was glad when she trusted him enough to eat what he had given her.

Joylynn's eyes widened. "Why, it is very good," she said in a surprised tone. "Thank you."

High Hawk smiled. "Now come for water," he said, taking her hand. "Then we will continue onward. Home is not far away now."

She went with him to the stream, while the warriors led the horses to the water a short distance away. Some of the animals snorted and shied away from it, while others joyously dipped their noses into the cold liquid and eagerly drank.

"A precaution must be made when stopping to quench one's thirst," High Hawk said, releasing Joylynn's hand. "As a child, I was taught to kneel on one knee with the right hand cupped to bring water to the mouth. Never lie flat on your stomach with your face to the water."

He looked past her, at his horse and hers, which were enjoying their drinks, then smiled at her. "Normally, a rider dismounts, holds the reins of his steed in one hand and lets the horse drink first," he said. "The horse then stands guard while the rider drinks."

"But this is not a normal night," Joylynn said, sighing. "You have a captive to keep an eye on."

"*Ho*, a captive," he said, then glanced over at his horse, and again into Joylynn's greenish-brown eyes. "Old people say that a horse is a far better watcher and more alert than a dog such as white people use. If it is a gentle horse, the reins can be held in the left hand, and the right hand used to drink more rapidly. If, however, the horse is fractious, the reins should be held with the stronger arm and hand."

"That is too much for me to remember just now," Joylynn said, sighing again. "Can I just bend down and take a quick drink?"

He laughed softly. "*Ho*, do as you wish," he said,

now only watching her. He watched as she held her beautiful long auburn hair back from her face with one hand while bringing the water to her perfectly shaped lips with the other.

She made not a sound as she sucked the water from her hand.

Although she seemed strong in so many ways, she was delicate, too.

He could not help being intrigued by her.

He hoped to learn more about her when they talked once they reached his lodge. There they could be alone together, with the entrance flap securely tied.

He hoped that he could persuade her to accept this new life that he would give her. He hoped that she would accept him as her man, for he felt toward her, a stranger, more than he had ever felt for any other woman. Within his heart he felt a caring he would not have thought possible for a woman of white skin.

He felt torn about having abducted her. A part of him did not want to think of how she must despise him for having taken her from her home, yet a part of him was proud that he had found her and done his father's bidding.

He would not allow himself to think of the bitterness his mother would feel about what he had done tonight.

Her thirst quenched, Joylynn pushed herself to her feet. As she turned toward High Hawk, she found him gazing at her in a way that made it clear he was attracted to her.

She wasn't sure how to feel about that. Up until now he had treated her gently. She had even begun to trust him.

Yet she must remember that she was not there of her own choosing. She was his captive. And would he not take full advantage of his power over her eventually?

She would not allow herself to think about it, not now, anyway. In time, she would find her way out of this predicament. She always had, except for that one day when she was brought to the ground by a madman who'd left his seed growing in her belly.

She swallowed hard and looked down at the ground, for whenever she thought of that child, she felt many emotions. She was determined not to keep the baby when it was born, but her decision ate away at her heart. It was painful to know that she must give birth, then give the child away to strangers.

"Is your thirst quenched?" High Hawk asked, bringing Joylynn's eyes back to him.

"Yes," she murmured, swallowing hard.

He looked over his shoulder at his warriors, who were still watering the horses, then nodded at Joylynn. "Sit with me as we wait for the steeds to be fully watered," he said, already moving toward a thick bed of grass along the embankment.

Joylynn went with him and sat down on the grass, her plan of escaping tonight abandoned, for she knew that there was no possible way to flee this man. He was determined to keep her, and so he would, until she finally found a way to get the best of him.

"You seem to place great value in horses, judging by the way you are taking such time to see that they are watered," Joylynn said, hoping friendly conversation would cause him to trust her. All she needed was the right opportunity and she would most definitely try to escape, even though he had warned her against it.

She had been a free woman for too long now to let any man hold her captive!

"Do you not place the same sort of value on your steed?" High Hawk said as he glanced over at her chestnut stallion, which was enjoying drinking from the stream along with the others. "It is a magnificent horse, but of course you do not need me to tell you that. How could anyone not see its worth?"

"Especially you, who do not hesitate to take any horse you want," Joylynn said sarcastically. She leaned closer to him. "Swiftie is mine. He has been mine for many years and will always be, so do not think that I will allow you to place him among your herd. Do not believe he is now yours just because you have me as a captive."

"Swiftie?" High Hawk said, lifting an eyebrow. "You call your steed by such a name as that?"

"He deserves the name, for he is faster than any other horse I have ever been on," Joylynn said. Her voice softened. "And what is wrong with that name? Tell me what you call yours. I'm certain what you chose is laughable to me."

"I have many horses, so I do not waste time naming any of them. One is as valuable to me as another," High Hawk said proudly. He gazed intently into her eyes. "But women need names. What is yours?"

"Like I said before, my name is none of your business," she said, yet she was weakening, for this Indian was causing her to feel things in her heart that were new to her. Just his nearness made her feel foreign to herself. And he was her captor!

She turned her eyes away, for she knew how foolish it was to think anything good about this man; surely he intended nothing good for her. More than likely he would place her among the other women and make her work in the fields, or make her carry his water and firewood.

To him, she was undoubtedly no more than a slave.

"If you do not give me your name, then I will give one to you, and that is what you will be called by my people," High Hawk said, watching her eyes as she brought them up and looked directly into his. "Should I start thinking up names now? Or will you share yours with me?"

"I would never want an Indian name like Sun

Flower or Dancing Snow," Joylynn said, lifting her chin defiantly. "They are ridiculous."

"Then what is the name your mother gave you, which you do not think is . . . ridiculous?" High Hawk said, his eyes dancing. He was enjoying this banter with a woman who had much spirit and pride.

"Joylynn," she said softly, realizing that she was being foolish, not telling him her name. She had more important things to be concerned about. "Joylynn Anderson."

"Joy is a word our people have used often when giving daughters names," High Hawk said, searching her eyes. "But Lynn? No. I have not heard such a name as that before."

"Joylynn is one name, not two," she found herself saying more softly than she wanted. She wanted to appear strong in the eyes of this warrior, not appear defenseless. She had looked after her own welfare ever since she had fled her tyrant of a stepfather.

"Joylynn," High Hawk said, slowly nodding. "That name will do. I will enjoy calling you that until later. Until you are with my people for a while. Then you will be given a name of my people."

"And so you plan to hold me hostage for a long time, do you?" Joylynn said, trying to act as though what he had said did not matter much to her. She now knew what his intentions were. He didn't plan just to keep her for a while, until she trusted him with her beautiful horse, and then let her return to her own world. He had abducted her to keep as his own.

"I do not like that word 'hostage,' or 'captive,'" High Hawk said. "It is not my habit to take either. And I do not see you as my captive. You are with me for a specific reason. The moon's glow showed me to you. Destiny made it so."

"A specific reason?" Joylynn gasped out. "Destiny? The moon showed me to you? What sort of nonsense is all of that? You heard my horse and came for it, to steal it, and then could not pass up the opportunity to take a woman to your lodge with you to do . . . to . . . do whatever you plan to do with me."

"Plan to do with you?" High Hawk said softly. He reached a hand out to touch her face, only to have her slap it away. "In time you will understand why I had to find you and bring you among my people."

"I will never understand why you abducted me," Joylynn cried. "It is wrong. All of what you have done tonight is wrong." She gestured with a hand toward the stolen horses. "Not only did you steal someone else's property, the horses . . . but . . . also me, a human. You are watering the horses, and me, as though we are your true possessions, when in truth, neither I nor the horses are yours."

High Hawk glanced over his shoulder at the muscular, handsome horses he had stolen, then turned his eyes back to Joylynn. "No matter how you see it, the horses are now Pawnee steeds, and there is a Pawnee saying that says, 'Take care of your horse, and he may save your life,'" he replied. "These horses will be better off with my people. We show respect for our steeds by saying, '*Heru atiku*,' which means, 'Greetings, horse.' We spend much time caring for our mounts. After a hard ride, a warrior will walk his horse for a while to allow it to cool down, and he will use a corncob to curry it. Tallow is rubbed on a horse's groin if it has been ridden for several days on long journeys."

Joylynn listened attentively, surprised to find what he was saying truly interesting. Indeed, she was finding everything about this handsome warrior fascinating.

His voice, his eyes, intrigued her no matter how hard she fought against such feelings.

Unconsciously, she leaned closer to him as he talked, as though his voice had put her in a trance.

"Different plant medicines are used to heal or alleviate ailments such as saddle sores and distemper," High Hawk continued. "It is said that a horse has understanding. If you see a horse put his head down and sidle along when he is ridden, someone is mistreating him. If you take care of him and have compassion for him, when you get on him he is going to want people to know he is proud. Horses are smart. When there are people about, he is going to nicker and hold his head up. That horse is going to try to make you look good to others."

He glanced again at Joylynn's steed, then into Joylynn's eyes. "Horses are creatures of *Tirawahut*, and they must be treated with respect," he said. "But there are always evildoers who will mistreat anything."

"Who is *Tirawahut?*" Joylynn asked.

"The Pawnee's Great Spirit, as your God is your Great Spirit," he said. Then he took her hand and helped her to her feet. "We can spend no more time watering the horses or teaching you the knowledge that you must have now that you are a part of the Pawnee's lives."

Frustrated at his including her as a part of his people, Joylynn went to Swiftie and swung herself into her saddle. She rode beside High Hawk as he led his warriors, with the stolen horses trailing behind them.

Everyone was quiet as they rode onward until up ahead Joylynn saw the Pawnee village. The moon illuminated many tepees in the shadow of a tall bluff, and glittered on the surface of a river rolling past not far away.

Fires flared before almost a hundred lodges, smoke spiraling lazily from their smoke holes. The tepees were arranged in a semicircle, with an opening left facing the river.

Joylynn was frightened at the prospect of facing

so many Pawnee. She had become accustomed to High Hawk and his warrior friends, but she knew how whites were resented among Indians. She hoped that this warrior who abducted her was of a high rank and would not be challenged by anyone.

She rode onward at High Hawk's side, feeling cold and trembling from fear.

CHAPTER SIX

Dawn was breaking along the horizon as Joylynn rode into the village with High Hawk close beside her. Upon arriving at the outskirts, she had noticed huge fields of corn, beans, squash and other plants.

Close by, where the river ran snakelike over the land, there were clusters of scrub oak with heavier timbers of elm, cottonwood and willow.

The village itself was clean and neat, hardly a tepee was soiled or yellowed with age.

People were awake now, women, children and warriors alike, coming to their entranceways, lifting their flaps, to see who was arriving so early.

Some of their eyes went immediately to Joylynn, studying her, while others, mainly the men, looked intently at the horses that had been captured and brought home.

The onlookers did not come out to meet High

Hawk and his warriors, but went back inside their lodges to prepare for the long day ahead.

The smell of food cooking over lodge fires made Joylynn's stomach growl even though she had recently eaten High Hawk's kind offering of what he had called *wasna*.

It had been satisfying to the taste, and had eased her hunger. Her belly now seemed always in need of nourishment, and she knew why.

The child.

She was now eating for two!

She sighed heavily because she was not only hungry, but also bone-weary and sleepy. She hoped that she could stay awake and alert long enough to ascertain whether or not she would be safe here with High Hawk.

She looked quickly at him as he stopped before one of the larger lodges of the village, while his warriors took the stolen horses to one of his corrals.

It was now only herself and High Hawk, and she could not help being afraid, even though he had been nothing but gentle toward her up until now.

She flinched when a small boy came from a nearby tepee and hurried to High Hawk. When he dismounted he gave his reins to the young brave.

High Hawk came to Joylynn and gently lifted her from her horse, then handed her reins to the young brave as well. The boy hurried around the tepee, to a small corral that Joylynn had seen earlier.

She wondered how many horses High Hawk owned. Was he one of the richest men in this village?

Wondering about his riches and power made her give him a sideways glance as he took her elbow and led her into the huge tepee.

It was obvious tonight that he had been in charge of the warriors who rode with him, for it was he who had given the commands.

But surely he was not their chief, for no one had addressed him as such, nor had he told her that he was a chief.

So she assumed that his riches made him a leader of sorts, and tonight he had become a richer man by the number of horses he had captured.

Had he gained even more wealth in the eyes of the Pawnee people because he had captured a white woman? She didn't see how capturing a woman could make any man look rich, or any way at all except cowardly!

"This is my home," High Hawk said, dropping his hand from her elbow. He leaned his rifle against the outside cover of his lodge, close to the door, then turned to Joylynn. "Do not be afraid. I mean you no harm."

"You mean me no harm, yet . . . yet . . . you take me from my home?"

She placed her fists on her hips. "Let me tell you something. I have come face to face with more danger in my life than you could imagine, and I have survived it all just fine. I shall survive your abduction, too."

Of course she knew she had just told him a lie, for she had not come out of the rape just fine. But she had to look strong and courageous in the eyes of this red man; perhaps then he would respect her.

But when she glanced up at him, she was uncertain how he had reacted to her statement.

It was hard to read this man. He seemed practiced at keeping his feelings to himself.

Her clenched jaw softened and her eyes wavered when he turned away from her and made no reply. Instead, he gestured toward soft pelts that were spread beside a slowly burning fire in the center of the tepee.

"Sit," High Hawk said, smiling to himself at the way this woman continually proved that she was not just any woman. Her fiery spirit fascinated High Hawk.

Ho, his mother was filled with much fire. She was in control of herself and all things around her.

But this white woman was different from his mother in ways that he liked.

He was going to enjoy having her with him!

Knowing she had no other choice but to do as he said, at least until she found a way to escape his clutches, Joylynn sat down on the pelts while he added wood to the fire.

He removed the binoculars from around his neck and set them aside, then sat down beside her.

Between them lay a beautiful rush mat with a variety of food in bowls and platters spread upon it. No doubt it had been brought there by someone when the approach of the horses was heard.

He offered Joylynn a wooden bowl and a spoon made of horn.

He nodded toward an earthen vessel shaped like a bread tray, filled with pieces of what she believed was more *wasna*, as well as ribs that looked delicious. In other bowls were foods that she did not recognize.

It was all tempting, yet not knowing what most of the dishes were, Joylynn hesitated, even though her belly was aching from hunger.

"Eat and then you can rest while I go and attend to some personal duties," High Hawk said, noticing that she hesitated to take anything in her bowl.

He thought it might be because she was afraid to eat food his people cooked. He hoped she was not so prejudiced that she believed his people's food was too dirty for her.

She *had* eaten the *wasna* he had given her.

As she continued to stare at the food, High Hawk pointed to one thing and then another.

"There you have pemmican, which is dried meat pounded into paste with fat and berries," he said. He pointed to something else. "There you have a brace of buffalo ribs, delightfully roasted."

Again he pointed to another bowl. "And here is something my mother made this morning," he said.

"This bowl contains a kind of pudding made of a delicious turnip of the prairie, finely flavored with buffalo berries, which resemble dried currants."

She started to nod and reach for some of the food, but stopped when he cut a piece of meat from the ribs and threw it into the fire.

He didn't explain his action, but she guessed that it was some sort of sacrifice he felt he must perform before eating.

As he seemed to be waiting for her to place food in her bowl, she hurriedly took small pieces of everything, then dipped some of the pudding into her bowl beside the other food.

She glanced up at him and saw that her behavior seemed to have pleased him, for he was smiling.

But his smile faded when an elderly woman came into the lodge, her look anything but friendly. She gazed down at Joylynn with contempt in her faded old brown eyes.

Joylynn was glad when the woman turned to High Hawk as he rose to embrace her. Joylynn could only conclude this was High Hawk's mother.

The woman wore an elaborately beaded ankle-length dress; her graying hair fell in one long braid down her back. Her face was lined with wrinkles, yet still beautiful.

But in her eyes a look of anger and utter contempt made Joylynn uncomfortable. Did she disapprove of her son bringing a captive home, or was it his kind treatment of his captive that angered her?

"Your father left right after you departed to check on a buffalo herd that had been sighted, and he has not yet returned," Blanket Woman said tightly. "I am getting concerned."

"*Ina*, Father has done this before," he said calmly. "He may be gone for many days."

"Your *ahte* is no longer a young man," Blanket Woman said. "His body is not as strong as it once was."

"Do not worry," High Hawk said. Then, just as he started to introduce Joylynn to his mother, Blanket Woman took him by an arm and led him to the entrance flap.

"Come outside with me," she said, yanking on his arm.

Trying not to be embarrassed by his mother's antics, High Hawk hurried outside, leaving Joylynn alone, her eyes wide at the confrontation between mother and son.

Joylynn was put off by the older woman. She was abrasive. She was someone who did not care whether or not she was humiliating her proud son in the presence of . . . of . . . a captive.

Joylynn listened as the woman scolded High Hawk. Her angry tone was evident, even though Joylynn knew that his mother was trying to keep her voice down.

But Joylynn could tell from all that the old woman was saying to High Hawk that she did not approve of his having brought her home with him.

Joylynn heard the woman tell High Hawk that he should not have a white woman in his lodge. He, who would one day be chief, should be keeping his lodge pure, for soon he would be choosing a wife to bear him children . . . to carry on their family bloodline because his crippled brother could not do so.

Joylynn realized from what she had just heard that High Hawk had no wife. Of course that should mean nothing to her, but strangely enough, somewhere deep down, where her desires were formed, she did care.

Feeling foolish for allowing herself to think such thoughts, she focused again on what the elderly woman was saying to High Hawk, and then anxiously awaited his response. But all that she now heard was silence. A moment later High Hawk came back inside the tepee and sat down beside Joylynn again, where he proceeded to eat without saying a word.

She knew that he had taken a scolding from his mother, but out of respect, had said nothing back to her.

The more time Joylynn spent with High Hawk, the less she saw him as someone who would enjoy taking a woman captive, yet . . . yet . . . he had!

Joylynn had also learned something else about her captor. She was in the presence of a powerful man who would one day be chief of his people. His mother had said as much.

Joylynn wasn't sure if this knowledge should

alarm her, or make her feel less threatened. It was surely up to him what her future would be now.

And what was this about a brother?

No sooner was the thought formed than the very person she was wondering about came into the tepee.

He seemed painfully shy in her presence; his eyes would not linger long with hers.

She could not help looking at his twisted body, for it was like nothing she had ever seen before. But she soon realized that he knew she was looking at his deformity, and, not wanting to embarrass him, she looked quickly away.

"This is my brother, Sleeping Wolf," High Hawk said, rising and placing a gentle arm around his brother's twisted shoulders.

High Hawk then stepped away from him and gestured with a hand toward Joylynn. "Brother, this woman is my captive," he said tersely. "Her name is Joylynn."

"You have brought a captive into your home?" Sleeping Wolf gasped, his eyes wide as he stared at Joylynn. When her eyes met his again, he saw in them compassion, not pity.

He could not help liking her immediately.

But not being used to kind treatment from strangers, and unsure how he should react to this captive, he turned and limped away, leaving the tepee almost as quickly as he had come.

High Hawk gazed down at Joylynn. "My brother

was born with an affliction that keeps him from doing as others do," he said sadly. "He cannot ride a horse. He cannot shoot arrows. He cannot do the things that he would like to do, the things that normally make parents proud. But we could not be any more proud of Sleeping Wolf if his back were straight and he could do as others do. He is someone well loved by our people. He is a man who never wants to be pitied."

Joylynn wanted to tell him that she did not pity his brother, but he suddenly turned and left before she could speak.

She watched for him to return, and when he didn't, she shoved the bowl of half-eaten food away and stared into the flames of the fire. She was feeling less and less threatened, except . . . for High Hawk's mother, who seemed to detest her mere presence. She knew she must be watchful of this elderly woman.

And how would High Hawk's father, a powerful Pawnee chief, behave toward her when he arrived home from his search for buffalo? Would he approve of her being there, or disapprove?

She looked slowly around her, at High Hawk's personal belongings. On a pole at the far back of the lodge was hung a shield painted with scenes of fallen buffalo, with arrows lodged in their bellies.

Beside this was another pole on which hung a quiver of many arrows; the quiver seemed to be made from the hide of a cougar.

Close beside these was a huge bow, with its string loosened.

Elsewhere around the inner circle of the room lay travel bags and other items for daily life. Rolled-up blankets and pelts were stored against the wall, ready to be used for bedding.

She wondered if she would remain in High Hawk's lodge while she was there as his captive.

If so, where . . . would . . . she sleep?

And . . . would he want to bed her?

She could only watch and wait . . . and hope that he wouldn't try to force her. One other man had, and she was living with the results . . . the child she was carrying!

She placed her hand on her belly, wondering what High Hawk would think, or do, when he discovered that he had stolen away a pregnant woman?

More importantly, what would his mother do? She already seemed to loathe Joylynn's presence. How would she react when she learned that her son's captive was carrying a white child in her belly?

Joylynn gazed again at the arrows in the quiver, then at the bow. She knew not the first thing about bows and arrows, but she wondered if she could use an arrow as a weapon against High Hawk if he were to threaten her.

The thought made her cringe. She realized that she did not want to kill him.

She waited and waited for his return, but he did not come back. Finally, she eased down on the blankets spread out beside the fire and fell into a restful sleep. She was awakened sometime later by the sound of a voice angrily calling her name.

CHAPTER SEVEN

Joylynn grimaced as she recognized the voice. It belonged to High Hawk's mother. Although it was obvious that the woman despised her son's captive, for some reason she had come for Joylynn.

She took Joylynn roughly by the hand and pulled her outside. "I am Blanket Woman," she announced as she took Joylynn behind a nearby tepee and gestured at a hole that had been dug there. "This is my personal cache pit. You will help me finish digging it."

Joylynn had no idea what a cache pit was, and when she asked Blanket Woman, the elderly woman tightly explained that it was the storage pit where her family's crops were piled after they were harvested.

It did not take long for Joylynn to understand why the older woman had asked for her help. It was grueling work, especially with the sun beating down on them as they worked.

Although Joylynn was angry at the older woman because of the way she'd been treated, she could not help being concerned about Blanket Woman's health as she labored to get the cache pit ready for the coming harvest.

Under the copper color of Blanket Woman's face, Joylynn saw a pronounced redness. Clearly the older woman was having trouble with the heat.

Sympathetic to all elderly people, Joylynn wanted to tell Blanket Woman to go and stand in the shade for a while. She could rest while Joylynn continued to prepare the storage pit.

But the loathing in Blanket Woman's eyes made Joylynn think better of offering her anything. Probably, Blanket Woman would laugh at her for trying to be kind. She seemed the spiteful sort, someone that Joylynn could never like.

"Watch what you are doing," Blanket Woman snapped as she paused. They were digging the earthen wall with hoes made of bone, stopping occasionally to carry away bowls full of earth. "If you do not do this in the right way, the wall will tumble back down and we will have to start all over again."

Joylynn paused and gave Blanket Woman a wary stare, taking time to wipe the perspiration from her brow. She could feel the wetness of her hair as it clung to her neck. Her dress was soaked and clung to her body, causing Joylynn to be afraid that someone might notice the slight swell of her belly.

She kept pulling the dress away from herself, but she was afraid that Blanket Woman was astute enough to notice her pregnancy.

"Are we almost through?" Joylynn asked, feeling bone-tired and sleepy.

She used to be able to ride all day, even into the night, without stopping to eat or rest.

Now? Because of her pregnancy, she could hardly go a few hours without needing both!

"*Ho*, we are almost finished. It should not take long now," Blanket Woman said, also wiping sweat from her brow. "Soon we will lay hides at the bottom, and the sides will be lined by grass to keep the contents dry."

Joylynn noticed that the cache was shaped like a bottle with a narrow neck, and decreased in size toward the top.

"To load the cache, a hide will be laid out near the pit so that one end will hang over the mouth. I will sit there while I place the harvest inside," Blanket Woman said, resuming digging and nodding to Joylynn to do the same. "Large baskets of corn will be placed there as well as many strings of braided corn. Also there will be a number of strings of dried squash. The braided corn will be laid on the floor and along the sides of the cache, the shelled corn will be placed inside that, and squash will be inserted in the middle."

She paused, wiped sweat from her brow, then resumed digging and talking as though she felt the need to talk to forget the drudgery of the moment. "After the cache is full, a circular cover made of thick skin from the flank of a bull buffalo will be placed over the top," she said. "Next I will lay down a layer of dry grass, and over this I will place puncheons, which are strong planks designed to make sure that if a horse steps on the cache, he will not go through it. Over the puncheon I will place packed earth, and above this, ashes and refuse to disguise the location of the cache."

"Why would you want to disguise where it has been dug?" Joylynn asked, again pausing to wipe perspiration from her brow.

"So that strangers who might come in the night to steal from the Pawnee cannot find it," Blanket Woman said, looking quickly over her shoulder and smiling when High Hawk came walking toward them.

He stepped up next to Joylynn and gazed at her. He saw her flushed cheeks and perspiration-soaked hair, but said nothing about it. It was good to have her there to help his mother. Blanket Woman seemed older of late, and not as able to do things as she did only a moon ago.

"And so there you are, sweat-free, doing nothing, while your mother and I are scorching hot from digging this damnable cache pit," Joylynn blurted out as she placed her left fist on her hip and glared at High Hawk. "I see now why you brought me to your home. I am to be your slave."

"No, I did not bring you here to be a slave," High Hawk said, impressed by her fiery spirit. He was amazed that she would stand up to him, her captor, when she had no idea what he might do to her for her defiant attitude. He gestured toward his mother, who had again paused to wipe sweat from her brow. "You are just doing what all Pawnee women do, and they are not slaves; or would you call my own mother a slave?"

"Well, yes, I would," Joylynn snapped back. "And must I remind you that I, Joylynn, am not Pawnee!"

He gave her a half smile, then walked away and entered the huge council house at the edge of the village, while Joylynn turned and gave Blanket Woman an angry stare. Then she went back to helping the elderly woman, because she knew she had no other choice. And the faster she worked and got this pit finished, the sooner she could rest.

After the last of the dirt was carried away and the cache pit was finally finished, Blanket Woman stepped up to Joylynn and took the bone hoe from her. "Go to the river and bathe with the rest of the women," she said tightly. "I shall join you there soon."

Joylynn's heart skipped a beat as she gazed at the river, where the other women were already gathered. Then she glanced at Blanket Woman, who was walking away from her with the digging tool.

Finally she looked down at her tummy. If she bathed in the river with the rest of the women, surely they would be able to tell that she was pregnant.

She thought of not going to the river, of returning to High Hawk's tepee instead, but knowing how vile she smelled, she knew she had no choice but to bathe.

"Come with me," Blanket Woman said as she returned to Joylynn, grabbing her arm. "You will bathe. You will not stink up my son's lodge."

Joylynn sighed and walked with her until they reached an isolated place in the river where the women were undressed and already in the water.

She stepped back from Blanket Woman, who was removing her own clothes, but Joylynn still made no move to unfasten her dress.

"You . . . will . . . bathe!" Blanket Woman snapped as she glared at Joylynn. The older woman stood there before her unashamed, totally nude. She grabbed the hem of Joylynn's dress and started to raise it up over her head, but Joylynn yanked it away from her.

"I refuse to go nude in the water with you women," Joylynn said, then ran into the water fully clothed.

She saw the incredulous looks the women gave her, but she ignored them and splashed herself with the wonderfully refreshing cool water. She dipped her hair down into it and rubbed her fingers through the wet strands.

She was the last one out of the water, for she was

truly enjoying the coolness and refreshing wonder of it.

When she finally left the river, she went back to High Hawk's tepee, glad that he hadn't returned yet.

She hurried out of her wet clothes and dug inside her travel bag, taking from it a clean dress. She removed her hairbrush from her bag and brushed her hair until it lay neatly over her shoulders, then shoved the brush back inside the bag.

Feeling so tired and sleepy, she spread out a roll of blankets at the back of the tepee, away from the fire, and lay down. Gratefully she breathed in the fresh air coming from where the lower part of the buckskin hide had been rolled up.

Then she noticed another change. While she had been gone, High Hawk had removed all of his weapons from the lodge. He had probably taken them to his parents' tepee for safekeeping. She supposed he had thought better of leaving them so handy for Joylynn's use.

She had yet to see her own rifle since she'd arrived at High Hawk's tepee. Surely he had put it, with the rest of his firearms, out of her reach.

Too tired to think any more about these things, she slept for a while, only to be awakened again by Blanket Woman, who'd brought a maize cake and shudock berries for her to eat.

After her meal, Joylynn stretched out again on the blankets and found comfort and solace once more in sleep.

She wasn't aware of High Hawk coming into the tepee and resting on his haunches beside where she lay. She didn't know that he reached a hand to her hair and ran his fingers through it.

"I have never seen anyone so beautiful," he whispered to himself. He smiled. "Or so feisty."

He liked both things about this woman. For now, she was his captive. But soon he hoped to change her status among his people!

CHAPTER EIGHT

Light spiraling down through the smoke hole above her awakened Joylynn. She realized that she had slept the entire night, and this time without nightmares.

She would have thought that her nightmares would have doubled as her mind replayed not only images of the highwayman and the rape, but also her abduction by the Pawnee. But in any case, she was glad that she had had a good night's sleep.

She turned slightly to the right, finding a blanket hanging on a rope strung from one side of the tepee to the other. High Hawk must have placed it there last night while Joylynn slept.

She was surprised that he had recognized her need for privacy. She was touched by his thoughtfulness.

Her pulse raced and she tried not to make a sound as she slowly lifted the blanket so she could look beneath it.

Her eyes went instantly to High Hawk, who sat before a newly built fire, his back to her.

He had no idea that she was awake as she slyly watched him while he prepared his hair for the day ahead of him. He was already dressed in a shirt and leggings of fringed buckskin that set off his splendid physique to advantage.

To Joylynn's eyes, he was uniquely handsome, and she had to fight the feelings that were growing within her.

She felt something for him that she had thought she would never feel for a man, especially since the horrible rape.

But she had never met anyone like him before . . . noble, gentle, and thus far, a gentleman as far as she was concerned. The blanket he had hung between their sleeping quarters proved just how gentlemanly he was toward her, making her almost forget that she was his captive.

She continued to watch him as he smoothed his thick, raven-black hair back from his face with deer marrow, then slid a beaded headband in place.

She drew in a quick breath, giving herself away. Her eyes met and held High Hawk's as he turned and found her there, obviously watching him.

But he didn't have a chance to say anything, for a woman's voice outside the tepee distracted him. "I have brought food for you and your captive."

He opened the entrance flap and thanked the woman as he took the platter of food from her.

Bringing it inside, he set it down on blankets spread out before the fire.

High Hawk turned toward Joylynn, who was still watching him. He smiled and beckoned with a hand. "Come. Sit and eat with me," he invited.

Dressed in the same clothes she had put on immediately after her bath in the river, and very aware of the wrinkles in her dress, Joylynn rose and sat down beside the platter of food, while High Hawk sat on the other side.

She eyed it all hungrily, seeing an assortment of vegetables, small flat cakes and fruit.

As High Hawk dished out the food on separate wooden plates, Joylynn hurriedly ran her long, slender fingers through her hair in an effort to remove the tangles from it.

High Hawk glanced quickly at her as he prepared their plates, wishing it were his fingers moving through her hair. He recalled how soft it was last night when he had taken the liberty to touch it while she slept.

He had ached to do more than that. He had wanted to kiss her!

But he was an honorable man and he would not take advantage of a woman as she slept, even if she *was* his captive. He knew most of his warriors would feel they could do as they pleased with a captive. But he wasn't just anyone. He was a man who would one day be a proud Pawnee chief. And he wanted the respect that was due an honorable, proud chief.

He wanted *her* respect!

Joylynn had not noticed High Hawk's longing glances. She was oblivious to everything but getting food into her stomach.

She took a plate from him and ate. As soon as her hunger abated, Joylynn eyed him cautiously.

"Has your father returned from the buffalo hunt yet?" she blurted out, bringing his eyes quickly to her. "I know that your mother was worried. I'm sure you were, too."

Surprised by her sudden question, and her apparent concern about whether or not his father had returned, High Hawk paused in his meal and gazed into her beautiful green eyes.

Then he shook his head slowly back and forth. "No, *Ahte* has not arrived home yet," he said. He set his plate aside without finishing all the food on it.

He glanced over his shoulder at his closed entrance flap, and then into Joylynn's eyes. "I am worried," he admitted. "Yet I have known my father to be gone for seven sleeps when hunting the buffalo. Surely he is all right now, as he has always been before."

"I hope he is all right," Joylynn murmured. She popped a blackberry into her mouth and enjoyed the tantalizing juices as she chewed.

Then she pushed her plate aside and gazed at High Hawk again. "Your mother and you have talked of your one brother," she murmured. "Are there any other brothers or sisters?"

"Our family numbers four," High Hawk said. "Only two sons were born to my *ahte* and *ina*. My brother, the older, has taken much time from my *ina*, because he was born with a twisted back. It is sad that he cannot do as others his age do. But I have tried to make up for it by taking him with me whenever possible."

"I'm sure he appreciates it," Joylynn said, finding it odd to be sitting there discussing such things with the man who was her captor.

But the longer she was with him, the less she felt like a captive.

It was as though she were just there as a friend, discussing things and enjoying his company.

But it was foolish to think that way, for she knew that soon he would be giving commands about the things he wanted her to do.

Yesterday it was helping to dig the cache pit.

Today? She hated thinking what the chores might be!

"I will always remember how my brother watched as I learned the skills of a warrior," High Hawk said softly. "Before I was twelve winters of age, I was assigned to stalk a deer. My brother tried to join me, but found it too hard and had to return home."

"What were you doing that was so hard for him?" Joylynn asked, leaning forward so that she could look more directly into his eyes.

"While stalking the deer, I had to move a small

bush before me, crawling, and pausing for long intervals as I watched the deer for signs of alarm. Lying flat, I waited to crawl again, doing so across long stretches of prairie. My brother's body would not tolerate any of this. Even I learned the excruciating patience that was necessary to stalk the deer."

He drew his legs up before him and locked his arms around them as he gazed pensively into the flames. "Entering my teen years, I was allowed to track bear," he said. "I am very glad my brother was not with me one day when I was doing so, for surely one or both of us would have perished."

"What happened?" Joylynn asked, her eyes anxious.

He turned his gaze toward her. "I rounded a point of rock high in the mountains and came face to face with my first grizzly," he said. "The bear rose, towering above me. In that brief moment of indecision, which only the eagle recognizes in the snake, I shot forward between the massive arms of the bear and plunged my lance into its heart."

Joylynn gasped and turned pale.

"I dodged the crushing sweeps of its paws, running, inches from death, until the grizzly finally fell," High Hawk said.

Seeing how impressed she was by this tale, he squared his shoulders and told her another. "Often I rode recklessly as I hunted buffalo with my lance," he said. "My friends and I drove turkeys from the mountain ravines onto the plains. Riding our ponies, we chased the turkeys until they tired; then we youths swept among the turkeys, snatching them from the ground."

"How interesting," Joylynn said. "I . . . I . . . remember my father bringing home wild turkeys for my mother to prepare. Thanksgiving was when they were the most sought."

"Thanksgiving?" High Hawk asked, raising an eyebrow. "What is this thing . . . Thanksgiving?"

"It was a time for giving thanks," she explained.

And then, knowing that she wouldn't be allowed to just sit by as the other women of the village worked, she asked, "What are my duties today?"

"The horse care falls to women," High Hawk replied. "They care for the animals each day, usually in the morning after their morning meal."

"What . . . is . . . required of them?" Joylynn asked guardedly, though she was sure she was up to this task. She knew everything about how to care for horses.

"The women take the manure from the corral and dispose of it in the river," he said, seeing that this comment made Joylynn wince. "Then they go to the coulees to cut grass, which they haul home on their backs and store for fodder. Sometimes the women cut cottonwood bark to feed the horses."

"And . . . which of those things . . . will I be made to do today?" Joylynn asked.

"All of it," High Hawk said matter-of-factly.

No.

She couldn't believe it.

She had never realized an Indian woman's life was so hard.

But she would not allow herself to look weaker than they. She would show High Hawk and everyone else that she could take whatever he and his mother dished out to her.

"And I assume you expect me to join the women even now?" Joylynn asked, challenging him with her eyes.

"*Ho*, now," High Hawk said, amused at how she was trying to disguise her dismay at what was expected of her today. "The women leave as soon as they have fed their husband and children the morning meal. I imagine most of them are already outside in their husbands' corrals, scooping up manure."

Although Joylynn had always taken special care of her own horse, never leaving manure standing in Swiftie's corral, the fact remained that it was only one horse's droppings. From what she had seen of High Hawk's corral, there would be a lot of manure to scoop up and carry away.

And that was only the one corral she could see.

"Do I have to clean all of your corrals?" she asked.

"One is all that will be required of you today," High Hawk said, rising and playfully holding aside the entrance flap for her. "The one behind my tepee."

"Well, thank *you*, kind sir," Joylynn said sarcastically, hating to leave the tepee without changing into clean clothes. She even had the private chore of relieving herself to see to, and wondered where on earth she might go in broad daylight to do that.

She would go into the thick shadows of the forest not far from his corral. She just hoped that the sentries wouldn't think she was trying to sneak away and come upon her in the middle of her personal chore.

She would never be able to live down the embarrassment!

But knowing how asinine it was to think of being embarrassed by anything while being treated in such an ungodly way, she lifted her chin and walked briskly past High Hawk. Then she realized that she was barefoot.

Sighing heavily, she turned and walked past him again into the tepee. After slipping her shoes on, she left again, her head held high.

She found a wooden bucket beside the corral, and a shovel made of bone. She was glad that the day was not yet unbearably hot, as it had been yesterday. She hurried through the chore, all the while imagining that the stink of manure was soaking right into her pores. It seemed to take forever before she had hauled the last load to the river and dumped it into the water.

She eyed the manure as it floated away, making a note never to put one foot in the river there, or downstream, where the other women were dumping their buckets of manure into the water.

She cringed when she wondered whether the manure might float down to where the women bathed daily. If so, might she step into a pile while walking out into the water for her bath?

She shook such a thought from her mind and returned the bucket to the corral. She took the time to stop and stroke her steed's sleek mane, seeing that someone was taking good care of Swiftie, and wondering who it might be.

Surely it was High Hawk, for he did seem to have a deep love of all horses. She was afraid that she had lost the horse to him, but she would change that when she found a chance to flee.

She turned when she felt someone's presence behind her.

She frowned when she found Blanket Woman standing there, her arms folded across her chest.

"What now?" Joylynn asked, sighing heavily.

"You do not think you are finished for the day, do you?" Blanket Woman snapped.

"No, so what is it you want of me?" Joylynn said tightly. "What chore must I do now to earn my . . . keep?"

Blanket Woman slapped the handle of a hatchet into Joylynn's hand and gave her a wicked smile, causing Joylynn's face to lose its color.

CHAPTER NINE

"Do not look as though I was going to use the hatchet on you," Blanket Woman said, cackling as she saw Joylynn's horrified expression.

"I did not think so," Joylynn said, trying to ignore Blanket Woman's continued obvious dislike of her "Are you going to tell me what I am to do, or am I supposed to guess? I'm not a mind reader, you know."

"The hatchet is used to remove bark from cottonwood trees," Blanket Woman said, this time matter-of-factly. She placed the handle of a basket in Joylynn's hand. "You are to bring the bark back in this basket and feed it to my son's horses." She harrumphed. "And also the one that you call yours."

"That horse *is* mine," Joylynn protested, not wanting to believe that Swiftie belonged to someone else. "It has been mine for many years. My horse and I went through all kinds of adventures together when I worked as a Pony Express rider."

"I know of such things as the Pony Express. But I have heard that only men carry the white man's written words from place to place, not women," Blanket Woman said, searching Joylynn's eyes. "Surely you lie to impress this old woman."

"I don't care what you think about anything I do or say. I did not tell you that to impress you," Joylynn said flatly. "It just slipped out, that's all."

But in truth, she *had* told the older woman about her being a Pony Express rider in order to let her know that she was dealing with a woman of strength, stamina and spirit.

Yes, it had taken all of those traits to ride for the Pony Express, and she would always be proud that she had been able to handle the job.

"Just . . . slipped . . . out?" Blanket Woman said, squinting into Joylynn's eyes in wonderment. "What is such talk as that?"

"White people's talk, that's what," Joylynn said, then turned and gazed into the forest of cottonwood trees and walked away from Blanket Woman. She was determined to get a good amount of bark in order to prove that she could do whatever task the older woman assigned her.

But when she started trying to cut long strips of bark from a tree with the hatchet, she realized how hard it was. The bark stubbornly clung to the tree's trunk, giving only an inch at a time as Joylynn tried to slice it away.

When the hatchet slipped, barely missing Joylynn's leg, she stepped quickly away from the tree.

She turned with a start when a twig broke behind her. Someone was approaching her through the trees.

Her eyes widened when she found High Hawk's brother coming toward her, smiling. She held the hatchet at her side as he kept approaching, his one leg dragging as he struggled to walk as straight as possible. It was obvious that he was embarrassed by his appearance. He looked into her eyes one moment, smiling, then down at the ground, his smile erased, the next.

"Good morning, Sleeping Wolf," Joylynn said as he stepped up to her.

She felt awkward, not knowing what else to say to him.

She could not help wondering what had brought him into the forest.

"I have come to help," Sleeping Wolf said, taking the hatchet from her. "I watched. I saw how hard it was for you to remove the bark. Let me do it for you. My mother need never know."

"I . . . I . . . don't want to be deceitful," Joylynn murmured. She stepped away from the tree as he came closer, but the first time he tried to cut a strip of bark from the tree, he dropped the hatchet and fell to the ground, groaning with pain as he grabbed at his back.

"Oh, no," Joylynn said, bending quickly beside him to help him up.

But before she had the chance, he managed to get to his feet and hurried away as fast as his crippled body would take him. Obviously, he was embarrassed at his failure to help her.

Too stunned at first to do anything but watch him, Joylynn then ran after him, hoping to soothe him. She was stopped when Blanket Woman stepped from behind a tree, blocking her way. Her eyes were filled with venomous anger.

"I saw what happened," Blanket Woman said, leaning into Joylynn's face. "I had come to check how you were doing, and what do I find? My crippled son trying to help you, then falling and embarrassing himself in front of you, a white woman."

"You look at me as though it is my fault," Joylynn said, taking slow steps away from Blanket Woman. "I didn't ask him to help me. He just came and took my hatchet, and before I knew it, he . . . he . . . was on the ground."

"Did you not hear me say I saw how it happened?" Blanket Woman said tightly. "I do not fault you for what he did, but I would fault you if you went to him and made him feel even more foolish."

"I would never do that," Joylynn said softly.

"Then turn around and go back to what you

were doing before my son interfered," Blanket Woman said, taking Joylynn by the arm and turning her back toward the cottonwood forest.

"I have to admit that I did not peel even one strip of bark from the tree with the hatchet," Joylynn said reluctantly. "I just couldn't do it. How on earth do the other women manage it?"

"It takes practice," Blanket Woman said, releasing her hold on Joylynn as they stepped up to the tree where Joylynn had done only a small bit of damage.

It did not take long for the older woman to cut several strips of bark, and she did not stop until she had many piled up on the ground.

"Shouldn't I be doing that?" Joylynn asked, her voice drawn.

Blanket Woman turned a glare Joylynn's way, then continued her work.

"Place the bark in the basket," Blanket Woman said, laying the hatchet at the bottom of the basket before Joylynn put the bark in it.

Blanket Woman placed her hands at the small of her back, stretched and groaned. "I have done enough of your labor today," she said.

Joylynn wanted to say that she hadn't asked Blanket Woman to do it for her, but she held her tongue. She was grateful for whatever help she could get.

Joylynn started placing the bark in stacks in the basket but stopped when Blanket Woman placed a sudden hand on her wrist.

Joylynn looked questioningly into the older woman's faded brown eyes.

"I have something more to say about Sleeping Wolf," she said tightly. "Stay away from him. Never give him cause to believe a woman can look past his twisted back. I don't want him to be hurt by rejection in the end."

"I . . . would . . . never do anything to hurt your son," Joylynn said, yanking her wrist away from Blanket Woman. "I like him as a friend. Surely he realizes that."

"Just listen to what I say," Blanket Woman said heatedly. "Heed my words, white woman. You must not talk to Sleeping Wolf, or encourage him, or you will pay dearly for it."

Joylynn had never done or said anything to this man that might make him believe she cared for him as anything but just a friend. Stunned by the warning, she stared into Blanket Woman's eyes.

When she saw fiery determination there, she knew better than to try to explain anything else about her feelings for Sleeping Wolf. The older woman was so blinded by her need to keep her son safe from a "woman's clutches," she did not know the truth when it was right in front of her.

Sighing, Joylynn resumed placing the bark in the basket, surprised when Blanket Woman began helping her.

"It is done," Blanket Woman said, placing her hands at her waist. She was obviously uncomfortable from the bending and stooping. "You carry the basket back to the village. There is no need to tell the other women that it was I who peeled the bark, not you."

Joylynn looked in amazement at Blanket Woman. Was the woman perhaps trying to make up for her earlier harsh words?

"The basket," Blanket Woman said softly, nodding toward it. "Get the basket. The other women should be home by now, finished with their chores for the day."

The more the woman showed such kindness, the more puzzled Joylynn became.

But she truly was happy for the change.

Could Blanket Woman, in time, be a friend to Joylynn? She desperately needed a friend in this place.

Although Joylynn was mesmerized by High Hawk, she could not let herself show him that she had feelings for him. She must never forget that she was his captive.

She wanted her freedom back, and she would have it, some way, somehow.

She thanked Blanket Woman, then walked to the village alongside her.

When the other women saw Joylynn with the basket of bark, they gave her looks of approval, some even smiling at her. Joylynn felt uncomfortable that she was allowing them to believe she had gathered the bark herself.

But since Blanket Woman had suggested the deceit, Joylynn took the credit that had been granted her.

She watched the women go to their husbands' corrals and place the bark there for their horses to feed on. Following suit, Joylynn went to High Hawk's corral and emptied her basket there.

She smiled when Swiftie approached the bark, sniffed, then turned his head away, as though putting his nose in the air over being offered such a thing to eat. He went back to where the grass was thick and nibbled on it.

"That's my boy," Joylynn said, going to him and patting his thick neck. "You know what's best for you, don't you?"

Swiftie whinnied, gave her a look with his big brown eyes, then resumed eating as Joylynn walked from the corral and hurried toward High Hawk's tepee.

She stopped when she saw the women gathering together with their clean clothes and bathing supplies, then walking in a group toward the river.

Knowing she was filthy after her long day of work at the Pawnee village, she hurried after the women.

She looked around for Blanket Woman, and when she didn't see her, wondered where she was. The day before, she'd joined the others to bathe. Had the old woman overtired herself doing Joylynn's work? she wondered, feeling guilty.

When they all reached the river, Joylynn again bathed with her dress on, ignoring the curious looks of the other women.

Ignoring them, Joylynn enjoyed her time in the water, making certain her hair got a good soaking, for she did not want to smell of anything but river water when High Hawk entered his lodge for the evening.

Although she did not want to feel anything special for this man, she could not fight off the spiraling need that sometimes overwhelmed her.

He made her feel like a woman in a way no other man had ever done.

And she knew that if he tried to embrace her, she would allow it. She needed to know if her feelings for him were true, or just a figment of her active imagination.

If she did care deeply for him, what was she to do when she found a way to escape him?

Could she flee if it meant never seeing him again?

Her thoughts were so full of High Hawk, she wasn't even aware that the women were leaving the water until she found that she was alone.

Since they were already on shore, dressing, she lingered in the water for a while longer. She did not want them to see what her wet and clinging dress might reveal.

Only when they had all headed back toward their homes did Joylynn leave the water.

When she reached High Hawk's tepee, she was glad to see that he wasn't there. She would have a moment of privacy to change into a dry dress, one that was not revealing.

Once she had on dry clothes, she realized how worn-out she was. Sleep seemed even more important than food, even though her belly was grumbling loudly.

She went back to her bed of blankets, stretched out and was soon fast asleep.

Again she was plagued by the same nightmare that had troubled her almost every night since the rape.

She cried out in her sleep, then awakened with a start, wet with sweat. As she sat up, she realized that eyes were on her.

She had forgotten to lower the blanket that gave her privacy while she slept. She looked quickly over to where High Hawk stood just inside the entranceway. He must have only now arrived back home.

High Hawk came quickly to her.

He knelt down beside her. "What has caused you to cry out in your sleep?" he asked, searching her eyes.

Her heart pounding, she turned her eyes away. There was no way on God's earth that she would tell him about the rape.

Oh, Lord, she had to escape before she got much larger, for she did not want this lovely man to know what she had endured at Mole's hands. It was something she did not ever want to say aloud to anyone.

She just wanted to have the child, hand it over to a preacher, then get on with her life. Until then, she had to continue guarding her secret in every way possible.

"Food is being brought for us," High Hawk said quietly, seeing that Joylynn didn't want to talk about what had disturbed her so.

He would take one day at a time and hope that she would be more open with him soon. He cared so much for her. He wanted to be the one who helped her get past her hidden fears, if she would only allow it.

Then a terrible thought came to him. What if her troubled dreams were caused by his having abducted her?

What if her fear was of him?

His thoughts were interrupted when a woman's voice spoke outside the tepee. "I bring food for you and the white woman."

He lifted the entrance flap and nodded a quiet welcome to the woman, who came into the lodge carrying a platter piled high with an assortment of meats and vegetables.

He took the platter from her, thanked her, then, as she left, placed the food on a mat beside the lodge fire.

Still without saying anything more to Joylynn, he

got two wooden plates and nodded toward them. "Come and sit by the fire with me," he said. "The night has turned chilly. The fire will feel good."

Joylynn gazed up through the smoke hole and noted that day had turned into night. She could feel the breeze as it came through the spaces where the bottom edges of the tepee had been rolled up.

She watched as High Hawk went and closed them, then came back and again nodded toward the food.

"Eat with me and then you can rest again, if you wish," he said thickly. "My mother told me that you worked hard today and that you must be as bone-weary as she."

Joylynn felt guilty about the older woman's tiredness, for it was surely because she had done some of Joylynn's work.

She swallowed hard, then went and sat down beside High Hawk. She realized how hungry she was when the aroma of the cooked venison and corn wafted to her nose.

"Thank you," she murmured when he gave her a plate filled with food. "I am quite famished."

He ate in silence beside her. He watched how hungrily she ate, but his mind kept drifting. He had searched for his father today and had not found him.

His mother even now sat crying beside her lodge fire, fearing the worst.

High Hawk would not give in to those same

fears. He continued to believe that his father would be home soon with an explanation for his delay.

"Has your father returned home yet?" Joylynn asked, as though she had read his thoughts.

All he could do was shake his head, his eyes revealing the despair he was feeling.

"I'm sorry," Joylynn murmured. "Truly I am."

"I believe you," High Hawk said. "I have been with you long enough now to know that you are not only a woman of strength and fire, but also compassion. Your compassion is appreciated."

"Are you going to search for him again?" Joylynn asked, thinking that the more often he left, the more likely it was she would find a way to escape.

But she felt guilty for thinking of herself when she could tell that he was so worried about his father.

"We will continue searching until we find him," High Hawk said tightly. "But I am certain he will come home soon on his own."

Her stomach comfortably full, and her eyes feeling tired again, Joylynn shoved her empty plate aside. "I truly must retire to my bed," she murmured. "May I?"

"You do not have to ask permission for such as that," High Hawk said. He nodded toward her bed of blankets, then followed her there.

For a moment she thought that he might be planning to go to bed with her, but he had only followed her in order to drop the blanket down, to give her privacy while she slept.

She climbed onto the blankets, once again grateful that he treated her with respect. She no longer felt threatened by him. She knew that if he had been going to take her, he would have done it already.

She snuggled onto her side on the blankets and fell into another deep sleep, but this time she dreamed sweet things . . . like riding Swiftie through a meadow of flowers with High Hawk at her side.

They were carefree and happy.

They were laughing.

And then a hawk suddenly swept down from the sky, searching for snakes and rodents, and spooked her horse.

She cried out in her sleep as she fell from Swiftie in her dream, then awakened in a sweat.

No matter that the blanket was there between them, when High Hawk heard her cry out in her sleep again, he could not help going to her to see if she needed comfort.

He hurried to the blanket and held it aside, his heart going out to Joylynn when he saw her leaning on an elbow, tears streaming from her eyes.

"You dreamed bad things again," he said gently.

"Yes, partly . . ." Joylynn said. The beginning of the dream had been so wonderful. She only wished that it could be true, that she could be with High Hawk, happy and carefree.

But it was never to be.

They had met only because he needed a captive.

She had been in the right place at the right time for him to capture.

High Hawk wondered what she meant by "partly," but he did not ask her. She was already lying down again, her eyes closed so she could go back to sleep.

He knelt beside her for a moment and watched her. Then he looked up through the smoke hole and saw the full moon gazing back at him. Again he was filled with concern for his father.

Where . . . could . . . he be?

Tomorrow the search for him would widen, but High Hawk could not go himself. He had duties to his people that kept him home, for while his *ahte* was gone for so long, he had to take over his father's duties as chief.

Ho, tomorrow he would send out his most skilled scouts, who best knew the art of tracking and searching.

If they did not find his father, then High Hawk would truly be worried that his *ahte* might never be home again among his people.

He dropped the blanket down, hiding Joylynn from his sight, but he would not leave her during the night hours.

He would guard her, not because he feared she might flee, but because he did not want someone to come in the night and take her away!

If white eyes knew, somehow, that she was missing, they might already be searching for her.

His jaw tightened. He would not lose this woman to anyone!

She . . . was . . . his!

CHAPTER TEN

Alone, having eaten the morning meal by herself, Joylynn found herself restless, but she was reluctant to go outside and discover what would be required of her today.

Blanket Woman seemed intent on making her work.

Joylynn was afraid that one of these days, while mingling with the other women, one of them would notice her belly and realize that she was with child.

Of course she knew that it would have to happen eventually, for as each day passed, the child grew within her womb.

But she had hoped to keep that knowledge to herself until she found a way to escape. Then nobody but herself would ever need know.

"Escape," she whispered as she shoved the empty wooden plate away from her.

She gazed over at the rolled-up blankets at one side of the tepee, knowing they were used for High Hawk's bed.

She crawled to them and ran a hand slowly over the bundle, then leaned low and smelled them.

A sensual craving that was unfamiliar to her swept through her at the scent of the man she should loathe, but now knew she secretly loved.

Everything about him spoke of gentleness and kindness, even caring.

He had never threatened her in any way, only treated her with respect.

She sighed and sat down by the fire, enjoying its warmth, for the nights and days had suddenly become cooler. She wished she could feel free to love that man, and he her. But the way they had come together was anything but normal, or right.

She was his captive.

He was her captor.

Such relationships should create hate, not infatuation.

But . . . she knew he felt something for her, too. Often she would catch him looking at her, so tenderly and, yes, so lovingly. She believed he regretted having taken her as his captive, yet if he had not, they never would have met. Like High Hawk, she truly believed now that it had been their destiny to meet.

Yet she was ready to turn her back on that destiny . . . on him. It just wasn't forgivable for a man to take a woman forcefully. She had rights, and they had been taken from her, not once, but twice.

Well, she would take them back.

"I have no choice but to find a way to leave," she whispered, tears suddenly in her eyes. "If only . . ."

Her thoughts were interrupted when she heard a soft voice, a child's, coming from outside the tepee. The child was singing what sounded to Joylynn like a lullaby.

She leaned her ear closer to the entranceway and listened more intently.

The child was singing, *"A-ho, I-lo, A-ho,"* and other Pawnee words unknown to Joylynn.

To her, those Pawnee words had no meaning, but as the child continued to sing, the lullaby seemed to take on a special significance, somewhat like "Hush-A-Bye" in the English language.

"Is she singing a lullaby in Pawnee, and if so, is she singing to a baby, perhaps her brother or sister?" Joylynn whispered.

Too curious to sit there any longer, she rose to her feet and lifted the entrance flap slowly so she could see the child.

The little girl, perhaps seven years of age, sat beneath the low-hanging branches of a cottonwood tree, a few feet from High Hawk's tepee.

Joylynn's eyes widened in wonder when she saw what appeared to be a doll, made from dried husks of corn, in the girl's arms.

As she sang, she slowly rocked her doll back and forth in her arms.

Recognizing maternal love in this little girl's tender song to her make-believe child, Joylynn slid her hand to her stomach.

She only now realized that although this was a child of rape within her womb, she could not help having feelings for it.

It was a part of her, wasn't it?

How could she not have feelings for it?

Tears filled her eyes again. What should she do when the time came for her to decide the fate of this baby? She knew that she should not want to keep the child, yet . . . yet . . . could she truly give it away? Once she held it in her arms, as this little girl was holding her pretend baby, could Joylynn turn her back on the tiny, defenseless creature?

Feeling someone's eyes on her, the child stopped singing and stared at Joylynn. Then she smiled the sweetest smile Joylynn had ever seen.

The little girl laid her doll aside and came to Joylynn. "Why do you have tears in your eyes?" she asked in perfect English. It seemed most of the people in this village could speak English. "Are you sad?"

"Not really," Joylynn murmured, wiping the tears away.

"Then why are you crying?" the child asked. "Are you lonely? You look lonely."

"Yes, I am lonely," Joylynn said, slowly smiling.

"But now that you are here, talking with me, I don't feel so alone any longer."

To Joylynn's surprise, the girl took her by one hand and yanked on it. "Come with me," she said. "You can play house with me."

"Play . . . house?" Joylynn said, walking with the little girl back to where she had been sitting beneath the tree. "Yes, I would love to play house with you . . . that is, if your mother wouldn't mind."

"*Ina* is busy grinding meal for tonight's supper, so she will not know what we are doing," the little girl said, softly giggling. She let go of Joylynn's hand and gazed up at her. "I know your name but you do not know mine, do you?"

"No, I don't," Joylynn murmured. "But I would like to, especially if we are going to play house together."

"I am called by the name Singing In Water," the child said, smiling widely. "I like your name. Do you like mine?"

"It's as pretty as you are," Joylynn said, her eyes moving slowly over the little girl. She was petite and pretty with big brown eyes, a round, copper face, and hair hanging in two braids down her back to her waist. She was dressed in buckskin, ornamented with beautiful beaded designs. She wore moccasins that went up to her knees, also beautifully beaded.

"Sit," Singing In Water said as she spread a blanket out for Joylynn. "Watch. I will show you how to play house."

Feeling lighthearted and gay for the first time in months, Joylynn plopped down on the blanket and watched what Singing In Water did next.

"You do this first," Singing In Water said. She scurried around beneath the tree and picked up some forked limbs that had fallen to the ground. "You stick these in the ground like this, and then watch what I do."

Joylynn saw how she pushed the limbs into the ground in the shape of a tepee, then disappeared momentarily inside her parents' tepee and came back with a small, old buffalo hide that she placed over the sticks, so that it looked like a small tepee.

"This is our home," Singing In Water said. "It is just big enough for us to go inside and sit. Will you sit with me?"

"If I can fit in," Joylynn said, laughing softly.

She crawled inside but had to keep her shoulders hunched over so that she would not push her way through the roof.

Singing In Water came in after her, carrying her pretend baby.

She sat down close to Joylynn, so close that Joylynn could smell the sweetness of the child's skin and clothes, like rainwater.

"On days when a lot of my friends play with me, we make a much larger house, and boys play with us," Singing In Water said. She placed a braid that had come over her shoulder behind her, so that it hung alongside the other down her back.

"You pretend to be families?" Joylynn asked, beginning to feel cramped in the small space. Her stomach was uncomfortable in her hunched position.

"*Ho*, and the boys go to their mothers to get a buffalo tongue that has been cooked, or some pemmican," Singing In Water said, slowly rocking her pretend baby back and forth in her arms. "We girls then spread clean grass on the floor of our home and put the food on it. We feast on the food, the boys on one side of the imaginary fire pit, the girls on the other."

"It sounds like so much fun," Joylynn murmured. She had never had any close friends to play with when she was a child because the farms the families lived on were too far apart.

"It is fun," Singing In Water said, then she handed the doll over to Joylynn. "Would you like to hold my baby?"

Joylynn was taken aback by the suggestion.

She stared at the strange-looking thing the girl called her baby, then did as she had seen the child do.

She slowly rocked it back and forth in her arms, seeing that this pleased Singing In Water. The child smiled even more broadly than before.

"Sometimes our dolls are made of rushes; oftentimes they are made by our grandmothers in the summer from mud," Singing In Water said. She shrugged. "I like all dolls. I love to think of when I will have a real baby of my own."

Singing In Water lifted an eyebrow. "Why do you not have a baby of your own?" she asked matter-of-factly. "You are of the age when you should, are you not? Do not white women have babies very often?"

That question took Joylynn aback. She could feel the heat of a blush rush to her cheeks, for how could she answer such a question? Here she was, holding a fake baby, while inside her belly lay a true one!

"Joylynn, where are you?"

The familiar, dreaded voice of High Hawk's mother penetrated the small tepee, but this time it was welcome. Joylynn was finding the little girl's questions uncomfortable.

"Oh, no," Singing In Water said, sighing. "High Hawk's *ina* is wanting you. She will probably put you to work again today. Do you mind working alongside the other women?"

"Joylynn!"

Blanket Woman's voice was more insistent, more shrill.

"I must go," Joylynn said, placing the doll in Singing In Water's arms. She leaned over and brushed a kiss across the child's brow. "Thank you. I've had fun."

"Me, too," Singing In Water said, crawling outside with Joylynn.

"There you are," Blanket Woman huffed. In her arms was a lovely white doeskin dress. Between her fingers she held a pair of beautiful moccasins. "Come back to my son's lodge. I have clothes for you."

Joylynn gazed at the clothes and then into Blanket Woman's eyes. "I have enough of my own dresses to wear, thank you," she said tightly.

"You will wear them no more," Blanket Woman said, going to Joylynn and thrusting the dress into her arms. "Come. I will bring the moccasins in for you. You will wear them, too, instead of your sort of shoes, which are ugly."

Joylynn gave Blanket Woman an angry stare, then, feeling the eyes of other women on her, she sighed and hurried to High Hawk's tepee with Blanket Woman on her heels.

Once inside, Joylynn turned and faced Blanket Woman. She shoved the dress back into the older woman's arms. "I refuse to wear this," she said tightly. "Why should I? I am not Pawnee."

"It is better that you wear something that makes you blend in with us Pawnee women," Blanket Woman snorted out. She shoved the dress back into Joylynn's arms. "Now. You . . . change . . . now!"

Understanding that she had no choice but to do as Blanket Woman said, and seeing that the older woman was back to her normal hateful self, Joylynn kept the dress in her arms, but she stood stiffly glaring at Blanket Woman. "Leave, and then I will change," she said tightly.

"I do not believe you will, so I shall stay until you are wearing the dress of my people and what you are wearing has been thrown into the fire," Blanket Woman said, angrily placing her fists on her hips. "Now, white woman. Change now!"

Joylynn felt cornered. She did not want this woman to see her belly, because when Joylynn was nude, there was no hiding that she carried a child within her womb. She lifted her chin angrily. "I . . . absolutely . . . refuse," she said. "You leave, and then I will change into this . . . this thing that you call a dress."

"And now you even insult what I have sewn?" Blanket Woman huffed. She stepped closer to Joylynn. "You take off that ugly white woman's dress or I will do it for you."

Truly believing that the older woman would carry out her threat, Joylynn realized that she had no choice but to risk Blanket Woman learning her secret. She laid the doeskin dress aside, then slowly pulled her own gown over her head.

Before she had it totally removed, she heard a gasp. She felt weak in the knees to know what had caused Blanket Woman's surprised reaction.

"You . . . are . . . with child?" Blanket Woman said, then rushed from the tepee, leaving Joylynn alone with her fears.

"Now what?" she murmured, slipping into the doeskin dress. Actually, she thought it soft and absolutely beautiful, not ugly.

She slid her feet into the buttery soft moccasins, then sank down on a blanket before the fire.

Oh, how she dreaded High Hawk's reaction to her pregnancy. If he had loved her at all, as she now hoped he did, surely that love would turn to hate, for had she not deceived him by disguising the truth about her condition?

CHAPTER ELEVEN

Blanket Woman could hardly get to the council house quickly enough. She was so eager to tell High Hawk the news, she barged inside and interrupted the council.

The men of the village were meeting to discuss her missing husband. Search parties had gone out in all directions again, and thus far, none had brought good news home with them.

Her husband was gone, perhaps . . . forever!

Ignoring the stares of the men who sat around the fire with her son, Blanket Woman stepped up to High Hawk as he rose quickly to his feet. "Come outside with me," she said, placing a hand on his arm. "I have something to tell you."

Seeing the anger in his mother's eyes, he stepped outside with her and placed his hands gently on her shoulders. She stared up at him with a familiar determination in her eyes. Never had he known such a strong-willed person. Yet he realized the white woman seemed to be just as determined.

But he would never compare Joylynn to his mother. There were vast differences in their personalities. There was a softness about Joylynn when she let down her guard with him.

His mother's softness had left her long ago!

"What do you have to tell me? What is so important that you would interrupt the council of warriors?" High Hawk asked.

"It has been proven to me today that you were absolutely wrong to bring the white woman to our village," Blanket Woman blurted out.

"And how was it proven?" High Hawk asked, weary of his mother's interference.

"She . . . is . . . with child," Blanket Woman said. Her words brought alarm into her son's eyes, and he jerked his hands from her shoulders. "It is ironic, is it not, that she is with child when your father's main purpose in having you abduct her was to prevent one more white child from being born into the world."

She clenched her jaw. "And here this woman is pregnant!" she said angrily. "I was right to counsel you against this abduction. I have been proven right!"

"How do you know that she is with child?" High Hawk asked warily.

"I took her a dress to wear, and when she disrobed, I saw her belly," Blanket Woman said bitterly. "I know when the swell of a woman's belly means that she is with child!"

High Hawk was so stunned, he was speechless.

Joylynn was not a married woman. She had not been living with a man.

So how could she be with child?

Had she been married? Had her husband died? Or had he been killed?

"You must return the white woman to her home," Blanket Woman said tightly. "It is bad enough that you stole her in the first place. But you cannot keep a captive who carries the child of a white man in her belly!"

"I will never take her back to the white world," High Hawk blurted out. "She is a woman alone in a harsh land. I cannot leave her vulnerable, especially now, now that she is with child."

Blanket Woman took a shaky step away from him, her eyes wide. She now knew the depths of her son's feelings for Joylynn.

"*Ina*, take your anger elsewhere today," High Hawk said, giving her a look she could not decipher. Then he walked away from her.

High Hawk hurried to his tepee.

He stopped just inside the entrance flap and stared down at Joylynn as she sat before the fire. She had not yet noticed that he had come into his lodge.

He knew that she must be worried about the outcome of his mother learning her secret.

Joylynn gasped when she turned and found High Hawk standing there. Quickly she moved to her feet. The moment she stood before him, his eyes went to her belly.

She knew the beautiful dress she was wearing clearly outlined the small mound of her growing baby. When he continued to stand there, staring at her belly, she was sure he realized that she was most certainly with child.

Suddenly he came to her and gently placed his hands at her waist. There was no contempt in the gaze he leveled on her. "Where is this child's father?" he asked thickly.

That question made Joylynn cringe. She couldn't tell him the truth, for she had never told anyone about the rape. She especially didn't want to tell this man, a man she was beginning to love.

When Joylynn refused to respond, High Hawk was torn. He was not certain how to feel about her. He had begun to love her, but now it was obvious she did not care enough about him to be truthful with him.

He gazed again into Joylynn's eyes, then turned and left the tepee without saying anything else to her.

Feeling as if she had lost the world, Joylynn crumpled to the rush mats, held her face in her hands and cried.

CHAPTER TWELVE

Joylynn now felt more uncomfortable with High Hawk than when he had first abducted her. He hadn't spoken one word to her since she refused to answer him about the baby. Awkward silence reigned between them.

Even now, as they ate their morning meal, she could hardly swallow the pieces of fruit. She ignored the meat altogether since her stomach was so tense.

She was frightened to learn what her fate would be. High Hawk had full control of her future, whether she and her unborn child lived or died.

Still, she couldn't believe he would harm her in any way. Perhaps his silence meant that he was making plans to release her.

"High Hawk!"

A voice outside broke through Joylynn's troubled thoughts.

She looked over at High Hawk. He had scarcely touched the food on his plate. Instead, he sat staring into the flames of the early morning fire.

The alarm in the voice of the warrior shouting High Hawk's name brought him quickly to his feet.

Joylynn watched him rush from the lodge.

She followed.

She stood back and watched as he talked with a mounted warrior. The rider was gazing with a troubled, sad expression down at High Hawk as he spoke.

When High Hawk turned from the warrior, his face was filled with pain and his eyes and hands reached toward the heavens, as though he was crying out to his Great Spirit. Joylynn knew that the news was not good.

She watched him hurry to his horse, then ride from the village with the warrior who had come for him.

Joylynn feared the worst . . . that his father had been found, and was perhaps dead.

CHAPTER THIRTEEN

His heart heavy, High Hawk rode alongside Three Bears to meet the warriors who were bringing his father home on a travois.

His *ahte* and those who rode with him had been found, and the news was not good.

Chief Rising Moon was badly injured and the others were dead.

Although terribly injured, Rising Moon had managed to stay alive until he was found this morning, hiding in the thick brush.

His wounds were too severe for him to last much longer. It was a miracle that he had survived this long.

Three Bears had told High Hawk that those who were slain now lay side by side in the shade of a tree, awaiting transport back to the village for burial.

High Hawk rode his horse at a hard gallop away

from Three Bears when he caught sight of the warriors who had found his father. They were coming slowly toward him, dragging the travois that carried his father.

When High Hawk reached them, they stopped.

High Hawk wheeled his horse to a stop, then leapt from the saddle and fell to his knees beside the travois. The sight that met his eyes was so terrible, his heart felt as though it was being squeezed inside his chest.

"Ahte," High Hawk said, trying to keep his emotions in check as he leaned down and placed a gentle hand on his father's cheek.

His father was covered up to his chin with a blanket, preventing High Hawk from seeing his wounds.

He focused on his father's eyes. As Rising Moon looked up at him, the light and energy seemed to have left his gaze.

"My son," Rising Moon said only loud enough for High Hawk to hear. He reached a trembling hand from beneath the blanket and gripped High Hawk's fingers. "I . . . will . . . soon be gone . . . from you. Mole. It was Mole who did this."

Rising Moon closed his eyes, choked, then cleared his throat and clung even harder to High Hawk's hand. "High Hawk . . . now . . . chief . . ." he said. His hand fell away as his eyes locked suddenly in death's stare.

Everything within High Hawk went cold when

he realized that he had just lost his beloved father. And at the hands of a villain everyone detested.

Mole!

He swallowed hard as tears rushed to his eyes. Only now did he realize that his father had named him chief even without knowing that High Hawk had succeeded in both challenges set to him by his father.

It had not mattered to his father whether High Hawk had or had not abducted a white woman.

Yet he had, and as a result, he was in the midst of a dilemma.

But for now, all he could think about was his *ahte*, and the pain he felt at knowing he would never hear his father's voice again, or know those moments of laughter when his father forgot the solemnity of being chief and reveled in the joy of having a son.

"Your *ahte* was shot many times, but he still managed to ride away from the shooter. He was finally stopped when he was shot in the back," Three Bears said thickly as he dismounted and knelt beside High Hawk. He placed a comforting arm around his best friend's shoulder. "Being so strong-willed, your *ahte* lived long enough to tell you that you are now our people's chief."

"That coward . . . shot . . . my *ahte* in the back?" High Hawk said between clenched teeth. A slow rage was building within him.

He knew the killer from other altercations. He

was a man who, until now, had always cleverly eluded anyone who would hunt him.

High Hawk reached a gentle hand to his father's eyes and slowly closed them. "*Ahte*, he will not get away with this," he said tightly. "*Ahte*, I vow to you that he will die!"

Distraught, feeling empty inside, High Hawk lifted his father from the travois and carried him the rest of the way to the village. His people were outside their lodges, waiting.

When High Hawk saw his mother break into a run toward him, he felt as though someone was stabbing away at his heart. On her face he saw the despair she felt over the loss of her beloved husband.

When Blanket Woman reached them, and High Hawk saw the sadness in his mother's eyes, he felt helpless. He did not know what to do or say to comfort her.

He winced when she started wailing and pulling at her hair. She continued doing this even when High Hawk carried his father's body into Two Stars's lodge, where the shaman would pray for him and stand by as Blanket Woman prepared her husband for burial.

Joylynn had heard the commotion and had gone outside.

She went cold when she saw High Hawk coming into the village, carrying his father's dead body.

Joylynn was touched deeply by the utter sadness she saw in High Hawk's eyes as he gazed momentarily at her before taking his father into the shaman's lodge.

She could not help sympathizing with the tormented woman who was now a widow. Although Joylynn had found it hard to like Blanket Woman, she did feel sorry for her in her time of grieving.

She gulped hard when she looked around her and beheld a full village of mourners who were also wailing.

She was aware of drums thumping somewhere in the village in a steady rhythm, adding to the sadness of the moment.

Even the children were no longer laughing. They were silent as they stood beside their mothers, tears streaming down their small, round cheeks.

Joylynn's heart skipped a beat when High Hawk left the shaman's lodge alone and came toward her. He stopped and gazed into her eyes, then brushed past her and went inside his tepee.

She wasn't sure what she should do.

She felt awkward standing there alone while everyone else was now grouped together in their sorrow in the middle of the village near the shaman's lodge. Joylynn knew she had no choice but to go back inside High Hawk's tepee.

She crept inside.

She found High Hawk sitting beside the fire, his face ashen and solemn, his red eyes filled with both anger and sadness.

She sat down, then finally found the courage to

speak to him. "High Hawk, I am so sorry about your father," she said softly. "How . . . did . . . he die?"

He turned to her and held her gaze steadily. "He was downed by a heartless man who has been named Mole because of the many ugly moles on his face," he said thickly. "My *ahte* was shot many times, even in the back. The other warriors who were with my father were also killed by those who rode with Mole. My men have gone now for our fallen ones' bodies."

Joylynn grew cold inside when she heard the name Mole.

She gagged, choked, and turned her head away as she stumbled to her feet.

The man who had raped her, who was the father of the child that grew inside her, had killed High Hawk's father.

Now she and High Hawk both had cause to seek vengeance against Mole!

High Hawk had heard Joylynn gag, had seen her turn her eyes quickly away from him. He was puzzled by her reaction.

He rose and placed a gentle hand on her shoulder, turning her to face him. "It seems you know this name. Why did you react as you did when I mentioned the man named Mole?" he asked warily.

She turned her eyes to him again, looked at him through a wash of tears, then reached for one of his hands and placed it on her stomach, where the child lay in the safe cocoon of her womb.

"This . . . the *child . . .* is why," she said.

Stunned to know whose child lay within her womb, he glared at Joylynn. "Were . . . you . . . that man's woman?"

"No, oh, Lord, no," she gasped out, her heart going cold at the thought. "That man was nothing to me. I hate him. He changed my life forever."

"How?" High Hawk asked, searching her eyes.

"He . . . ambushed me one day and . . . heartlessly raped me and . . . left me for dead," she said, tears spilling from her eyes as she spoke the horrible words aloud.

It had been enough to see the rape over and over again in her dreams. But to speak of it was like living it all over again.

"Raped?" High Hawk gasped.

He reached out and brushed tears from her cheeks with the pads of his thumbs, then took her hands and urged her to sit beside the fire again with him.

He sat there and listened to the story of how she had been a Pony Express rider, and then how Mole had stopped her one day during her ride, and raped her.

A bitter rage toward Mole filled High Hawk anew when he imagined such a thing happening to his woman.

Yes!

His woman!

He loved Joylynn with all his heart. He was actually relieved to finally know exactly how she had come to be pregnant. And he felt deeply the pain that madman had caused her.

"Yes, raped," Joylynn said softly, lowering her eyes. She rose to her feet and turned her back to High Hawk. "Afterward, he choked me. He thought I was dead when he rode off. But I wasn't. I had enough breath left in my lungs to survive the terrible rape."

Suddenly she felt strong arms around her.

She melted into High Hawk's embrace as he turned her toward him.

While she sobbed and cried, he held her ever so lovingly.

When he placed a finger beneath her chin and gazed down into her eyes, she saw cold determination. "The man will die for sinning against you and my people," he said angrily. "He does not have much longer on this earth."

"He cannot die soon enough," Joylynn said, sighing when High Hawk held her close, proving that she had nothing to fear from him any longer.

She could feel his love for her in the tender way he held her and talked to her.

"Although I am now chief, and I have the last word in everything at my village, I will not promise anything except this. Mole will die a horrible death when he is found," High Hawk said thickly.

For now, that was enough for Joylynn.

134

Despite the terrible circumstances that had brought them together, she found herself rejoicing.

Yes, even though High Hawk understood that she was with child, and knew who the father was, he had not turned away from her. She knew now that she was much more to this handsome warrior than his captive. She was not just a woman he had brought home to his people as some sort of trophy.

She knew now that he loved her, as she loved him.

She savored his embrace, for who was to say what tomorrow would bring to either of them?

CHAPTER FOURTEEN

Sleeping Wolf had been up all night mourning his beloved father. Now he sat before his morning fire, his eyes swollen from crying, his heart feeling empty at the loss of his *ahte*.

He still could not believe that someone had callously murdered Rising Moon. He had been shot more than once in the belly, and when his father had found the strength and willpower to wheel his horse around and ride away from the ambushers, the man called Mole had shot him in the back.

It was incredible that his *ahte* had lived as long as he had, but being the strong-willed man he was, he had pretended to be dead while Mole and his men kicked his body to see if he was alive.

"I cannot stand thinking about it any longer," Sleeping Wolf whispered to himself as tears again rushed from his swollen, bloodshot eyes.

No. He could not stand to just sit there any

longer, burying himself deeper and deeper in grief. He had to do something to avenge his father!

And although he knew it was practically impossible for him to ride a horse, he knew what he had to do.

For once, he would prove to everyone that he was not the weak man they all thought him.

Ho, he was determined to do something that would make him look strong and vital to his people. He would prove that he was worthy of having been born into a family such as his.

Sleeping Wolf groaned as he pushed himself up from the rush mats upon which he had been sitting. He was already dressed in a fringed buckskin shirt and leggings.

His waist-length black hair was held back with a beaded headband that his mother had made just for him. She had used beads that he had picked out, most of which were bright in color.

He groaned as he dragged himself to his small cache of weapons. All of them had been gifts from his *ahte*, even though he knew this son could never leave the village on a horse, to use them for the hunt, or for the defense of their people.

They were just symbols. Possessing these weapons made Sleeping Wolf at least look like the warrior he could never be.

His jaw tight, he sheathed his sharp knife to the right side of his waist, where it would be easier to grab once he found that horrible man called Mole.

He had never seen the man. But his description was all that Sleeping Wolf needed in order to find and kill him. He was a man with many moles on his face; Sleeping Wolf had heard they were sickening to look at.

"I will find you and kill you. You will regret the day you downed my father and so many valiant Pawnee warriors," Sleeping Wolf whispered, grabbing up his favorite rifle from those his father had placed there for him.

He struggled as he filled the chamber with bullets, then smiled when he had accomplished the feat. It was hard for him to do anything except eat and sleep.

His right hand gripping the rifle, Sleeping Wolf turned and walked as determinedly as possible toward his entrance flap. It was too early in the morning for anyone to be up and about, especially since the people of the village had mourned their losses long into the night. He had sat by the huge outdoor fire with them, but being so weary and tired, he had returned to his lodge before anyone else.

He had not slept, only listened to the wailing and crying as the drums beat out a steady rhythm into the night. He had never spent such a mournful night as last night. And he would make certain Mole would not be responsible for any more nights like this. By nightfall, he would be dead.

Stepping outside, where the sun was just barely creeping up over the horizon, sending its beautifully colored sprays of pink and orange across the land, Sleeping Wolf stopped to look around him and to listen.

Everything was still.

Even the trees stood with not a leaf stirring.

And then he heard a soft wailing sound coming from Two Stars's lodge.

His mother was still in the shaman's tepee, at her husband's side. Sleeping Wolf was sure she had not slept at all last night either.

He could imagine her there now, preparing her husband for burial. Everything she did would be imbued with the loving care and dedication of a wife.

"*Ina, Ina,*" he whispered to himself, wishing there was some way for him to go and comfort her.

But he knew there was not one person on this earth who could take away her sorrow.

She was a woman without a husband now. He was sure her heart was feeling even more empty than his own.

He then slid his gaze over to his brother's tepee. Slow spirals of smoke came from the smoke hole. He was not certain whether that meant his brother was already up, or whether his lodge fire was still burning enough to send off smoke.

His heart went out to High Hawk, for although he was a strong man, he had adored his chieftain father, and in addition to his sorrow he had to shoulder the responsibilities of seeing to the safety and welfare of many people.

"You will do it well, my brother," Sleeping Wolf said, smiling with pride in High Hawk. His brother had never pitied him, but had made Sleeping Wolf feel as though he was his equal in so many ways.

"You were kind to do that when all who saw me knew it was not so," Sleeping Wolf said, then turned and walked toward the corral behind his brother's tepee. Although Sleeping Wolf had never gone on a horse-stealing expedition, he knew that his brother's steeds were also his.

In all ways his brother had been generous to him. But he needed more than High Hawk had given him now. He needed to know the pride of being the one to avenge his father's death!

He chose a horse, but not a saddle. A saddle was too heavy for him to lift, so he moaned and groaned and struggled to mount the steed bareback.

Suddenly he slipped and fell hard on his back. He cried out at the pain that shot through him.

He heard footsteps and saw Three Bears running toward him. The warrior knelt down at his side.

"Sleeping Wolf!" Three Bears gasped. He had just stepped from his lodge to stretch his arms and legs before preparing for another day of mourning.

"Sleeping Wolf, what were you trying to do?" Three Bears asked. He was not sure how to help the other man, for it seemed that Sleeping Wolf was in too much pain to be moved.

"Mount . . . the . . . steed," Sleeping Wolf gulped

out, wincing when renewed pain struck his back like a hot poker.

"But why?" Three Bears asked, gently slipping an arm beneath Sleeping Wolf in an effort to help him up from the ground.

But he withdrew his arm quickly when merely touching Sleeping Wolf's back made him cry out with renewed pain.

"I wanted to avenge my *ahte's* death," Sleeping Wolf said weakly. He was acutely embarrassed that once again he had failed to act like a man.

The fall and the resulting helplessness made Sleeping Wolf feel more useless than ever before.

"But you know . . ." Three Bears began, but he stopped before saying the words that he knew would hurt his best friend's brother . . . that Sleeping Wolf knew he could not do as most warriors did, even so simple a thing as mounting a horse.

"*Ho*, I know," Sleeping Wolf said thickly, knowing what Three Bears had been about to say.

"I will carry you inside your lodge, then go for Two Stars," Three Bears said. He forced himself to ignore Sleeping Wolf's cries of pain as he picked him up. Sleeping Wolf seemed no heavier than a feather since he was so slight in build, without an ounce of muscle anywhere on his body.

Sleeping Wolf closed his eyes to the humiliation of being carried like a baby. Soon Three Bears placed him on the bed of blankets in Sleeping Wolf's lodge.

"I would rather be by my fire, not in my bed," Sleeping Wolf said weakly, and Three Bears carefully moved him to a blanket near the fire pit.

"I will return shortly with Two Stars," Three Bears said, then left the tepee in a hurry.

Sleeping Wolf soon heard voices and recognized his mother's among them. Three Bears was telling her what had just happened to her older son. Sleeping Wolf hung his head in shame and sobbed. Once again his mother would be reminded that one son was proud and strong, while the other was weak, an object of pity, and so very useless.

He did not even look up when she came into the lodge and sat down beside him. She cradled him in her arms as if he were nothing more than a baby.

"My son, my son," Blanket Woman said softly. "Why would you do such a thing? You know you are not able."

Her words made Sleeping Wolf's embarrassment and shame twofold. He began crying as his mother held and comforted him.

"I only wanted to help," he sobbed out. "I wanted to be the one to find my *ahte's* murderer. But all I succeeded in doing was make myself look a fool. I will never live this down. Never."

"You will, as you have always done before," Blanket Woman murmured. "Everyone understands. Do not feel ashamed because of what life has handed you. I am so sorry, my son, for it was surely something I did while carrying you in my womb that caused you to be so different from your brother."

She continued to hold and rock him. He sobbed and clung to her until Two Stars came.

Blanket Woman moved away from Sleeping Wolf and watched as Two Stars ministered to the few bloody scratches on her son's face and hands.

She could not help being afraid for this son. She was not certain if he could live with the humiliation of what had happened today.

She knew now that she must keep a much closer eye on him.

She would move him into her lodge after she saw to her husband's burial.

She dropped her face into her hands and sobbed as she felt the world slipping away from her. She had always been so strong, so courageous.

Today she felt neither!

CHAPTER FIFTEEN

Joylynn sat in High Hawk's tepee alone. After he had heard about his brother's fall, he had gone to sit with Sleeping Wolf along with his mother.

Joylynn was feeling lonely and worried. Since early morning she had experienced slight cramping in her lower abdomen.

But then each time the ache would go away again, and she would put it out of her mind.

But now she was suddenly cramping again, and this time it was much worse.

She winced when a sharper pain shot through her belly, and then she felt a damp heat between her legs.

Her heart pounding, she reached her hand up inside her dress and found wetness there. She drew her hand out and gazed at it, panic filling her when she found it covered with blood.

She tried to get up, to go seek help, for she was

afraid she might be losing the baby, but her knees buckled. The pains came now at short intervals.

She held on to her stomach, sobbing, screaming when she saw the blood beginning to seep through her clothes.

"Help me!" she screamed, sweat pearling her brow as she felt an intense pressure at the bottom of her abdomen.

When two women came running into the tepee, they didn't have to be told what was happening.

They saw the blood.

They saw how Joylynn was holding her belly.

"I will go for Two Stars," one of the women said, leaving the tepee in a rush.

"I am Pure Blossom," said the other one as she knelt down beside her. "You will be all right. Two Stars will make it so."

"The child . . ." Joylynn panted. "I am . . . losing . . . the child."

"*Ho*, I believe you are, but *you* will be all right," Pure Blossom said, trying to reassure her. "Two Stars will make you as comfortable as he can until the child slides from your body."

Joylynn gripped Pure Blossom's hand. "I'm afraid," she said, her voice breaking. "There is so much blood. . . ."

"You will be all right," Pure Blossom repeated gently.

Two Stars hurried into the tepee, carrying his bag of medicines.

Pure Blossom stood away from Joylynn to make room for the shaman as he knelt down beside her.

He pressed gently on Joylynn's abdomen, then gave her a look of concern. "The blood and the position of the child tell me it will soon be released from inside you," he said, taking her hand. "I will keep you safe, but there is nothing I can do for the child. It is being born too soon to live.

"Pure Blossom, go and get water and soft doeskin cloths," Two Stars said. "Go and tell High Hawk what is happening."

Pure Blossom nodded and left.

High Hawk had already heard.

He came into the tepee and sat on the opposite side from where Two Stars sat, waiting for the child to be pushed from Joylynn's body, which happened only a few seconds later.

Two Stars wrapped the fetus in a blanket, while High Hawk held Joylynn's hand.

Two Stars then handed the aborted fetus to Pure Blossom as she stepped into the tepee with water and cloths.

"Take it away," Two Stars said softly.

It was then that Blanket Woman came into the tepee, her eyes soft and gentle as she gazed down at Joylynn.

She laid a hand on Two Stars's shoulder. "I will see to the rest," she said. She glanced at High Hawk. "You can leave now with our shaman. Joylynn will be all right. I will make certain of it."

Joylynn was surprised that Blanket Woman was being so kind, but perhaps she shouldn't have been. Hadn't Joylynn's body made certain the white child would not be born to her? Wasn't that what Blanket Woman had wanted all along?

"*Ina*, thank you," High Hawk said as he gave Joylynn one last loving look, then rose and left the tepee with Two Stars.

"Pure Blossom, help remove the dress so I can wash Joylynn," Blanket Woman said, already squeezing water from a soft doeskin cloth.

Once her clothes were removed and Blanket Woman was gently washing her, Joylynn closed her eyes and fought back the tears that were stinging the corners of her eyes. She was no longer in pain except inside her heart. Although she had planned to give the baby away, a part of her was overwhelmed by sadness.

She squeezed her eyes tightly shut so that Blanket Woman wouldn't see the tears and tried not to think about what it would have been like to have kept and raised the child. She had always dreamed of having children. Now . . . would she ever?

Cleansed of all signs of the miscarriage, and now dressed in a soft doeskin gown that one of the women had brought, Joylynn could not help smiling at Blanket Woman as she gently drew a blanket up over her.

"You are so kind . . . to . . . do this for me," she

said softly. "Any other woman of the village could have done it."

"You are in my son's lodge. It is my responsibility to care for anyone who shares it with him," Blanket Woman said, smoothing Joylynn's perspiration-dampened hair back from her face. "Even you, a woman I had not ever thought to be kind to. But I do not like seeing anyone suffer. I am happy to have helped you."

Joylynn started to thank Blanket Woman, but was stopped when Two Stars came back inside the lodge, High Hawk with him.

High Hawk knelt on the far side of Joylynn, while his mother and Two Stars knelt on her other.

Two Stars brought a wooden cup of what looked like broth up to Joylynn's lips. "Drink," he said. "This will make you rest and sleep."

Welcoming the very thought of escaping a world that had cheated her of a child she now knew she could never have given up, Joylynn smiled and took the cup. She drank the sweet liquid from it.

She didn't dare ask what it was made of. She would just welcome the sleep it brought and hope that when she awakened, things would be better for her.

She was glad of one thing . . . that Blanket Woman seemed to feel differently about her. She might even be a friend now, not a foe.

"I will leave you alone now," Blanket Woman said, nodding over at High Hawk as a silent way to say that he should leave, too, but High Hawk ignored her and continued to sit there as Blanket Woman left with Two Stars.

Joylynn was already feeling groggy from whatever had been in the sweet drink. She gazed up at High Hawk, so glad when he bent low and brushed a soft kiss across her lips.

But the words he murmured next puzzled her, and her eyes widened.

"You may leave the village as soon as you feel like traveling," High Hawk said thickly. "You are no longer anyone's captive. My father wished your capture, not I. I am now chief, and I am not someone who wants white captives, especially not a woman like you who seems to love her freedom so much."

He then explained to her why he had abducted her in the first place, that he had done it for his *ahte*.

Joylynn fought sleep now; she wanted to stay awake a while longer, while High Hawk was there. He was so close she could smell the sweet freshness of his skin.

"Do you understand now why I took you from your home?" High Hawk asked.

"I believe so," Joylynn said. "And I am so glad that it was not because you hate white women enough to take one captive."

"I normally do not have any feelings for white women," High Hawk said, taking her hand and gently holding it. "Not until you."

"Are you saying that you have . . . special . . . feelings for me?" Joylynn murmured, already knowing that he did.

It was in his every gesture, word and gaze.

"I have from the beginning," High Hawk said, slowly nodding. "When I first saw you, I knew that destiny had brought me to you, not my father. I have loved you from the moment our eyes met."

"You love me that much?" she asked, swallowing hard.

"*Ho*, that much," he said fervently.

"And I feel the same about you, High Hawk. I do not want to leave you or your village, ever," Joylynn said. She was feeling so sleepy, she could hardly keep her thoughts straight, yet she knew enough to understand that everything transpiring between them was good.

"Surely it is the drug my shaman gave you that causes you to say such things to me," he said. His heart was pounding hard at the possibility that she truly had meant her words.

"No," she murmured. "It is not the drug. I have spoken from my heart. I am oh, so very weary of living alone . . . of hiding, which I was doing because of the child I was carrying."

"You do not ever have to hide again from anyone. Nor do you have to live alone," he said. "If you truly wish to stay among my people, they will welcome you here."

"It is not your people who make me want to

151

stay," she said, smiling slowly at him. "It is you. Do you not believe me when I say I love you?"

Suddenly she couldn't fight off sleep any longer.

She wasn't even aware of him placing his arms beneath her and taking her from the blankets to hold her on his lap.

He wrapped his arms around her and gazed down at her loveliness.

He prayed it was not the medicine she had been given that had caused her confession of love.

He would wait until she was herself again and then see if she still wanted him as much as he wanted her.

CHAPTER SIXTEEN

Joylynn was sitting beside the lodge fire, slowly brushing her hair. She gazed into the dancing flames, smiling, for she had finally regained her full strength after losing the child.

She had thought she would bounce back quickly, because she had never had trouble regaining her strength after being ill.

But it was now four weeks since the miscarriage and only now was she feeling like her old self again. In fact, she wanted to join the search parties that went out almost daily as the hunt for Mole continued.

During her recuperation, Joylynn had not been able to help the women as they harvested the crops, picking everything in the huge garden and storing the crops in cache pits.

She felt guilty about not having helped when she

knew how hard a task it had been, especially for someone of Blanket Woman's age.

The guilt came because Joylynn now felt she was a part of these people's lives. She hoped to be the wife of their chief, and soon would be using the stored food herself, once she began cooking for High Hawk.

That thought made her grimace a little, for she had only recently learned how to cook after hiding herself from humanity.

She doubted that she was even close to being the sort of cook a powerful chief would want as his wife.

But she did not doubt for a minute that Blanket Woman would take it upon herself to be sure her younger son had healthy meals, for she coddled both her children.

And now Blanket Woman would have more time for coddling them since she no longer had a husband to feed and clothe.

Chief Rising Moon was missed by everyone but Joylynn. She had never known him. But she knew both his sons, loving one herself, and she had thought of Sleeping Wolf often during her recuperation. She knew he was fighting his own battle to regain what strength and pride he'd had before his fall.

Thus far, he had not left his tepee. His mother had joined the women harvesting crops by day, and

154

then sat vigil at her older son's bedside each night. Two Stars sat with him through the day.

Joylynn believed that such continued attention from his mother and the shaman only made Sleeping Wolf feel less a man. She truly believed that the more everyone coddled him, the more he felt the despair of his condition.

Joylynn had wanted to go and talk with him, but when she even hinted at doing this, Blanket Woman scolded her and told her to stay away from her older son. Was it not enough that she had put a spell on her other son? she demanded.

Her hair finally brushed, Joylynn began twisting it in one long braid down her back. She had noticed that many Pawnee women wore their hair in that style. Wanting to be accepted by them, she wore her hair in the same way and continued to wear the lovely soft doeskin dresses that several women had been kind enough to give to her. Joylynn knew that their young chief had hinted that they help her however they could. And because they admired and loved Chief High Hawk so much, it had not taken much encouragement to prompt them to do as he asked.

Hearing someone entering the tepee, Joylynn turned her head.

When she saw Blanket Woman carrying in a tray of food, she had mixed feelings.

Sometimes Blanket Woman was kind to her,

even sweet, while at other times she was tight-lipped and reserved. Some days she came and went without even a word being spoken between Joylynn and the mother of the man Joylynn would forever love.

"How is Sleeping Wolf today?" Joylynn asked, even though she knew that Blanket Woman resented Joylynn's mere mention of her elder son.

Blanket Woman placed the wooden platter of assorted foods beside Joylynn, then sat down next to her. She nodded toward the food. "Eat," she said, plucking up a handful of berries herself and eating them quietly, one at a time.

Accustomed to this woman's uneven temperament, Joylynn shrugged. "All right, don't tell me," she murmured. "But thank you anyway for bringing me breakfast."

Blanket Woman picked up a tiny slice of venison, nodded and continued to eat in silence.

"My son Sleeping Wolf is well enough in one way," she said suddenly. Joylynn was so surprised, she almost choked on a berry as it slid suddenly down her throat without her chewing it.

Blanket Woman glanced at Joylynn. "But weaker in the other," she murmured.

"What do you mean?" Joylynn asked.

"It is in Sleeping Wolf's head and heart that his weakness lies," Blanket Woman said, her faded old eyes revealing the grief she still felt at the loss of her husband. "He cannot forget his humiliation. He desperately wanted to find the criminal who killed his father."

"I'm so sorry," Joylynn said, understanding now what Blanket Woman meant about Sleeping Wolf. Joylynn had seen so much in Sleeping Wolf's eyes the few times she met him. There was such despair in their depths.

"I fear so for him," Blanket Woman said, her voice breaking with emotion. "For he seems to carry such a weight on his shoulders. He seems to carry a greater burden than his brother, who is now responsible for our people's welfare."

"I so wish that things could be different for Sleeping Wolf. From the little I know of him, I can tell what a loving person he is," Joylynn said, fearing that she was treading on shaky ground, saying so much about the son Blanket Woman protected with her very being.

When Blanket Woman only gave her a sideways glance, then continued to eat from Joylynn's plate, Joylynn knew it was time to talk of something else.

She felt safe enough mentioning the other brother, for by now Blanket Woman knew that there was nothing she could do to come between Joylynn and High Hawk.

Nothing!

"When do you expect High Hawk to return home?" Joylynn asked softly. "I am anxious to tell him I feel strong enough to ride again. I want to go with him on the next search, if he hasn't found Mole's hideout yet."

"High Hawk left at daybreak," Blanket Woman said, her voice drawn. "He will search again today as long as there is light to see. He cannot seem to rest until he finds and stops that man who killed not only his father, but many beloved warriors of our band."

Blanket Woman then turned to Joylynn. "And you are not strong enough to ride a horse. Must you always be reminded that you are a woman, not a man?" she said gruffly. "You must do as women do, not men, and no woman accompanies the warriors on search parties."

"I might be a woman, but I have the same hate and need for vengeance as does your son," Joylynn said, trying to control her irritation at the woman who still tried to make her feel useless. "I know now, though, that today I have no choice but to wait. I have no idea where High Hawk has gone."

Blanket Woman gave her an annoyed stare, then emitted a low "Harrumph," rose, and left without another word.

The day turned out to be a long and boring one for Joylynn. The women did not yet include her in any of their daily activities; they still did not think she was strong enough to help them.

Joylynn had taken a walk down by the river,

stopping to run her fingers through the sand as she watched fish jumping from the water, then falling into it again.

She was reminded of those times she had fished with her father, how at first she was squeamish about putting a worm on the hook.

But once she got past that, she had caught as many fish as her father, never forgetting the perplexed look on his face the first time she pulled an eight-pound bass from their pond.

Ah, that fish had tasted good that night along with corn on the cob, her mother's canned green beans, and sliced tomatoes fresh from their garden.

"That was so long ago," Joylynn whispered as she sat beside the lodge fire. She gazed up through the smoke hole and saw the orange glow of sunset as the day waned.

The sound of horses arriving outside made Joylynn's heart skip a beat. "High Hawk," she whispered, relieved that he had returned home.

"I hope it is he," she whispered, jumping to her feet.

Breathing hard, her hair loose and long down her back, she ran outside barefoot just as High Hawk came into sight with several of his warriors.

When he saw her standing there, the sunset casting dancing shadows on her, he smiled and waved, then rode up to her and dismounted.

The smile had given her some hope that perhaps he had found the scoundrel, but soon she knew that the smile was meant only for her and conveyed how happy he was to see her.

High Hawk swept Joylynn into his arms and hugged her as a young brave came and took his horse's reins, then led it to the corral.

"Did you . . . ?" she asked, not finishing the question, for he was already answering it.

"He still eludes our search," High Hawk said, his smile fading. "But he cannot hide forever. One day, *ho*, one day he will be mine!"

"And mine," Joylynn said, reminding him that she wanted a role in Mole's comeuppance.

"*Ho*, and yours," High Hawk said, sliding an arm around her waist and walking with her into the tepee.

Joylynn stepped away from him and gazed into his eyes. "High Hawk, I am strong enough now to ride my horse," she said. "I want to ride with you the next time you leave to continue your search. Please let me go with you. Please?"

"No woman should do this," he said, placing a gentle hand on her cheek. "And I have never seen anyone more womanly than you."

Joylynn found herself blushing, a rarity for her.

She smiled, then spoke with determination. "Must I remind you how I made my living before Mole interfered with it?" she said softly. "I did the work of a man, not a mere woman. I rode many miles a day on my steed to deliver the mail.

160

Doesn't that prove that I am strong enough to go with you?"

High Hawk saw her determination, and he knew she was stronger than most women, not only in body, but also in mind. He had never met such a strong-willed woman as Joylynn. She even surpassed his mother in that capacity!

But his mother could not even saddle a horse, much less ride one.

"All right," he said, nodding. "I will let you ride with me tomorrow. I have returned home to rest and to pray. I must leave you for now, to tend to something, but I will return later. By then you should be asleep."

He brushed a kiss across her brow, gave her a lengthy hug, then left, leaving Joylynn as alone as before.

Remembering the hug, and the feel of his lips as he brushed kisses across her brow, Joylynn hungered to have his lips elsewhere, on hers. She sat down beside the fire.

She wanted more now than ever to be his wife.

She had never thought she would find a man who would make her want to give up her life of freedom, but High Hawk did.

A part of her still hankered to return to the world of the Pony Express rider. Yet a bigger part wanted to act like a woman now . . . a woman who wanted a man, not dust on her face and mud on her clothes after riding all day on her horse.

She wished that Mole could be found, for while he was out there, wreaking havoc on other innocent people, High Hawk's thoughts were mainly centered on him. And Joylynn wanted to talk with him about something besides Mole.

She wanted to talk to High Hawk about *their* feelings—hers and High Hawk's—for one another!

"And I will," she whispered to herself. "Soon."

In fact, she was determined to wait up for him tonight, even if she was awake into the wee hours of the morning, to finally tell him her truest, deepest feelings about life, about *him*.

CHAPTER SEVENTEEN

Joylynn decided to take a swim in the river to pass away some time while waiting for High Hawk to return.

Swimming in the river reminded her so much of swimming in the pond on her father's farm years ago.

To be assured of privacy, she planned to go farther along the bank than the place where the women bathed.

She would not allow herself to think of the danger, namely Mole.

If he had an ounce of sense inside that grotesque head, he wouldn't come anywhere near the Pawnee village.

After grabbing up a soft buckskin towel, she paused at the entrance flap, having second thoughts about what she was planning. Was it truly wise to go so far from the village alone?

She set her jaw firmly. Yes, she would go and have that swim; she was no longer a captive. She could come and go as she pleased.

She hoped that by the time she returned to the tepee, High Hawk would be there. She wanted to smell clean and sweet when he arrived, for she was hoping for something more than kisses tonight from the man she loved.

She wanted his lips.

She wanted his arms.

She blushed as she thought of what else she wanted from him, for never in her entire life had she had such sensual thoughts about a man.

And after the rape, she had wondered if she would ever want a man to hold her in his arms, to press his naked flesh against hers.

But High Hawk's gentleness, his utter handsomeness, his muscles, his long and flowing raven-black hair, had made her forget her doubts about wanting to be with a man. In truth, she actually ached for him.

She shook her head. "What am I thinking?" she whispered to herself as she opened the entrance flap, holding it aside long enough to take a look outside. No one was aware of her scrutiny. They were too busy doing what they did each evening before the moon replaced the sun in the sky.

She was glad to hear the laughter of the children again. It had been hushed for too long after their chief's death.

He was buried now.

Slowly everything in the village was getting back to normal. Yet on some faces, she still saw the pain of recent loss . . . a husband, a brother, a cousin. . . .

Not wanting to think any more about gloomy things, longing to find joy in her life, not sadness, she stepped out of the tepee. When she began walking in the direction of the river, she noticed some women gazing at her with various expressions on their faces.

Some showed resentment that she was still among them. Those who had befriended her smiled and nodded.

The warriors seemed not to care one way or the other that she was there. They did not even seem to notice the direction in which she was walking.

Their attitude demonstrated that she *was* a free woman and could do anything she pleased.

High Hawk had told her that she was no longer his captive. She could leave if she wished. But High Hawk now knew that Joylynn had no desire to leave. He knew that she loved him.

She had hoped they could express their love for each other with more than mere words tonight. Perhaps that might still be possible. But first she had to be patient. He had been adamant that there was something else he had to do.

She thought it was to spend time in prayer, for he had said he needed to pray before leaving again to search for Mole.

The shine of the river was visible now as she

made a left turn away from the village. She searched for any sign of High Hawk. She had no idea where he went to pray. She hoped that one day she would know everything about him.

She walked onward beside the pristine river. In the clear water she could see the shadows of brook trout, and dragonflies sometimes dipped down close to the water. She smiled when she saw a wood turtle meandering along the embankment toward the brush a few feet away.

She was reminded of the pet turtle she had kept in a fish bowl when she was twelve years old. She had loved watching it, but she had begun to feel sorry for the turtle being imprisoned in such a way, so she had taken it to the pond and freed it.

She would never forget how quickly it went into the water and was lost to sight. She had understood then that it was wrong to keep anything captive, not even something whose companionship gave her such joy.

As the sun lowered farther in the sky, warning that Joylynn did not have long to enjoy her time in the water, she stopped. She looked over her shoulder to see if anyone was about, but spotted no one.

She looked to her left, at the thick brush that grew up to the forest's edge. She saw no movement there either.

She looked straight ahead again and saw nothing but the banks of the river. At last, she felt secure enough to undress.

She pulled her dress over her head and shook her moccasins from her feet. Only then was she aware how cool it had grown now that the sun was only a vague, purplish shadow along the horizon.

She hugged herself as she ran into the water, glad that it still held the warmth of a long day of being bathed in sunlight.

Joylynn dove into the water and began swimming. It gave her such a free feeling, something she had so enjoyed as a teenager. The water felt delicious on her body. She giggled when a tiny fish came up and nibbled on her leg.

She watched it swim away, probably disappointed that it had not found something to eat.

Joylynn resumed swimming, then suddenly realized how far she had traveled. She was far away from where she had left her clothes, and the sky would soon lose its light altogether.

She started to turn around and swim back to where she had entered the water, then stopped when she caught the scent of smoke. A thin spiral rose from a spot up ahead where there was a bend in the river.

Curious, yet knowing there could be danger so far from the village, she swam quietly onward to the bend in the river. When she reached it and could see where the smoke came from, she gasped and stopped, standing on the sandy river bottom.

It was a small frame lodge made of willows. Outside the entrance of the lodge, past the buffalo robe that was being used as an entrance flap, was a fire built in a circle of smooth, round rocks.

Her eyebrows rose when she saw a large rock in the center of the fire, glowing red from the heat.

She searched further and saw a clump of clothes and moccasins lying near the small lodge. Someone was there.

"A man's clothes," she whispered to herself, knowing now that she should turn around and swim quickly away, for where there was a man, a stranger, there might be trouble for her, a woman alone.

But just as she started to swim away, she stopped. She heard a voice singing something soft and low, as though in meditation, or prayer.

And then the voice was stilled and in its place came the sweet sound of what she thought might be a flute. Its melody was haunting and beautiful, making Joylynn believe that surely no one evil could play such enchanting music.

Her curiosity growing, Joylynn fought off the voice speaking in her head that said, "Go now, leave." And then she was glad that she had ignored it, for she saw with whom she shared this beautiful early evening. Her heart leapt inside her chest when High Hawk crawled out of the lodge.

Joylynn felt a strange, sensual melting inside when High Hawk stood up and the sunset's glow fell on his naked, copper body.

She watched him stretch his arms above his

head, making even more of him accessible to Joy-lynn's feasting eyes.

She saw the rippling of his muscles, from his head to his toes. The way his hair fell down his back as he gazed heavenward made her long to run to him and run her fingers through it. She loved his hair, every inch of it!

She even saw that part of a man she thought she would always fear after being raped so viciously.

But seeing High Hawk's full anatomy only awoke a strange hunger inside her heart, a hunger only he could fill.

She looked suddenly away from that part of him and again gazed at his sculpted face. How on earth could he be so handsome? So alluring? Such a wonderful specimen of a man?

She had seen many a man in her time, especially when she was a Pony Express rider, but none could compare with High Hawk.

So far he had not spotted her, for she was standing in the shadow of a low-hanging willow tree. She wasn't sure what she should do. He had come to this secluded spot for privacy and prayers; wouldn't he see her as an interference?

But if he was finished praying, and had come out to dress for his return home, perhaps he would welcome her.

Suddenly her heart seemed to drop to her toes when High Hawk broke into a run and dove into the water and began swimming in her direction.

He seemed so intent on his swim, he had yet to realize that he was not alone in the river.

As he grew closer to Joylynn, she wasn't sure what to do.

Allow him to see her?

Or go farther back into the shadows of the tree, then swim hurriedly around the bend that would take her from his view?

Might he not like it that she had come to his private place?

Or would he marvel at her being there? Would he come to her and welcome her in ways that she was longing to experience with him?

Just watching him, being this close to him in the water, caused her to freeze. And then suddenly it was too late to leave.

High Hawk had stopped suddenly, his eyes on her. "Joylynn?" he said, his eyes widening. He reached his hands to his wet hair and smoothed it back from his face. "Joylynn, you are so far from the village. Did you come this far because of me? How did you know where I was?"

"I decided to take a swim," Joylynn murmured as he swam toward her, his eyes never leaving her. "I guess . . . I . . . swam much farther than I realized. I had no idea you were here. I thought I was swimming where I could be alone."

He swam to her, then stood up, his eyes searching hers. "Do you not understand the danger of what you have done?" he asked, reaching a hand

170

out to her. "It might have been another man in the sweat lodge, not the man who loves you."

"But it is you," Joylynn said, her voice sounding strange to her. She was feeling emotions that she had never felt before in her entire life.

"*Ho*, it is I," High Hawk said, smiling slowly at her.

His arms went around her and drew her against his body, where she could feel every inch of his flesh, even that part of him that she most definitely did not fear.

Instead, she ached to have him inside her. She needed him. Here was someone who could fill her every need and desire.

This was someone she loved with all her heart!

And . . . he . . . loved her!

"I love you so," she murmured, melting inside when he brought his lips down on hers in a passionate kiss. His arms held her so tightly against him, she could feel his heartbeat blending with her own.

Both were pounding hard.

Their bodies strained against each other.

Their lips trembled with the emotion that was awakened within them.

And then High Hawk suddenly pulled Joylynn fully into his arms and carried her to the shore near his makeshift lodge.

He found a place of soft moss beneath a willow tree and spread Joylynn out upon it, then knelt down over her, straddling her with his knees.

"I have wanted you in this way for so long,"

High Hawk said, brushing her wet hair back from her face. "Have you wanted me as much? I have seen it in your eyes. I have heard it in your voice, that you did."

"I did not know that such a want . . . a need . . . existed until I met you," Joylynn said, reaching up and touching his thick black hair, then twining her arms around his neck.

"Are you saying that you want . . . to . . . make love?" he asked huskily, his eyes searching hers. "You want me in that way?"

"Oh, Lord, yes, yes, yes," Joylynn cried, her eyes closing in rapture as he slid a hand over one of her breasts, cupping it, causing an exquisite sensation of bliss.

Her head was spinning with ecstasy, especially when he lowered his lips to that breast and flicked the nipple with his tongue.

Joylynn was aware of a tingling sensation that filled her very being. The feel of his lips and tongue on her breast was wonderful.

He lifted his head and gazed into her eyes. "Are you well enough to do this?" he asked, proving again to Joylynn the gentle man that he was.

She had already given herself over to him, yet he hesitated and wanted to make sure she was able to make love after the miscarriage.

"*Ho*, yes, I am very well," she murmured. "Oh, High Hawk, do make love to me."

He needed no more encouragement. He had

waited so long for this moment. From the first time he had seen her that night in the moonlight, he knew that only she could satisfy the part of him that had been so long unfed.

And he was right. As she clung to him, her every secret place became his. He swept a hand down between them and found her hot, moist center.

And when she wrapped her legs around his waist, as though knowing what he needed, he took his manhood in one of his hands and slowly slid his heat up inside her warm, waiting folds.

He slid the hand back up and, as he began his rhythmic thrusts, placed it on one of her breasts and softly kneaded.

He groaned against her lips as once again he kissed her with a fierce, possessive heat.

Joylynn writhed in response and gave herself up to the rapture, drawing a ragged breath when he slid his lips down and rolled her nipple with his tongue.

She clung to him and floated, it seemed, above herself, as once again he touched her lips with his, wonderingly.

Waves of liquid heat pulsed through High Hawk's body. He stopped his rhythmic strokes for a moment to gaze at her. Her hair, the color of flame, lay softly around her shoulders.

Her eyes, the color of grass, gazed back at him, hazed over with the rapture that his thrusts were causing.

Her breasts were small, but high and full, the nipples a deep, smoky pink.

Joylynn gazed back at him, her pulse racing at seeing his dark, stormy eyes and the rapturous gaze he was giving her. Just looking at him made the raging hunger grow more intense within her.

And then he kissed her again, with a lazy warmth that left her weak, while his lean, sinewy buttocks continued to move, bringing with each thrust a feverish desire to reach the final peak. She knew it would be something she would never forget, not for the rest of her life.

Erotic heat knifed through her body, stabbing deeply into her secret places as the pleasure built and spread within her. She was flooded with emotions, all because of how she felt for this wonderful Pawnee chief.

She clung and moved with him as he groaned against her parted lips, whispering how dearly he loved her.

Suddenly explosive colors filled Joylynn's head as the fulfillment of their togetherness finally claimed her. She arched her back, clenched her fists as she continued to hold her arms around his neck, and cried out with a passion that matched his own. She felt his body quiver and quake when he reached his own highest peak of pleasure.

Shaken with the passion he had just found in this woman's arms, High Hawk held her for a while longer, then rolled away from her and stretched out on his back. The moon had risen, illuminating the sky with its bright fullness; the stars were like sparkling sequins against the backdrop of night.

The glow from the fire burning in front of the small lodge fell on Joylynn's body as High Hawk turned and gazed in wonder at her.

"My love for you is forever," he said huskily, with passion still glazing his eyes. "We will marry soon. Is that your wish?"

"I want nothing more from life than you and . . . and . . . bearing you children," Joylynn said, tears filling her eyes at the thought of the child she had lost.

She wanted many children to help erase the thought of the one she would never have.

"I, too, want children," High Hawk said thickly. "One in your image—"

"And several in yours," Joylynn said, giggling.

When a breeze came across the river, brushing over her bare flesh, she shivered.

"I see that you are cold," High Hawk said. "Come with me. I will place my buffalo robe around your shoulders until we go for your clothes."

Joylynn went with him and was glad when he took the buffalo robe that had been used for the entrance flap of the small lodge and gently placed it around her shoulders.

She watched him dress, finding it strange that she hadn't felt at all uneasy around him. She felt no awkwardness as she watched him slowly cover his naked body with his clothes.

Then he came and sat beside her, cradling her against him with one arm as they gazed into what remained of the fire.

Joylynn still marveled at the large rock that sat in the midst of the fire. It had lost its bright red color as its heat lessened, for the fire was burning lower and lower.

She looked over at High Hawk. "What is this small lodge for?" she asked softly.

"It is what my people call a sweat lodge," he said, gazing over his shoulder at it. "It is a place built for the purifying of one's body, and for prayer. I built this sweat lodge myself today. In it I took my whistle made from the wing bone of an eagle. I endured the purifying sweat as I sang sacred songs and played music on my whistle."

"I noticed a large rock in the fire, glowing red," Joylynn murmured. "What is its purpose?"

"Inside the sweat lodge is a small circle made from rocks," he said, nodding. "I took hot stones from the outdoor fire, like the one you saw, which I did not use, and once inside I poured water over the stones, making steam fill the lodge. I purified myself with the steam and sage that I spread on the floor, and when I was finished I dried my body with the leaves of the sage. When I came from the lodge, even before I entered the river, I felt pure and clean."

"And then you saw me," Joylynn murmured. "Did seeing me disturb what you had just done? Did my presence take away the purity you found in the sweat lodge?"

"Seeing you was the perfect ending to an evening of prayer and music," High Hawk said, taking one of her hands. "You make me complete, my woman."

He leaned closer to her and drew her into his embrace. He kissed her, causing the buffalo robe to fall from her shoulders.

He spread the robe out across the grass, then leaned over her and kissed her again. One of his hands slid his fringed breeches down so he could enter her again, making love this time slowly and sweetly.

The cry of a loon wafted toward them from across the river just as they again came to the final throes of their passion.

Stunned that she had actually made love twice in one day with a man, Joylynn giggled as he rolled away from her, leaving his hand resting across that part of her body that still throbbed from their lovemaking.

When he began slowly stroking her love bud with his fingers, arousing in her a renewed rapturous bliss, she grabbed him around his waist and drew him atop her.

Again they found ecstasy, then lay on their backs, breathing hard, their faces flushed.

"Tomorrow you will be too tired to leave on another hunt for that dreaded outlaw," Joylynn said. She instantly regretted her words when she realized that bringing Mole into this special moment might have broken the spell that had been woven between her and High Hawk.

When he reached for her and lifted her onto his lap, she knew that nothing could spoil these special moments between them. He sat up, facing the river, his hands molding her breasts as she slowly rocked with him.

"Nothing will keep me from the hunt," High Hawk said, bending low to brush a kiss across first one of her breasts, and then the other. She closed her eyes and threw her head back in rapture.

Then she realized that he had just said he was definitely going on another search for Mole tomorrow.

She gazed into his eyes.

She took his hands from her breasts and held them.

"My wonderful Pawnee chief, my adorable love, I ask you again, please allow me to go with you tomorrow," she murmured.

When he didn't say anything, only drew her close and hugged her, Joylynn decided not to pursue the matter now.

She just relaxed, giving herself up to enjoyment of these moments with the man she loved.

Tomorrow, though?

She would be mounting up along with High

Hawk, and would leave the village with him to hunt for Mole, no matter how the women gasped at her bold actions.

They surely had already learned that she was different from most women they had ever known.

That thought made her smile and lean closer to High Hawk and bury her nose in the hair that lay in front of his shoulders. "I so love your hair," she whispered, slowly stroking her fingers through it.

She gazed up at him. "I . . . so . . . love you," she murmured, smiling at him.

When he smiled back at her, with such love and adoration in his eyes, her night was complete.

But there *was* tomorrow, and she most definitely would not take no for an answer when she mounted her horse to join the hunt with High Hawk and his warriors.

CHAPTER EIGHTEEN

It seemed like a dream to Joylynn that High Hawk was actually allowing her to ride with him and his warriors on this newest search for Mole and his outlaw friends. Upon first arising this morning, High Hawk had told her that he had one more place in particular that neither he nor his warriors had yet searched. It had come to him in a dream, which had awakened him with a start.

She was riding on her beautiful chestnut stallion, High Hawk on his best steed. They were far from the village now, after eating a good morning meal. It had to be enough nourishment to last for a while, for once they began traveling this morning, High Hawk said there would be no stopping. His dream was leading him onward, and he did not want to waste any time.

It was still early; the sun was barely creeping up

from behind the trees. The air was crisp, with a hint of the cold weather that was to come.

Joylynn wore a long-sleeved buckskin dress, which was heavier and warmer than doeskin.

She wore the same sort of headband that High Hawk and his warriors wore in order to keep her long hair back from her face as she rode beside the man she loved. It was a plain band of buckskin, with no fancy beading on it.

She had twisted her hair into one long braid down her back.

But High Hawk and his warriors wore their hair loose and free. High Hawk's was blowing in the breeze, away from his muscled, bare shoulders. Joylynn gazed at him with admiration, proud that he was the leader of a fine, peace-loving people.

She hoped that this was the day they would find Mole. The evil man seemed to have nine lives. He was so elusive, no one ever saw him unless he wanted to be seen.

But today? Ah, yes, today she believed that he would finally get his comeuppance. High Hawk was convinced that his dream would lead them to their quarry.

Suddenly Joylynn's gaze was drawn to the side of the trail. Far to her right were two animals that she had never expected to see together.

A skunk and a porcupine were approaching each other warily, oblivious of the thundering of the horse's hooves. They were only interested in each other.

They then turned and backed toward each other, the porcupine preparing to strike with the deadly spikes of its tail, and the skunk with its stink.

The porcupine looked over its shoulder before striking, and the skunk discharged its spray full in the other animal's face.

But at the same moment, the skunk was struck by the porcupine's quills, and the skunk squealed and fled. Meanwhile, the porcupine was gagging, coughing and retching as it ambled away into the brush in the opposite direction.

"I saw it, too," High Hawk said.

She was glad to see him smiling, for up until now, he had been deadly serious.

"I have never seen the like," Joylynn said, laughing softly. "I hope never to be attacked by either of those animals, for their ways of protecting themselves seem lethal, indeed."

High Hawk started to respond, but the sound of a horse approaching from the other direction caused his jaw to tighten. He drew rein, and his warriors followed his lead as Three Bears, whom High Hawk had sent on ahead to scout the area, came riding hard toward them.

When Three Bears reached them and drew up, breathing hard, Joylynn saw that his eyes sparkled with a strange sort of victory.

"Your dream told you truths," Three Bears said, smiling widely. "Mole is where your vision said he would be."

Then his smile faded. "But he is not alone," he said thickly.

"I knew he would not be alone," High Hawk replied. "In my dream, his outlaw friends were with him. They were sitting around a fire, eating their morning meal. Were they eating when you spied them?"

"*Ho*, they were eating, and if you inhale deeply enough, you will even now smell the scent of smoke and cooked venison from their campfire," Three Bears said. He leaned closer to High Hawk. "But there are more than his outlaw friends sitting around the fire with Mole."

"Who else?" High Hawk asked, lifting an eyebrow. "I saw no one else in my dream."

"Your dream must have ended before the pony soldiers entered it," Three Bears said guardedly.

"Pony soldiers?" High Hawk and Joylynn said almost at the same time.

"Pony soldiers are with the outlaws?" High Hawk asked, gazing past Three Bears in the direction of where Mole was camping with his outlaw gang.

"*Ho*," Three Bears said. "From where I watched in hiding I could hear them planning an attack on our village."

Joylynn's heart was racing. She never would have believed that any soldier under the command of a decent colonel would ally himself with the likes of Mole.

How could it be that Mole and the soldiers were coming together to fight the Pawnee? Just the thought of the United States government going back on its word to live in peace with these Indians made her skin crawl.

She knew how the government had duped the red man before, time and again, and how so many Indian tribes had suffered cruel raids. Even children had been killed in those attacks.

Now was she to witness the carnage she had read about?

Was she to die at the hands of people of her own skin color because she had aligned herself with the Pawnee?

The thought of dying alongside High Hawk did not frighten her as much as it made her feel keen resentment toward the lying white men who just could not stop until they killed every Indian on the face of the earth.

She had lived among the Pawnee long enough to know what a peaceful, loving people they were. They wanted nothing more from life than to live in peace, and to raise their children.

"Is it possible the white chief in Washington has decided to go against his treaties with us?" High Hawk demanded, doubling a fist.

His people had been promised they would not be bothered as long as they walked the road of peace.

His father had walked that road, just as High Hawk planned to walk it.

But now?

What was High Hawk to think?

What was he to do?

"I must see for myself," he said, reaching a hand to his rifle, which was sheathed in a gunboot at the right side of his horse. "If it is true, we have no choice but to kill those who plot with Mole."

He glanced at Joylynn. "Under these circumstances, my woman, I want you to return to the village," he said firmly. "I will send you there with an escort. I do not want anything to happen to you."

"Please don't ask that of me," Joylynn said, pleading with her eyes as she gazed into his. "You need all the help you can get if the soldiers are plotting against you. And if they are sitting with Mole and his outlaws, eating with them as though they are kindred souls, then you know they have nothing good on their minds. I want to help you stop what has just begun around that campfire. Anyone who would side with Mole has to be as bad as he."

"I hope you understand why I must take care of this now before any of my people are harmed," High Hawk said thickly. "If the soldiers are there plotting with Mole when we arrive at the campsite, they must be among the casualties."

"I understand," Joylynn said, her voice tight. "And I will be at your side to help you. You need as many people fighting with you as possible. I am a crack shot. My father taught me well."

"But you will be firing upon people of your own skin color," High Hawk said.

"They might be of my color, but inside their hearts, they are not the same as I," Joylynn said, placing a gentle hand on his face. "I love you. I love your people. I must do what I can to help."

High Hawk took her hand and kissed its palm, smiled, then released it.

He turned and gazed over his shoulder at his warriors, whose eyes were lit with the fire of eagerness for what lay ahead of them. "My woman stays with us," he said, his eyes moving from man to man to see how each felt. "She will be among us as we attack."

He saw a look of astonishment in some of the men's eyes, and looks of pride in others'. He thanked destiny, which had brought him a woman of such courage, who would risk her life for him, and for his people.

His gaze met Joylynn's again. "Come, we have business to attend to," he said, then looked over at Three Bears. "You ride on one side, while my woman rides on the other, until we get close enough to stop and leave our horses behind. You know when that should be, since you have seen the camp. Tell me when we should halt our steeds."

Three Bears nodded and smiled, then sank his heels into the flanks of his horse as High Hawk and

Joylynn rode away with him, the other warriors riding behind them.

The farther they rode, the more frightened Joylynn became. She was going to be part of an attack, and not only that, she would be fighting against people of her own skin color! Once it was over, would she regret her actions?

Or would she be proud to have helped such a fine people as the Pawnee?

She knew the answer to that without thinking about it. She would be proud to help High Hawk and his people.

They rode onward for a while longer, until the smell of smoke from the campfire became stronger.

Then Three Bears raised a fist into the air, turned to High Hawk and nodded. They all brought their horses to a stop.

Joylynn could not help it; her knees were strangely rubbery as she dismounted and grabbed her rifle from the gunboot at Swiftie's side. It was her own rifle, which High Hawk had given back to her after declaring her no longer a captive.

All of the horses were picketed amid thick grass and left to feast upon it while the Pawnee warriors, with High Hawk in the lead and Joylynn at his right side, moved stealthily and quietly onward, some with bows and arrows at the ready, others with loaded rifles.

Joylynn's heart raced as they grew close enough to the camp that she could hear the loud laughter of the men. They must be telling jokes around the campfire, or even laughing at the fate of the red men, women and children whom they planned to ambush.

She had no doubt that was the plan, which made it easier for her to do what she knew she must at High Hawk's side.

She looked heavenward and whispered a prayer, then stopped when High Hawk reached out and grabbed her arm.

"We must hurry into the trees and let their dark shadows hide us from the white men," he said to Joylynn, only loud enough for her to hear.

He did not have to speak commands aloud to his men. They were practiced at this sort of ambush. They knew they could not give the white eyes the chance to flee. If any white eyes escaped, they would carry the word of this attack back to the one in charge of the pony soldiers.

Silently High Hawk motioned a halt when the men at the campfire came into sight. They were getting ready to mount up.

Joylynn's eyes widened when she saw how many soldiers had aligned themselves with Mole and his murdering, thieving outlaws.

And when she saw a pile of firearms that was be-ing distributed by the soldiers to the outlaws, she knew there was a collaboration between these murdering thieves and someone in the army. She wondered how far up the chain of command the corruption went.

"My prayers were not ignored. *Tirawahut*, my people's Great Spirit, told me where to come today," High Hawk whispered as he leaned closer to Joylynn. "My dreams brought me here just in time!"

"I am sickened by what I see," Joylynn whispered back. "Did you see the rifles? How many there are? The soldiers had to have brought them there, to give to Mole and his men. I am certain they are army-issued rifles."

"I see it all and I am here to stop it," High Hawk replied, studying the white men now as they loaded their rifles, laughing, boasting of the Pawnee scalps they would take, the squaws they would rape.

He turned back toward Joylynn. "You have time now to return to the village," he said, his voice drawn. "If you stay, you will see things that may give you nightmares for the rest of your life."

He looked at the rifle she clutched hard in her right hand, then gazed into her eyes again. "Especially if you kill people whose skin is white like yours," he said. "Turn away now if you feel you should. I would understand."

"I would never turn away from doing justice," Joylynn said, her eyes filled with loathing for those who were planning to kill innocent people. She searched his eyes. She squared her shoulders. "And I am not afraid."

High Hawk smiled. "I saw much courage in you the night we first met," he said. "You are like no woman I have ever known, and you are mine."

"*Ho*, yours," Joylynn said, proud to be using an Indian word now and then, for when she did, she knew she pleased High Hawk.

He reached a hand to her cheek, then nodded. "It is now time," he said softly.

The attack happened so quickly it seemed like a blur to Joylynn. The Pawnee warriors fired upon the outlaws and their allies. The soldiers grabbed their firearms and tried to defend themselves, but to no avail.

Suddenly there was silence. There were no more reports from the rifles. There was no sound of arrows whizzing through the air. There were no more cries of death.

All who had been plotting against the red men were quiet. Their voices would no longer mock the Pawnee before they killed innocent villagers. None of those who spoke of raping a downed Indian woman were alive to brag about such a deplorable act again. No Indian child would die at the hands of these fallen men today!

But Joylynn had not gotten off one round of gunfire. Once the attack began, she had frozen. Her eyes wide, she had watched it happen, and then it was over.

A warrior rushed over to High Hawk. "One escaped," he said breathlessly. "Two of our warriors have gone in pursuit of him."

Joylynn hardly heard what he said, for her eyes were on Mole. He lay there, quiet, covered with blood.

He was obviously dead.

His reign of terror was over.

He would no longer ambush innocent people, both red and white-skinned.

He would no longer rape helpless women!

She turned her eyes away, for seeing him again brought the rape rushing back into her mind as though it had just happened.

Her hand went almost automatically to her belly. The loss of her child still tore at her soul.

If not for that man, she would have not been pregnant. She would not have aborted an innocent baby!

But if not for him, she would have never met High Hawk. Even now she would be riding Swiftie on her route for the Pony Express.

She never would have known the bliss and joy of being with High Hawk. She would have had no need to hide away from humanity until the child was born. She would not have been at that cabin that night when High Hawk rode by.

"Joylynn?"

High Hawk's voice interrupted her troubled thoughts. She turned quickly toward him.

Her eyes were wide and tears spilled from them as she gazed into his.

"You cry," High Hawk said, wiping tears from her face with his thumb. "Do you regret having stayed? Do you regret what you now see?"

"No. It is just that seeing Mole again has brought such terrible memories to mind," she said, glancing again at the outlaw's body.

"He will not touch you again, nor will he harm innocent white people, or red," High Hawk said.

He gazed past her into the darker depths of the forest, then into her eyes again. "One soldier escaped," he said. "That means trouble for my people."

"What do you mean?" Joylynn asked.

"If the escaped soldier is not found, he will carry news of today's ambush to those in charge," High Hawk said. "I must see that my people do not suffer because of what had to be done today."

"What can you do?" Joylynn asked, placing a gentle hand on his smooth, copper cheek. She ached inside to see the torment in his eyes.

"We must return home quickly and prepare my people for a quick departure to a place where they can hide from the pony soldiers," High Hawk said. "*Ho*, when that soldier arrives at his fort and explains what happened today, the pony soldiers will come in large numbers, looking for High Hawk and his warriors. Not only that. They will slaughter my entire Wolf band."

"Your warriors will surely find him," Joylynn said, horrified at the thought of what High Hawk now feared.

"Even so, once the bodies of these downed soldiers are found, I fear there will be trouble," he said. He gazed at her rifle and saw that it had not been fired. "I am glad you did not fire upon the whites. That means that if they ever catch us, they cannot fault you for what happened. They will, instead, see you as my captive and will take you with them, thinking they have saved you from a 'savage.' "

Joylynn dropped her rifle and flung herself into his arms. "I can never leave you, not for any reason," she sobbed, clinging to him. "You are my life, High Hawk. You are my very breath and heartbeat."

"As you are mine," he said, gently holding her. "That is why we must leave quickly for the mountains. I have always known this would happen, that a time would come when my people would be forced to seek shelter away from the white eyes. I have searched and found the place where more children will be born into our band, and where those who are children now will grow up and have children of their own."

"You already know where you will go?" Joylynn asked. "You knew this might happen?"

"Always," High Hawk said, again drawing her close and hugging her.

Suddenly there was the sound of horses arriving.

Joylynn's heart skipped a beat. Had the sound of gunshots brought someone to investigate already?

But soon the two warriors who'd been sent to find the escaped soldier came into view. They rode up to High Hawk.

"He is long gone," one of them said. "We traced his tracks, then lost them in the river. He has apparently gotten far ahead of us."

"Then we must hurry home and prepare for our departure immediately. Once that soldier arrives at his fort, and reports what happened, the white eyes will be out for blood . . . *ours*," he said. "Hurry home. Prepare your families quickly for departure. You know where we are going. I have met in council with you and told you."

He turned and looked at the stack of rifles, and at others lying beside the dead men.

He gave his warriors a tight-jawed look. "Before we head for home, gather up all the rifles you can find among the dead, as well as those stacked there. They are now ours. If the white eyes find us, we will use their own firearms against them."

The warriors nodded, and after gathering up the rifles, hurried to their picketed horses.

Joylynn took one last look at Mole, not allowing herself to again relive the rape, then smiled and ran alongside High Hawk until they reached their horses.

Soon they were riding hard toward their village, knowing that time was now their enemy.

"Although I hate to leave the village where my people have lived for generations, where our ancestors are buried, the place I will lead my people to now is a paradise," High Hawk said to Joylynn. "It is a place where our children will be born and raised without the fear of white eyes waiting to shoot them in the back."

"Wherever you are will be the right place for me, a true paradise," Joylynn replied, smiling. His answering smile brought a wonderful warmth into her heart, helping erase the memories of blood and death they were leaving behind them.

CHAPTER NINETEEN

The village was a sad sight to behold. Only yesterday the Pawnee had been a content people. With their crops harvested and placed in cache pots, with much meat put aside, as well as warm clothes made from newly tanned buckskin, they were well-prepared for the cold winter ahead.

But now as she stood watching, she saw nothing but fear and despair as the villagers ran here and there, getting ready for their flight into the mountains.

Joylynn would never forget how High Hawk had explained their journey to his people after they'd returned to the village. "Send your conscious minds ahead to the mountain that now beckons us, for that is where we will have a peaceful life without interference ever again from our enemies. I have been there, my people. My spirit mind, my dreams, led me there. I was told that this is the true home of the Wolf band, my beloved people. That is where we will go as quickly as you can load your belongings on travois and packhorses."

Frantic activity ensued when everyone disbanded after the announcement. The people rushed into their lodges, taking what they could from them.

Joylynn had helped load High Hawk's mother's personal belongings, piling everything on a travois, all the while glancing at Sleeping Wolf, whose fear was evident on his face. He had watched, wild-eyed, as everything he knew changed before his very eyes.

She would never forget how Sleeping Wolf had gone to his brother, his body all twisted, one leg dragging behind him, and looked into High Hawk's eyes for answers.

Tears had filled her eyes when High Hawk had taken his brother into his arms and comforted him as one would a small child. Afterwards, Sleeping Wolf seemed comforted and unafraid as he tried to help his mother with the final preparations.

Clouds had suddenly covered the sun, and there was a hint of rain in the air as thunder boomed far off, coming from the very mountains in which they would seek shelter and make their new home.

A chill wind came to Joylynn, causing a shiver to ride her spine, even though she wore a coat made of warm bearskin.

She hugged herself, still watching the frantic activity around her, wondering if High Hawk regretted having slain the soldiers. But what else could he have done when they were planning to annihilate his people?

He was a wise leader, one who thought over all decisions before acting on them. Since he had already chosen a place to take his people when the time came to leave their home, he had known he could escape the soldiers' reprisals.

Tired already, even before they had begun the rigorous trek up the mountainside, Joylynn had taken a short rest. She stood just outside High Hawk's tepee now, listening to the echoes of thunder, a reminder that a storm could threaten their journey.

She hugged herself and gazed heavenward, sighing with relief when the clouds slowly moved onward. The sun came out again, and the sky turned blue. Even the thunder had ceased to rumble in the distance.

Hearing High Hawk's mother's voice, Joylynn turned and saw her hurrying to High Hawk, who was instructing a warrior about the people's horses. Even now the horses were being taken from the personal corrals of the village, while other warriors had gone where the other steeds had been hidden, gathering them together for the long trek to their new home.

"High Hawk, what of the food stored in the caches?" Blanket Woman asked, stopping and gazing up at her son, who now carried more weight on his shoulders than had ever been required of her chieftain husband.

Her husband had struggled to keep his people safe from the white pony soldiers and outlaws. He had always feared that one day they would be forced to find a new home, or die, or worse yet—be penned up like animals on a reservation.

Her husband had kept his Wolf band of Pawnee in their home, where so many generations of their people had been born and died, but he had also sent his second-born son away more than once to seek a new place for his people should danger ever threaten them.

That place had not been found during any scouting trip, but instead, had come to High Hawk in a dream. He had followed that dream and found the place of his people's future. He had kept the location locked inside his heart until only recently, when he had known it was time to share this knowledge with the warriors of his village.

They were sworn to secrecy.

That had kept the knowledge of their new home safe.

High Hawk knew that once he took his people there, they would not have to concern themselves about such men as had been slain today.

But Joylynn feared there was no place that could not be found by men who were determined to find it. She only hoped that many generations of Pawnee would be born before the people of her own race finally found them.

"Son, there is much food in our people's caches this year," Blanket Woman continued. "Must it truly be left behind?"

High Hawk placed a gentle hand on his mother's bent, frail shoulders. "*Ina,* you and the other women are to take from your cache pits only what can be carried on the travois and packhorses. Some household items might have to be left behind in order to make room for the food we must take with us."

He looked at the women who had come and circled round him after hearing Blanket Woman's question.

He glanced from one to another, hating to see the fear in the eyes that until today had been filled with peace and joy.

He could not fault himself, but instead blamed those white eyes who just could not allow the red man to live how they had lived for generations.

The red man wanted nothing from white people but to be left alone on land that had always been his, but such was not to be. Every day, new interlopers arrived on Pawnee soil.

The treaties that had been signed by the white chief in Washington were like falling leaves, fluttering around on an autumn day, having no true meaning any longer.

They would tumble in the wind, drying up more as each day passed, soon to break up into tiny bits and pieces, to be lost in the dirt upon which people walked and rode their steeds.

"Each of you decide what is best for your family to take to our new home," he said solemnly. "But I must remind you, food is most important of all those things. Know this: Soon winter snows will fall, so no crops can be planted when we first arrive at our new home. Take food to eat and seed for spring planting. Think and choose wisely, for your family's future depends upon your decision."

He gestured a hand toward them. "Go, time is wasting," he said tightly. "We must hurry to leave this place, where our hearts will remain behind us. But your souls will soon be at peace when you see where your new home will be established. I have seen. I know. It is nothing less than a paradise."

This made the women's eyes light up. If their beloved young chief said their new home would be a paradise, they believed him. They knew him to be truthful in all things. They trusted him in all things.

"Children," High Hawk said, his voice carrying to the ears of the young ones, who seemed stunned by what was happening, their eyes revealing their confusion. "Go into the garden and fields and make certain there is no stray corn left there, nor any remains of the recently harvested crops. We want to leave nothing there for the soldiers."

What he said next caused the women to stop almost in mid-step and turn to look at him once again with shock in their eyes.

"You women, burn the caches of corn and vegetables that you cannot take with you so that no white man or soldier can profit from your hard work," he said firmly.

Joylynn was as stunned by his order as the women.

She recalled the hard work of making the caches and then filling them with corn.

As each moment passed, the truth of what was happening seemed to cut more deeply into the hearts of these wonderful people.

She tried to put from her mind the sadness of it, the heartache. Instead, she hurried with Blanket Woman toward the older woman's personal cache pit.

"We must first take food to sustain us through the winter, and carefully choose the seeds we take with us for our future crops," Blanket Woman said. "For corn, we must select the very best from the braided strings. We need five braided strings of soft white and thirty ears of yellow, and ten ears of gummy corn."

Blanket Woman huffed and puffed as she hurried onward, explaining what they must take in order to have everything that would be needed for their new homes, and in their new gardens.

"Joylynn, while selecting corn with me, choose only good, full, plump ears," Blanket Woman said. "And take only kernels in the center of the cob, rejecting the large at one end and the small at the other. In shelling the seed corn, remove the kernels from the cob with your thumb. Since seed corn can be kept for two years, all families reserve enough for two crops. So shall we today."

They hurried to where the cache pit had been hidden. Joylynn tried to remember all the instructions as she helped uncover the pit.

She smiled over her shoulder at a young brave who brought a horse with a travois dragging behind it. The travois would carry the food that was taken from Blanket Woman's personal cache pit today.

Blanket Woman thanked him, and he began helping dig through the twigs and leaves that had been lain on top of the cache pit, to conceal it from anyone who might happen along.

When the cache pit was open, Joylynn worked tirelessly alongside the young brave and Blanket Woman, marveling at the old woman's stamina as she continued to take the stored vegetables and fruit from her cache pit. She loaded it all on the travois in bags.

Clothes, blankets, lodge coverings and other belongings had already been loaded on another travois and on the packhorse's backs. They were ready for the long climb ahead.

Joylynn turned and gazed at the mountain that was their destination. A sense of dread filled her soul, for she knew that some of the passes would be narrow and steep. Could the packhorses make the dangerous climb? Could all the people, some of whom were frail with age?

Those people would travel by way of travois, too, as would Sleeping Wolf, since he was not able to ride, or even walk for any amount of time.

Blanket Woman hugged the boy who was helping them and thanked him in the language of the Pawnee.

He smiled and ran to help others.

"We have chosen the most excellent of seeds to start our new crops," Blanket Woman said, groaning as she placed a hand at the small of her back. "And we have enough packed to sustain us until the new crops can be harvested next year."

Blanket Woman turned to Joylynn. Her eyes wavered as she gazed at the younger woman. "Thank you for helping," she said, her voice breaking. "I am beginning to understand why my son loves you. Although you were born into the white world, your heart beats with the feelings of us Pawnee. My son High Hawk is a very astute man. He saw in you what I stubbornly would not allow myself to see."

"That's because you and your people have been given cause not to trust anyone whose skin is white," Joylynn said. She was ready to hug this woman who was admitting things Joylynn knew were hard for her to say. The moment Blanket Woman had first seen Joylynn, there had been hatred etched in her eyes.

But now? Joylynn saw something very different. She saw kindness. Joylynn hoped that in time Blanket Woman would love her as she would have loved a daughter.

Finally everyone was ready to leave. Before their departure, Two Stars said a prayer aloud to *Tirawahut*, asking for a safe journey.

Other prayers were said by various people, and High Hawk's voice joined them, reaching for the heavens.

Tears came to Joylynn's eyes at the injustice of it all. Like so many Indians before them, the Wolf band was being forced to leave their home, taking with them their cherished memories of the time when no white people walked on Indian soil. They would have to leave behind the life they had loved, with only the faint hope that they could reestablish it where they were going.

And they set out with the possibility that even their new home might be invaded eventually by the evil of white men who would not leave them in peace.

"It is time to go," High Hawk said, looking over his shoulder at his brother, who lay on a travois. In Sleeping Wolf's eyes was a deep sorrow at leaving behind the only home he'd ever known.

High Hawk was swamped with guilt at the knowledge that he was, in part, responsible for this flight into the mountains. Yet he knew he was not truly to blame. He had avenged his father's death.

He could not have done anything less. Nor would any of his people. And he could not stand by while white soldiers plotted the deaths of his people.

Because they had aligned themselves with the white devil, they, too, had had to die.

The procession was long and quiet as the Pawnee began their long journey.

Joylynn had spotted her binoculars in one of High Hawk's bags. Knowing that a close watch must be kept for pursuing soldiers, she had taken the binoculars and hung the leather strap around the pommel of the saddle on her horse.

She wanted to do everything in her power to help keep these people safe!

CHAPTER TWENTY

Still feeling useless and more dispirited than ever before in his life, Sleeping Wolf lay on the travois, glancing over and over again at the steep drop-off at his left side.

Today as the journey contined, once again the Pawnee were traveling along a narrow mountain pass. Everyone was quiet and alert, for one wrong slip of a horse's hoof and someone's life could be lost as he or she went tumbling down the mountain.

Sleeping Wolf knew that the warrior who rode the horse to which Sleeping Wolf's travois was attached held his reins firm and steady. His eyes were kept straight ahead as he watched the trail for dangerous spots.

As always since the journey to their new home had begun, Sleeping Wolf was on a travois pulled by the very last horse in the procession. He had requested this position, saying he enjoyed the scenery better if he didn't have to be between other travois and packhorses.

But he was not enjoying anything except the eagles that occasionally soared in wide circles above him. He felt more and more in the way, especially knowing that he was slowing his people down since he could not ride a horse.

The long days on the travois gave him too much time to think about the worthlessness of his life. There was nothing positive he could add to the lives of his people.

Instead, he needed someone to look after him all the time. His mother, upon whom most of the burden fell, had surely grown tired of her nuisance of a son, but worked hard to cover up those feelings by overprotecting him.

No, he could not hunt to supply meat for his mother's cook pots. . . .

He suddenly saw a soaring gathering of bald eagles above him, their huge, widespread wings casting massive shadows onto him. One by one the mammoth birds came close, then circled back.

Suddenly he had a strong desire to join them!

They seemed to be beckoning him!

"I am coming," he whispered as he watched them soar now below him, beside the mountain, instead of high in the sky.

They would sweep up close to the side of the mountain, then fly again further away from it. He could feel their eyes on him when they came closer.

He knew that they wanted him to be a part of their flight today!

His heart pounding, he gazed up at the warrior on his horse before Sleeping Wolf's travois. He was ignoring the eagles, instead still carefully watching where he was traveling.

Ho, everyone was too intent on navigating this narrow pass to notice Sleeping Wolf. He gazed at the birds again as they soared above him, and then again swept down lower to fly alongside the mountain.

With a peaceful, serene smile on his face, feeling triumphant for the first time in his life, Sleeping Wolf threw off his blankets. At last, he was actually doing something that he wanted to do, and without the help of his mother, shaman or chieftain brother. As quietly as possible, he rolled gently off the travois and immediately found himself tumbling down a steep incline, then falling free, like the eagles he had been watching. They were flying and soaring above and then beside him, their eyes ever watching him.

He was an eagle . . . flying!

He could not walk without much effort, but he could fly effortlessly!

He smiled as he continued to fall, his long black hair blowing away from his shoulders, his face feeling the soft sweetness of the air, his heart filled with joy, for he was now free . . . free . . . free!

When he finally came to an outcropping of rock, he hit it with a hard thud, dying immediately with a smile on his lips.

CHAPTER TWENTY-ONE

Having finally cleared the dangerous path he and his people had been riding on, High Hawk sighed deeply. He was relieved that there had been no mishaps. Now there was more earth than rock on their right side, and they could travel more safely. High Hawk's first thoughts were of his brother. He had not been able to check on him for some time because everyone had to ride in single file. High Hawk was at the head of the procession, Sleeping Wolf at the tail.

He felt that his brother needed some reassurance, for this morning, before they had set out on another day's grueling journey, he had seen something in Sleeping Wolf's eyes that he had never seen before. Total defeat.

And High Hawk understood. Sleeping Wolf was the only one besides the elderly and ill who traveled on a travois to their new home. If he had felt useless before, he must feel doubly so now.

High Hawk no longer knew what to say to his brother to lift his spirits. Sleeping Wolf seemed to have retreated to his own little world, one of stark loneliness.

And the way their mother constantly coddled him, treating him more like he was a baby than a grown man, had made Sleeping Wolf feel even more helpless. He had grown tired of not only her, but also her voice, Sleeping Wolf had confided to High Hawk. He craved to be alone. To him, that was better than being treated like a child.

High Hawk nodded a quiet hello to those he rode past as he moved down the line to see how his brother fared. Surely it had frightened him to be riding on a travois so close to the steep drop-off.

Perhaps now that their path was not so treacherous, Sleeping Wolf would feel less anxious. Perhaps he would even smile when he saw his brother High Hawk.

High Hawk looked over his shoulder and saw Joylynn glance back at him, as though she had known he was going to look at her.

Last night, beneath the stars, he had wanted her ever so badly.

But everyone lay in close proximity of each other. Their blankets were arranged as close as possible to the campfire, in order to make certain no mountain lion could come upon them as they slept and drag them away.

A fire always kept the night's animals away, for a fire was something unknown to them, and the unknown was feared by all beings; not only animals.

He gave Joylynn a smile, then turned and made his way again down the line of people. He was almost at the end of the procession, where he hoped his brother lay as comfortably as possible on the travois.

High Hawk had seen to it that he would rest on many blankets and pelts, in order to cushion his twisted back.

His mother had placed one of her more beautiful blankets on him, taking the time to lovingly tuck in the sides before they headed out this morning.

High Hawk nudged his steed with his heels and rode onward, nodding a hello to the warrior whose horse pulled Sleeping Wolf's travois.

Then High Hawk's heart went cold as he saw that the travois was empty, the blanket that had covered his brother dragging on the ground beside it.

"Sleeping Wolf!" High Hawk cried. He shouted at the warrior. "Stop! My brother. He is gone!"

The horse that was transporting the travois stopped, as did all the others ahead of him.

The horror in High Hawk's voice had caused everyone to stop and gaze at him, alarm on their faces.

Having heard, Joylynn rode quickly back to join High Hawk.

When she reached him, she dismounted and stood with him as he looked back in the direction they had traveled.

"He must have fallen off," Joylynn said, pale at the thought of what might have happened.

She looked quickly at Blanket Woman as two warriors escorted her there, one on each side of her, steadying her as they gripped her elbows.

"My son!" Blanket Woman cried as she stared at the empty travois, then looked in desperation at High Hawk. "He . . . is . . . gone. Where, High Hawk? Where is he?"

High Hawk went to his mother and embraced her as the two warriors stepped away from her. "Somewhere behind us," he said thickly. "He must have rolled off. We shall go and find him and bring him back."

"But if he fell off, why did he not cry out and alert someone?" Blanket Woman said, kneeling down beside the travois and running a hand across the indention of her son's body in the blankets.

Then she looked quickly up at High Hawk again. "He must have been injured by his fall from the travois," she said, tears spilling from her eyes. "He must have been knocked unconscious, or he would have alerted us that something had happened to him."

"*Ina*, the fall off the travois would not be far

216

enough to knock my brother unconscious," he said gently. "Probably, he did not want to cause any more problems after he slipped from the travois, so he decided to just lie there until someone discovered he was gone."

"But why?" Blanket Woman asked, pleading with her eyes. "Why would he feel he could not let anyone know he'd fallen off the travois?"

"*Ina*, I do not have any answers, and as long as we stand here talking about it, he is still back there, alone," High Hawk said. "*Ina*, I will go now. I will find and bring my brother back."

He shouted at several of his warriors, then mounted his steed as Joylynn mounted her own. They rode off down the trail, back over the land they had just traveled, but no matter how far they rode, they did not find any trace of Sleeping Wolf.

Joylynn sidled her steed over closer to High Hawk's. "I'm afraid to say what might have happened," she said, her voice drawn.

"Say it," High Hawk said, looking intently into her eyes.

"Back where the path was so narrow, where we rode beside a steep drop-off, he might have fallen to his death far below," Joylynn said, her voice breaking. "I fear that is what happened, High Hawk."

"But he surely would have cried out as he fell," High Hawk said, kneading his brow in frustration. "Someone, especially the warrior who was transporting him, would have heard."

Joylynn swallowed hard. "Do you think he did not want to be heard?" she asked guardedly. "He has been so despondent of late. Could he have . . . ?"

"Suicide is a sin unforgiven by *Tirawahut*, so I do not believe my brother would risk that," High Hawk said softly.

They rode onward, to where the land dropped off steeply at their right.

But this part of the journey had been long; they would have to travel a full day to retrace their steps beside the drop-off.

High Hawk decided to turn back and carry the news of his brother to his mother. He was almost certain Sleeping Wolf had perished by falling over the cliff.

He rode silently beside Joylynn, followed by the other warriors, and when they reached those who awaited news of Sleeping Wolf, his eyes went straight to his mother. He knew that she must have guessed the news was not good, or he would have had Sleeping Wolf with him.

Seeing the absence of her elder son, Blanket Woman began wailing and pulling at her hair, while others joined her in crying and praying aloud.

High Hawk dismounted and went to his mother, gathering her gently into his arms. "We could not find him," he said thickly, only now thinking about the mountain lions who might have been the cause of his brother's disappearance.

He would not speak of that possibility to his mother.

He would keep that thought to himself. He prayed that his brother had not been killed by a hungry mountain lion.

"Why can you not find him?" Blanket Woman cried, pulling away from High Hawk's arms. She glared at him. "You did not look hard enough. He is alive, High Hawk. He . . . has . . . to be alive!"

He gently gripped her shoulders. *"Ina,* we searched everywhere and found no traces of him," he said. "Please try not to let this make you ill. We have a distance to go before we reach our new home. You must be strong in order to endure the days and nights ahead."

"How can I feel anything but this terrible emptiness?" Blanket Woman said, again pulling free of her son's grip.

She glared at Joylynn, who was dismounting from Swiftie. She went to Joylynn and spoke into her face. "All the sadness that has entered my life in recent weeks is your fault," she said through clenched teeth. She doubled her fists at her sides. "Until you came into our lives, all was well. I believe that the very night my son brought you among the Pawnee people was the night my husband died. You are a jinx . . . taboo! You are responsible for uprooting my people from their homes . . . and also now for my elder son's death." She opened one fist and gestured toward Joylynn. "Go away! Leave us be! You are bad for the Pawnee, especially for my family. One by one, my family has been taken from me since you arrived at our village. You are bewitched. Leave! Go back where you belong, and that is not among people with red skin."

Joylynn's face drained of color under the assault from High Hawk's mother. For a while, back at the village, she had thought she had finally made peace with the woman.

But now she seemed to hate her more than ever. It was evident that Blanket Woman blamed all her people's recent misfortunes on Joylynn.

High Hawk stood stunned by his mother's fury. Not one word of it was truth. Joylynn had been stolen away in the night and taken to his village. She most certainly had not gone there of her own choosing.

What happened after that had had nothing to do with her. She was innocent of all the things Blanket Woman was accusing her of. He hoped that his people understood that, and realized that his mother was speaking out of grief.

He turned from his mother and reached out for Joylynn. She went to him and, sobbing, flung herself into his embrace. "I'm so sorry about everything," she said between wrenching sobs. "But I am not to blame. Please make your mother . . . your people . . . know that I am not to blame for any of it. Oh, please make them understand."

High Hawk held Joylynn tenderly close in his arms. He fixed his mother with a firm stare as he looked over Joylynn's shoulder at her. "*Ina*, you have said much today that should not have been said," he chided. "I understand your grieving, but I cannot understand why you seem intent on blaming everything on my woman."

Blanket Woman grabbed at her throat as she gasped and took a shaky step away from High Hawk. "Your woman?" she demanded in an almost strangled voice. "After all of this, you . . . still . . . plan to take her as your wife?"

"She will be my wife as soon as we arrive at our new home," High Hawk said, challenging his mother with his eyes for the first time ever. He had always showed her full respect. But her time to be respected seemed to be running out.

Blanket Woman covered her mouth with a hand and turned to fall upon Sleeping Wolf's blankets on the travois. She wrapped herself in the blankets, sobbing out Sleeping Wolf's name. "Where are you?" she cried. "Why did you leave me? Why?"

Joylynn clung to High Hawk as everyone stood quiet now. The wailing and praying had stopped after everyone saw Blanket Woman's grief and heard how she felt about the future bride of their chief.

It was apparent that the others in the band did not agree with Blanket Woman, for Joylynn had proven to them that she was a woman of heart, someone vastly different from any white people they had ever known before her.

Suddenly several bald-headed eagles swept down from the heavens. They flew above High Hawk and his people for a while, then soared away again, soon lost to view behind a fluffy white cloud.

"I feel my brother among them," High Hawk suddenly said, causing Joylynn to ease from his arms and look into his eyes.

"You felt him among the eagles?" Joylynn asked, searching High Hawk's eyes.

"When eagles come together like that in such a great number, they bring a message from *Tirawahut*," High Hawk said, searching the sky. He wanted to see the eagles again, but there was no trace of them.

"And that message is?" Joylynn murmured.

"A message of love and reassurance," High Hawk said thickly. "My brother's love."

Joylynn was astonished at how High Hawk received such comfort in the mere appearance of eagles. She hoped that in time she could believe as he did, for she saw such peace in his eyes.

She gazed down at his mother. The older woman still wept as she clung to the blankets upon which her eldest son had lain.

Joylynn wanted to go to the elderly woman and pull her into her embrace, but she knew better. Blanket Woman blamed Joylynn for all the recent misfortunes that had befallen the tribe.

Joylynn wondered how she could ever change Blanket Woman's mind now. She truly doubted that it was possible.

And if not, would Blanket Woman make Joylynn's marriage to High Hawk miserable?

She set her jaw, knowing that she would not allow anyone to stand in the way of her happiness with High Hawk. She had waited a lifetime for a man such as he, and she would never give him up. Never.

A chill coursed through her veins when she found Blanket Woman gazing at her with utter contempt.

She knew now that Blanket Woman would not stop at anything to keep her only remaining son free of this white woman she despised with every fiber of her being!

CHAPTER TWENTY-TWO

Having no choice but to resume their journey without Sleeping Wolf, the Pawnee continued on the frighteningly steep path up the mountainside.

Joylynn turned to prayer to find the courage to keep climbing, and to cope with her deep sadness over Sleeping Wolf's death.

Feeling that another tragedy could happen at any moment, especially since the soldiers might be closer than anyone thought, Joylynn had hung the binoculars around her neck in order to take an occasional look far below. She dreaded seeing any movement by men who might be searching for High Hawk and his people.

As Swiftie climbed slowly up the mountain pass, Joylynn clung to the reins with one hand and looked through the binoculars with the other. She slowly scanned the land far below her, able to make out objects despite the distance.

Her heart seemed to leap into her throat when she spotted something. She could hardly believe her eyes when she saw soldiers advancing on the mountain; they had almost reached the foot of it.

Even more astonishing was *who* she saw riding with the soldiers. The cigarillo glow first drew her attention, and then she looked intently at the one who smoked it. It was none other than the man she'd thought had died during the ambush on the outlaws and soldiers.

It . . . was . . . Mole!

"Mole," she whispered, growing cold at the sight.

But he had been among the casualties on the day of the attack.

"How could it be?" she whispered, trying to see the man more closely as he continued to ride with the cavalry. His size, his bearing, his mannerisms made her certain that it was he.

But how on earth could it be Mole? They had left him for dead! Blood had almost totally covered him as he lay lifeless on the ground among his outlaw friends.

No doubt most of the blood on him had come from men who had died beside him. His own wounds, if any, could not have been fatal.

Lowering the binoculars from her eyes, she looked ahead at High Hawk, who rode in front of her along the narrow path; they had thought it best to ride in single file. She hated having to tell him that not only had she seen soldiers advancing on the mountain, but the cold-blooded murderer of High Hawk's father had once again cheated death!

"High Hawk," Joylynn called, drawing his attention quickly to her. He looked over his shoulder. "I hate to tell you this, but . . . but . . . a number of cavalrymen are advancing quickly on the mountain, and not only that, but . . . Mole . . . is with them."

She saw the incredulous look that flashed in High Hawk's dark eyes, how his lips parted in a gasp, as the realization of what she had said hit home.

"It cannot be Mole," he said, carefully turning his horse to face Joylynn's. "He died. We saw him die. We saw the blood. My warriors checked on him to be sure he was dead."

"I remember that they only rode up to him and gazed down at him, assuming he was dead because of his stillness, and . . . and . . . all of the blood. They did not actually check him for a pulse beat," Joylynn said. "I, too, thought we were finally rid of that horrible outlaw. But I know that the person I saw through the binoculars, riding with the soldiers, is none other than the man we all hate."

Moving Swiftie forward cautiously, Joylynn rode up next to High Hawk. She lifted the binocular strap over her head and handed them to High Hawk.

"Place these before your eyes and look through the lenses," she said tightly. "You, too, will see the soldiers and the one civilian with them. Mole."

High Hawk lifted the binoculars to his eyes.

Joylynn saw him stiffen when he, too, saw Mole, as well as the soldiers who were advancing on the mountain.

They were out for blood!

The blood of High Hawk's Pawnee people!

"It does seem to be he," High Hawk said tightly, then lowered the binoculars and handed them back to Joylynn. "That means only one thing."

"What?" Joylynn asked fearfully as she slipped the leather strap about her neck again so that the binoculars now nestled against her breast.

"We must stop him. We must stop them all," he said harshly. "Now. Today. We cannot allow them, especially that mole-faced man, to get any closer to where we are traveling. My people deserve peace in their lives, and they cannot have it as long as the pony soldiers and that evil man, pursue us. They have but one goal on their minds . . . the death of the Pawnee."

His eyes softened. "And you," he said, reaching over and gently touching her face. "They also want you to die along with us."

"*Ho*, it does seem so," Joylynn said softly. "It was not enough for Mole to rape me and try to strangle me; he will not stop until he knows I am dead. He must have seen me with you the day of the attack. He knew then that he would not rest until I was dead."

She reached for his hand. "But what can you do

now?" she asked, her voice drawn. "We are halfway up the mountain. They are far down below us."

"They are not far enough away to escape me," High Hawk said stiffly.

"So what are you going to do?" Joylynn asked, truly afraid to hear his answer. She just wished they could go on and forget the men who were down below them. But she knew that was impossible.

Those soldiers, and Mole especially, would never stop until they found the Wolf band of Pawnee and made certain its members, including her, never walked the face of the earth again.

"We must finish what we started," High Hawk said with determination. "We must make certain they are stopped."

Joylynn and High Hawk were too involved in what they were saying and what was happening down below to have noticed High Hawk's mother approaching them to see what was causing the delay.

Blanket Woman was just now stepping up beside High Hawk's horse, drawing his and Joylynn's attention to her.

"What is wrong?" Blanket Woman asked, looking slowly from High Hawk to Joylynn, and then back to High Hawk. "Why have you stopped while the others are going onward? Why did you not send word for everyone to stop?"

High Hawk and Joylynn gave each other questioning glances, and then High Hawk dismounted and placed his hands gently on his mother's shoulders. "*Ina*, you are very astute," he commented. "While others have not noticed that I stopped to talk with Joylynn, you did."

"Are you saying that you wish I had not noticed?" Blanket Woman said, giving Joylynn an ugly glare, then again looking into her son's midnight-dark eyes.

"Everyone will soon know why I have done this," High Hawk said, sighing. "*Ina*, the soldiers are advancing on the mountain down below. They must be stopped."

Blanket Woman's eyes widened and her lips parted in a soft gasp. "How can you do that?" she asked, her voice trembling. "We are so far into our journey to our new home. If you stop and battle with the white-eyed pony soldiers, will that not threaten everything you had planned for your people? My son, why do you not just forget about those soldiers? They will never find us."

"But there is one man with them who will not rest until he does find us," High Hawk said, easing his hands from his mother's shoulders. "That man is the one who killed your husband."

"But you said he was dead," Blanket Woman gasped, her old eyes filled with a sudden uneasy fear.

"We thought he was, because he managed to fool us into thinking he was dead," High Hawk said as Joylynn dismounted and stood at his side.

"*Ina*, you are to go on with the rest of our people to our new home while I and some warriors will

backtrack and do what we must to stop the soldiers," High Hawk said, searching his mother's
eyes when he heard her gasp again with fear.

"*Ina*, this is the only way it can be done," High
Hawk continued, still trying to make her understand how it must be. He was chief. His word was
final. "As I was telling Joylynn, I will take some
warriors with me and backtrack until we come to a
place where we can shoot down at the soldiers.
You and the rest of our people will move quickly
onward toward our new home. It will be a safe
haven, where no soldiers will be able to find you."

Blanket Woman's eyes filled with tears. She
grabbed High Hawk's hands, desperately holding
them. "No," she cried. "You cannot do this. You
cannot go and draw fire on yourself. You will not
return to your mother and your people alive. My
son, you . . . will . . . die."

"*Ina*, I must go," High Hawk said firmly. "There
is no other way. And I am skilled in ways of eluding
those who hunt our people. Trust me. Go now with
the rest of the Wolf band. I will join you all again
soon."

"I must go with you and your warriors," Joylynn
blurted out, drawing High Hawk's eyes as well as
his mother's.

"No!" Blanket Woman shouted. "You will be the
cause of my son's demise. You cannot be allowed
to ride with High Hawk and the warriors. You will
be in the way, and . . . it . . . is taboo."

Blanket Woman broke into tears. She sobbed into her hands, her body trembling from crying so hard. "I have already lost one son on this treacherous journey," she said. "I . . . cannot . . . lose another."

High Hawk swept his mother into his arms in an effort to comfort her. "*Ina*, I am my people's leader," he said softly. "It is up to me to guard them against all harm. That is what I am doing today. If I do not do this thing, I will be forced to step down as chief, for I would be a coward not to do what I can to protect them."

"I know you believe what you are going to do is right, and I will no longer argue against it," Blanket Woman said, easing from his arms and gazing up into his eyes. "But, High Hawk, please do not allow that woman to go with you. She has brought ill fortune into our lives. Why can you not see that?"

Ignoring what his mother said about Joylynn, knowing she spoke out of jealousy, High Hawk looked slowly at Joylynn. He knew that it would be all but impossible to keep her from going with him. He could see the determination in her eyes.

And he liked that about her.

Her determination.

Her pride.

Her courage.

He gazed into his mother's eyes again. "I cannot deny this woman the chance to best that man whose face is ugly with moles," he said tightly. "He harmed Joylynn in the worst way. He raped her.

And he survived the recent ambush. He cannot be allowed to bring doom to my people, for it is he, *Ina*, not Joylynn, who has brought so much heartache and pain into our lives."

Blanket Woman walked away from High Hawk and Joylynn without another word. She stretched out on the travois where she was riding, pulled a blanket completely over herself, and hid her face.

Joylynn and High Hawk saw her do this, then gazed into each other's eyes.

"She will soon realize it is too hot to keep the blanket over her face, as she will realize one day that what I must do now is the right thing for our people," High Hawk said, taking Joylynn's hands in his. "Are you truly certain you wish to accompany me?"

"I am truly certain," Joylynn said, squaring her shoulders. "I could not stay behind, afraid of what might be happening to you. I must be at your side and know, firsthand. Thank you for allowing it."

He hugged her, then walked away and, with Three Bears accompanying him, managed to go to everyone and explain what must be done. Fear was evident in his people's eyes, yet, knowing that their chief was a great leader, they trusted his decisions.

Having chosen the warriors whom he wished to accompany him down the mountainside, High Hawk led them and Joylynn back down the path on which they had traveled.

Hearing the thundering of the hooves, Blanket

Woman lowered the blanket away from her face. She turned and saw the last of the warriors as they disappeared from sight around a slight bend in the mountain pass.

"*Tirawahut*, please keep them safe," she whispered, tears falling from her eyes. "*Tirawahut*, please bring my only remaining son, High Hawk, back to me. If I should lose him, I would lose my reason for living."

Still crying, she stretched out on the travois, clinging to it as the warrior who was dragging it continued along his way.

The Wolf band was fleeing discovery by the white eyes. The looks of hope on all their faces had changed to fear, for once again, their universe was being torn apart by the soldiers under the command of the great white chief in Washington!

CHAPTER TWENTY-THREE

It was more dangerous than Joylynn had imagined as they backtracked along the mountain pass.

She kept an eye on the location of the soldiers and the outlaws with her binoculars. She felt sad to think about what lay ahead. More soldiers would have to die. Although High Hawk was a man of peace, his hand had been forced now more than once, in order to preserve his people's right to live. The cavalry seemed intent on wiping the Pawnee off the face of the earth.

Joylynn held tightly to her reins with her left hand, while with her right she held the binoculars steady as she peered through them.

Before her eyes was the man she hated with a passion.

She still did not see how he could be alive, but there he was, riding on a horse, a cigarillo hanging from the corner of his mouth, his eyes, which she remembered as being almost bottomless, seeming to know she was looking at him. The way he held his head now, it seemed as though he was looking directly into the lenses of the binoculars.

She even saw a mocking smile flutter across his lips as he took his cigarillo from between them and flipped it over his shoulder, onto the path he and the others were traveling.

Her heart thumping, Joylynn lowered the binoculars, then gazed slowly up at the sun, which stood at the midpoint in the sky. Had it reflected on the glass, sending a message to Mole that she was there, staring at him?

She had to be more careful. If Mole hadn't seen the reflection in the glass this time, he might the next.

"My brother . . ." she heard High Hawk gasp.

She looked quickly at him and saw tears filling his eyes as he leaned over and stared down the side of the cliff.

Joylynn followed the path of his eyes.

Her heart ached with sadness when she, too, saw Sleeping Wolf. He lay on a slight outcropping of rock just below them.

Everyone dismounted at once.

Forgetting the soldiers and outlaw down below, Joylynn watched as several warriors helped High Hawk retrieve his brother. They brought his body up and laid it out on the rock floor.

Joylynn watched High Hawk as he knelt beside his brother and placed a gentle hand on his cold, copper cheek. He knew that he could not wail and pray aloud to the heavens over his loss, for the sound would echo and travel down below where the white men could hear him. That was all they would need to know they were on the right track.

Joylynn became aware of the sound of splashing water. There was a waterfall somewhere near.

Would that not be the perfect place for Sleeping Wolf's burial? It would not be wise to carry him back to his mother. She would not want to see how the fall had further disfigured him. His face was now covered with dried blood, his eyes frozen as they stared straight ahead.

High Hawk had not been able to close them when he'd tried.

"High Hawk, wouldn't it be wonderful to bury your brother beside a waterfall?" Joylynn asked as she knelt down beside him. "One is near. I hear it. It would be so peaceful there for your brother. He would not be alone. He would have the music of the water with him at all times."

High Hawk smiled at her. "*Ho*, that is where we will take him," he said, then lifted Sleeping Wolf into his arms and walked until they found the waterfall.

They didn't have any digging tools, so they had to depend on a thick cover of stones and rocks to protect Sleeping Wolf's body from being disturbed by animals. It had not been bothered on the narrow ledge. No animals could have gotten down to him.

It was as though *Tirawahut* had guided his fall

and seen that he fell where his body would be safe until his brother found him.

Now Sleeping Wolf's body was fully covered and prayers were being said over it.

Then Joylynn exclaimed at the sudden appearance of many eagles flying low overhead, as though they had come to say a final good-bye to Sleeping Wolf.

They continued circling until Joylynn watched one peel off from the others. It settled into a nest on a slight outcropping of rock near the waterfall.

She gasped when she saw several heads pop into view.

"Baby eagles," she said, drawing High Hawk's eyes there, too.

"My brother loved eagles," High Hawk said, sliding an arm around Joylynn's waist. "Sleeping Wolf will be at peace here where eagles nest. His spirit will fly forever with the eagles."

"It is so sad that your mother can't be here for Sleeping Wolf's burial," Joylynn said, wiping tears from her eyes.

"She *is* here," High Hawk said thickly. "In spirit she is here and always will be for her firstborn son."

He wiped tears from Joylynn's cheeks; then everyone returned to their horses.

They traveled onward until they had descended far enough to get a better view of the men in pursuit of them.

The soldiers not only carried firearms in their

hands; they were also dragging a cannon along behind them. Apparently, they had planned to kill many Pawnee at once with balls from the cannon.

"We have no choice but to stop them," High Hawk said tightly. "And now, not later."

"Are we close enough to fire down on them?" Joylynn asked.

She felt nothing in common with the men below, even though they were people of her own skin color. But that was the only thing they shared. Inside, they were completely different. The hearts of these men were filled with darkness; they took joy from killing innocent Indians—men, women and children alike.

In her heart was kindness toward all people except those who lived to murder and maim anyone who got in their way.

She knew that this time she could not freeze when it came time to shoot. Each shot was important.

This time, they could not allow anyone down below to survive.

High Hawk could not risk any more soldiers getting close to his mountain, not until his people were safely hidden away in their new stronghold.

"This is where we must make our stand," High Hawk said, drawing rein and stopping his horse. Everyone halted behind him.

In silence they dismounted and picketed their horses.

In silence they drew their weapons from their gunboots.

No arrows would be used this time.

Only guns.

Joylynn grabbed her own breech-loading rifle from her gunboot. She opened the rifle breech and placed cartridges in it, cocked the firearm, then eased the hammer into place.

She followed alongside High Hawk to the place where they could get the best aim and a clean shot.

They all stretched out on their bellies on the hard rock. They took aim.

Joylynn felt strange as she began firing at her own kind, but this time she did not freeze as she had the other time. She kept reminding herself that these soldiers were collaborating with outlaws.

She was fighting not only for her own survival, but for all of High Hawk's people. They were innocent of any wrongdoing, yet they were being hunted down like mad dogs.

She loved these Pawnee people.

She would do everything she could to defend them.

Her pulse racing, she took a more steady aim this time. She saw Mole firing steadily at her and the others. Thus far none of the Pawnee warriors had been hit, but many soldiers down below were dropping from the gunfire.

"You can't have nine lives," Joylynn whispered to herself as she held her aim steady on Mole.

She fired.

She saw his body lurch.

She had hit him.

She smiled victoriously when he fell from his horse. She saw him hit the ground, and watched carefully for any movement.

Seeing none, she was certain this time that he was dead!

She continued firing until no one was left alive down below.

Joylynn lowered her rifle and stood up.

As she continued to stare at the bodies lying so quietly on the ground, she was once again swept by a feeling of disbelief at her role in this attack, but then she recalled how so many soldiers said, "The only good Indian is a dead Indian."

Those soldiers had not known the sort of people the Pawnee were. They were devoted to their families, loved their children, were doing what they had to do to survive.

The white man was trying everything he could to stop their survival.

Laying her rifle aside, Joylynn lifted the binoculars to her eyes and surveyed the death and devastation below. She had to make certain they were all dead, especially Mole.

She saw a lone soldier move slightly, and realized that he could only be about eighteen years of age. She was torn about what to do, for she had not known the soldiers could be so young.

She hated to think he might have been downed by her own bullet.

Yet he was still alive.

She flinched when she saw him look in her direction.

She knew he could not see her, but she could look into his eyes. There was a pleading look on his face, as though he knew he was being observed.

Suddenly she realized that she could not leave this young man to die a slow death, and she certainly could not shoot another bullet into him. Nor could she allow anyone else to. Surely this young man had survived for a purpose.

"High Hawk, look through the binoculars," Joylynn said, quickly handing them to him. "A . . . a . . . young man, oh, much too young to be with the soldiers, has survived. Look. You will see. Please, we can't shoot at him again. Somehow . . . it . . . doesn't seem right."

High Hawk was torn, too, when he looked through the binoculars and saw the boy's age. There were so many of his own young braves of that age who would have gladly taken up arms to defend their people just as this young man had probably believed he was doing. He had not realized he was part of a plan to completely annihilate the red man.

"We will go get the young brave and take him to our shaman," High Hawk said, handing the binoculars back to her. "If he survives, he survives. If he does not, he does not. We will take him with us. Time will tell what his true fate is meant to be."

"What if he lives and is well enough to return home? Will you allow it?" Joylynn asked, remembering how it felt to be a captive.

"Should he survive, I will accompany the young man back down the mountain and hope that he will be so grateful for having been allowed to live, he will not spread the word as to where he has been. I will blindfold him so that he will not know the paths that could lead him back to my people."

Having heard High Hawk's plan, some of his warriors came to him, frowning. They told him that they did not agree.

High Hawk ignored them, taking other men with him to get the lad. Joylynn accompanied them, for she felt she must take one last look at Mole, to make certain this time that he was dead.

CHAPTER TWENTY-FOUR

Joylynn was stiff with apprehension as she approached the bodies of the soldiers and Mole. All were dead except for that young soldier. She and High Hawk went immediately to him and looked down at him from their saddles, finding him unconscious, but breathing.

High Hawk and Joylynn dismounted beside the young man while the warriors rode slowly around the campsite, checking the dead to see if there might be others who were alive.

"He must be worse than I thought," Joylynn said as she knelt on one side of the young man, while High Hawk knelt on the other. She glanced up at High Hawk. "Is . . . he . . . dying?"

"No, I do not think so, for the wound that I see is not serious enough to kill anyone," High Hawk said as he ripped the boy's torn pants away from his wounded leg. "He must have fainted from fear of all that happened here, for no bullet entered his leg. It just grazed the flesh."

"But there is so much blood," Joylynn said, shuddering at the sight. Not wanting to see all of the dead, not even Mole, she did not look past the young man. She knew that when Mole fell from the horse, he had already been dead from the direct hit to his chest.

She swallowed hard, still in disbelief that she could have shot anyone in cold blood, yet she had. She had downed more than one man today with the accuracy of her aim.

She kept telling herself that she had saved innocent people by having done this. Had these men been allowed to live, they would have hunted down High Hawk's band of Pawnee until they found and killed them.

"Blood does spill even from a wound such as this, but it is a little wound compared to others," High Hawk said. "He is awakening."

High Hawk and Joylynn watched the young man's eyes slowly flutter open. Fear appeared in them when he saw High Hawk, an Indian, kneeling beside him.

In his panic, he had not yet noticed Joylynn.

He was trying to stand, but fell back down when he tried to put weight on his wounded leg.

"Please don't be afraid," Joylynn murmured, bringing his wide eyes to her as he sat there, trembling. In them she saw surprise and curiosity.

She watched his eyes slowly move over her, noting that she was dressed in Indian attire.

"You are white," he gulped out. "Yet . . . yet . . . you had a role in what happened today? You . . . helped . . . the Indians? You are even dressed like . . . an . . . Indian."

"Yes, I am dressed like an Indian, and yes, I helped them," Joylynn said tightly. She saw how those words made him flinch. "But must I remind you where you were going? You were with a group of men who were on the trail of Indians, were you not? You would have helped kill them once you found them, wouldn't you?"

"Yes, it was part of the plan," he said, then lowered his eyes and began crying. "But it was not out of hatred that I would have done it."

He looked with desperation up into Joylynn's eyes. "I . . . I . . . joined the cavalry to get money for my mother, to help her put food on her table after the death of my father," he sobbed out, the tears seeming to be born of true regret. "Then . . . then . . . just before I was told that I had to go with these . . . these . . . soldiers on a search for a band of Indians who were responsible for several soldiers' deaths, I . . . received . . . word that my mother had died. I am now alone in the world. I did not want to be part of this mission, for I have never hated Indians. In fact, I don't understand why the government hates them so much. The

Bible says that all men are created equal. It's in my Bible that I carry with me at all times."

Joylynn saw a small Bible thrust into one of his back pockets, then again gazed into eyes that were as blue as the sky. His blond hair was worn long, to his shoulders.

"You sound like a religious person," she said.

"Yes, ma'am, I am," the young man said, wiping tears from his cheeks with the backs of his hands. "It . . . has . . . always been a dream of mine to be a preacher."

"What is your name?" Joylynn asked softly, glad that this young man was not among the casualties. She would not allow herself to think that there might have been others killed today who had just been following orders, who hadn't wanted to participate in a massacre of Indians at all.

She had to put such thoughts from her mind. She could not allow her guilt to become unbearable. She had participated in today's attack to assure the survival of a wonderful, peace-loving people who were being hunted down and slain as though they were nothing more than lowly snakes crawling over the ground.

"Ma'am, my name is Andrew," the young man said. The fear in his eyes had eased, since thus far neither the Indian nor the kind woman seemed to want him dead. "Andrew Roddick, but I am mostly called Andy."

"Are you hurting badly . . . Andy?" Joylynn asked softly, looking at his bloody wound.

"It does hurt, but I can bear it, ma'am," Andrew said. "Thank you for askin'."

"How old are you, Andy?" Joylynn asked.

"Eighteen, ma'am," Andrew said. "I was the youngest of my troop. Mama didn't like me joinin' up with the cavalry, but I convinced her that the money would be good. I had meant to send her my money as soon as I was paid. She . . . just . . . didn't live long enough to get it."

Finding his story so sad, Joylynn nodded, then turned to High Hawk. "Can we talk?" she asked, searching his eyes. "Away from the young man?"

High Hawk nodded and stepped away from Andrew with Joylynn. The youth continued to watch them as they put their heads together, talking softly so he would not hear.

"As you suggested earlier, I think it is a good idea to take the young man with us. When he is well enough, he can return to his own life," Joylynn murmured, her gaze locked with High Hawk's. "I doubt he will have anything to do with the military again. I think that if we give him the chance, he will actively pursue the ministry."

High Hawk turned and gazed at Andrew, saw the pleading in his eyes as the young man looked back at him, waiting to hear what his fate would be.

"He will have to prove that he is worthy of being

set free," High Hawk said tightly. "Come. We will tell him what we expect of him and then see how he reacts to our decision."

Joylynn smiled, then walked back to Andrew with High Hawk.

Both knelt down beside him, one on each side.

"Young man, it is up to you whether or not you will be freed to seek your dream of being a preacher," High Hawk began. "We will take you to our people. You will travel with us to our new home. In time, if you have proven that you can be trusted, and that you seek only to lead the life of a preacher instead of a soldier, you will be set free."

"Do you mean . . . you . . . are not going to kill me?" Andrew gulped out, looking quickly from High Hawk to Joylynn. "Even knowing that if we had found your people first, instead of your finding us, we would have massacred them? Even so, you would still give me another chance at life?"

"You say that you want to be a preacher," Joylynn said, bringing his eyes to her again. "Young man, we will help you get that chance."

She placed a gentle hand on his cheek, which was rough with a stubble of blond whiskers. "Are we right in trusting you?"

"Yes, ma'am," Andrew said, his eyes brightening. "I'll not let you down. Honest. I promise. Cross my heart and hope to die."

Joylynn had often used that same term when she

250

had promised her father something. A smile fluttered across her lips.

The smile was quickly erased when Three Bears rode up to her and High Hawk.

"Mole is not among the dead," he announced. "I searched the bodies twice. He is not there."

Panic hit Joylynn in the pit of her stomach.

How could he have escaped again?

She had seen the impact of the bullet as it hit his chest. She had seen him fall to the ground, surely dead.

Could she have been wrong?

Had she so badly wanted the man to be Mole that she'd imagined it was he as she took aim at him?

She looked quickly at Andrew again. "Andrew, was an outlaw called Mole a part of your group?" she asked, searching his eyes. "There were many civilians among the fallen who we know were outlaws. Was the outlaws' leader, a man with many moles on his face, among those who were searching for the Pawnee?"

A perplexed look came into Andrew's eyes. "I didn't know everyone," he said. "I stayed to myself mostly, reading my Bible. So I just can't say."

Joylynn didn't know how to take his answer. Was he telling the truth? Yet why wouldn't he?

Oh, surely she couldn't have imagined that the man she'd seen was Mole.

She would never forget his ugly face, his leer, the

251

emptiness of his eyes, and that cigarillo she'd seen him smoking today before the attack.

"I've got to see for myself," she said, rushing to her feet.

Breathing hard, her face flushed, she ran from one fallen man to the other, feeling more and more sickened by the blood and gore, but concentrating on only one thing.

Mole!

She had to find the man she'd thought was Mole!

How could she have been mistaken?

After searching each of the bodies and finding none that resembled Mole, she concluded that one of two things had happened.

Either he had survived and was even now fleeing, or . . . it had not been him at all!

Feeling dispirited, she went back to where Andrew sat. High Hawk was caring for his wound. She had not realized that he knew the skills of medicating wounds. Was there anything he could not do?

She knelt beside Andrew as High Hawk covered the wound with a mixture of buffalo fat from the food he carried in his bag and sweet grass he found on the ground. He then sprinkled on the powdered root of the ocotillo plant, which he carried, too, in his bag for such times as these, when he or his men might be injured.

She marveled at this man's knowledge of so many things as he gently wrapped the wound with a small strip of doeskin.

"He is well enough now to travel with us as we return to our people," High Hawk said.

Seeing Andrew shivering, and uncertain whether it was because of the chill of the late afternoon, or fear, or pain, Joylynn took a blanket from her saddlebag and slid it around the young man's shoulders.

"Thank you, ma'am," Andrew said softly. "I'm strong enough to ride, even with my leg bandaged. My injury shouldn't get in the way.

"Again, thank you for your kindness," he added softly.

A part of Joylynn wondered whether this young man might be skilled at duping people, for how could he have not noticed Mole among the outlaws? She could have sworn that Mole had been there, and that she had killed him. But if he'd merely been wounded, he would have had time to escape while she and the others were riding down to the scene of the ambush.

"Gather together what firearms you can carry on your steeds; then we must hurry back onto the mountain and catch up with our people," High Hawk instructed his warriors. "Hurry. We have a long trip ahead of us before we will be reunited with our loved ones."

He looked at Joylynn. "Can you ride the night through?" he asked. "I would like to continue until we reach my people."

"I'll be all right," Joylynn murmured. She glanced

over at Andrew. "Can you ride the entire night? Are you in too much pain to travel so long?"

"I'm from a farm," Andrew said proudly. "Before my pa died, I was in the fields with him day and night until crops were planted. At harvest time, we worked long hours, too. Yep, 'cept for my leg, I'm as fit as a fiddle and I can stand pain. I got many a snake bite when I was workin' the fields. I learned to tolerate even that sort of pain in order to stay with Pa until the work was done."

Hearing that he was raised on a farm made Joylynn feel a strange sort of camaraderie with him, for she had been the son her father had never had, and she worked long hours with her father, as well, during planting and harvesting time.

But she didn't share this tidbit with Andrew, not yet. She wanted to be sure that he was a truthful person, who was not lying to save his neck. She hoped that he was sincere about wanting to be a preacher.

"Bring the young man a horse," High Hawk shouted at his braves. "But leave the rest. We cannot take horses with us, although I hate to leave a steed behind. But in these circumstances we would be slowed, trying to get them up that narrow pass while keeping ourselves and our horses from sliding to our deaths."

"Sliding . . . to . . . your deaths?" Andrew gulped out. "Is where we are going to travel so dangerous?"

"Very," Joylynn murmured. "But if you are being truthful about your belief in God, you don't have anything to fear. He will keep you safe."

She gave him a lingering gaze. "He allowed you to live today while others died, did He not?" she murmured.

Andrew swallowed hard, nodded, then got up and limped to the horse that was brought to him.

High Hawk helped him into the saddle, then mounted his own steed. "Let us leave this place of death," he shouted, riding off with Joylynn at his right side.

Andrew soon caught up and rode on High Hawk's other side. With eyes straight ahead, the group rode for the mountain pass they had only a short while ago left behind them.

Joylynn was bone-weary from the long day of riding and fighting. But she had to find the courage and strength to ride for many more hours.

She gazed heavenward and said a silent prayer for strength, and for reassurance that the young man was not lying through his teeth in order to save his hide!

As she rode onward, she again thought about Mole. Could he even now be hiding and watching her, another plan hatching in that evil mind of his?

That thought made her shudder.

CHAPTER TWENTY-FIVE

A soft breeze whispered through the canyon as High Hawk and Joylynn edged their horses closer to each other while riding into the hidden valley that was to be their home.

Finally they had arrived.

A beautiful stream, its water clear and sparkling, lay just beyond, and a great herd of deer were drinking from it.

Groves of trees were set back from a grassy meadow. Overhead they saw flashes of color as birds flew by, chattering and playing.

Somewhere in the meadow, a field lark sang, high and musical.

And as High Hawk led his people across the lush grass of the meadow, brown flocks of quail rose from it, fluttering away, only to resettle again nearby.

"I have never seen anyplace as beautiful as this,"

Joylynn murmured as she drew rein beside High Hawk. "It truly is a paradise."

She was aware of the Pawnee people coming in from all sides, stopping to take in the grandeur of their new home.

"Do you hear the whispering of the wind blowing all around us?" High Hawk asked, lifting his chin and inhaling the sweetness of the air. "To me it is the voices of my ancestors saying this is where I will have a son!"

Joylynn's eyes widened just as he turned to her with a wide smile. "A son," she said, her pulse racing.

Yes.

Ho.

They would now have time to marry and make that son, as well as many more children they both would adore.

Then her smile waned as she recalled her recent miscarriage. Did that mean she could not carry any child full term?

The thought made her feel sick to her stomach. If she was not able to give High Hawk a son who would one day be chief after him, would he still want her as his wife?

"We will be married soon after the hunt," High Hawk said, reaching over and taking her hand. "The hunt is necessary to replenish our meat supply. The women must prepare it for use during the long, cold months of winter that lie ahead of us. With the vegetables each woman has brought from her cache pot, and with fresh meat prepared for storage, there will be enough to sustain us until new crops are planted in the spring."

He looked over his shoulder where they had left the canyon walls behind, then gazed into Joylynn's eyes again. "Canyon walls can be climbed, but not these," he said. "These walls and this land belong now solely to the Pawnee."

He slowly eased his hand from Joylynn's. His jaw tightened as he looked again at the hidden valley. "Let the white man try to disrupt our lives again," he said fiercely, then turned to Joylynn again. "If they do try to come, they . . . will . . . die."

Joylynn knew that he had already placed many sentries at strategic points along the high canyon wall. They could see all movement down below during the daytime hours, and could hear all sounds when darkness enveloped the land. If even a wolf or mountain lion crept close, these trained sentries would hear it.

Joylynn remained where she was while High Hawk rode to a spot where he could be seen by all of his people.

He drew rein and smiled at each of them, then spoke. "My people, I have brought you to where my dreams led me," he said. "This is your home now. No one will disrupt your lives again. No one will threaten your young sons or daughters. I promise this to you, my people, and you know I always keep my promises."

While he was talking and instructing his people, Joylynn's eyes shifted to Andrew. After finally getting several nights of good rest while on their journey to this new home, he looked his age again. Before, after being wounded and traveling without rest, the young man had seemed to have aged overnight.

Even Joylynn had felt as though she had grown older from the long, hard ride without sleep, rest or a warm meal to please the stomach.

After they had finally caught up with their people, it had been heavenly to finally feel safe enough to stop and rest a full night before heading out again along the narrow passages that had brought them to this hideaway.

She knew that many of the Pawnee people were still wary of Andrew, although their shaman had befriended him. She had seen Andrew and Two Stars often discussing religion, and she had seen Andrew hand his Bible to Two Stars after reading special verses to him.

She knew that Two Stars was quite taken by the young man and the passages that had been read from the Bible to him.

Joylynn wasn't sure how to take Andrew's friendship with the shaman. Was the young man getting on the good side of Two Stars in order to gain the trust that might lead to his quick release?

Or did Andrew truly care about the older man?

In time, Joylynn and everyone else would know the truth behind the young man's behavior.

She only hoped that he was not making a fool of such a wonderful man as Two Stars.

Hearing the rushing sound of a waterfall near the spot where the new village was going to be built, Joylynn remembered another waterfall, another time.

She swallowed hard as she thought about Sleeping Wolf's poor, twisted body being covered by stones. His burial had been near a waterfall, where he would hear it for all eternity.

He was also close to where eagles nested. Joylynn smiled at the remembrance of the nest of eagles, where the small heads popped up for food when their mother came with a tiny morsel for each.

She glanced over at Blanket Woman, who now stood beside the travois on which she had traveled. Joylynn was glad to see hope in her old eyes now, instead of the sadness that had been there as she mourned her elder son's death. Joylynn would never forget the look on Blanket Woman's face, when she had been told that his body had been found and buried. Blanket Woman had been beside herself that she had not been at the burial of her son. She had been desperate to say final words to him and pray over his body.

For Blanket Woman, the rest of the journey had been miserable as she lay on the travois with a blanket drawn over her face. But she had been heard. Her wails and prayers had reached into everyone's hearts.

Joylynn was glad when Blanket Woman stopped her open grieving and rejoined humanity, throwing the blanket aside and eating again, yet still saying nothing to anyone, not even her chieftain son.

But now? Joylynn could see a tentative joy in Blanket Woman's eyes as she gazed upon this new land that was so beautiful and filled with peace.

High Hawk was still telling his people what was to be, now that they had arrived.

Soon after, they cleared a large piece of land for their lodges and began building new tepees, placing them in a tight group at the lower level of a slope in the well-watered valley.

A large fire was built in the center of the village, where even now the elderly men, who were not strong enough to help cut wood, or build homes, sat smoking their long-stemmed pipes. In their eyes was a revived look of hope.

Joylynn pitched in and helped plant poles into the ground to support the lodge coverings. She smiled at High Hawk, who worked alongside her.

The children romped and played, some running after beautiful butterflies, others chasing quail from the high grass.

The deer that Joylynn had seen upon her arrival were farther down the stream, but not drinking. They watched with large brown eyes as they observed, for the first time in their lives, animals that walked on two legs, not four.

"They are beautiful, are they not?" High Hawk asked as he came and stood beside Joylynn.

"Do you ever hesitate to kill them?" Joylynn asked.

"One cannot afford such hesitation, not when so many people's lives depend on the meat and pelts of the deer," High Hawk said, watching as the creatures finally bounded away and were lost to sight amid a thick stand of cottonwood trees.

He looked to his left, then to his right, where tall pines stood like sentinels near the canyon wall.

He felt safe here, and content.

Then he reached his hands to Joylynn's waist and drew her into his embrace. "I have neglected you," he said regretfully. "But once the hunt is behind us, you will be the sole center of my attention. You will see that the waiting was worth it. I plan many good things for you on our wedding day."

"You are everything to me," Joylynn murmured, placing a gentle hand on his cheek. She laughed softly. "So you have something special planned for me, huh?"

"You will see," he said, his eyes twinkling. "My neglect of you will end after the hunt. Until then, though, my people's welfare comes first. They all need warm homes, and new cache pits are being dug for the food that will be stored there."

Joylynn groaned at the memory of helping his

mother dig her cache pit. "Again?" she said, but her tone was teasing, not whining.

"One more time you will help my mother prepare her cache pit, but after this, when new crops are harvested, you will dig one for our own food," he said. His eyes twinkled. "Maybe by then you will be so heavy with child, the other women will offer to dig our pit for you."

Again Joylynn worried about being pregnant again, unsure of whether she could carry a child full term.

But when he drew her closer and kissed her, everything but High Hawk and the joy she felt with him was forgotten.

"I have missed you . . . in . . . that way," she whispered against his lips. They had not been free to make love since their first time together. "You know what I mean, don't you?"

"*Ho*, as I have missed you in that way," High Hawk whispered back to her. "Once the Wolf band is settled into a normal way of life again, I will satisfy your hunger, over and over again."

"As I will yours," Joylynn said, blushing when she heard footsteps behind her. She turned and found Blanket Woman standing there, her hands on her hips.

"One cannot get tepee poles in the ground when kissing seems more important," Blanket Woman said, glaring at Joylynn. "When will you prepare mine? This old woman is anxious for her first lodge fire."

Joylynn wanted to tell her that everyone was anxious for the same, but she kept her thoughts to herself.

She wondered, though, if she and High Hawk's mother would ever be on friendly terms.

"*Ina*, this is your tepee we are building, not ours," High Hawk said, reaching for his mother and embracing her. "I know how anxious you are to feel that things are normal again in your life. But everyone else feels the same way, yet I have heard no one but you complaining."

"I disappoint you in so many ways," Blanket Woman said, sudden tears in her eyes. "I will try not to, my son. I will try hard not to."

"*Ina*, you are loved so much by this son, do not worry about trying so hard to do things that you think will please me," High Hawk said. He leaned back from her and gazed into her eyes. "*Ina*, we have a new chance at life here where no white man's feet have left any prints. It is a time to rejoice. Smile. Take heart. All is good."

Blanket Woman flung herself into his arms. "I will not complain ever again," she said, a sob catching in her throat. "I . . . I . . . sometimes feel so sad and bitter over the loss of land that was ours from the beginning of time, then the loss of my husband, and finally my firstborn. It is hard for this old woman to forget the losses that bring such pain to my heart."

"I will help you forget if you will only let me," High Hawk said. He looked at Joylynn, who was listening to the conversation between mother and son. "And so will this woman who will soon be your daughter."

Blanket Woman looked at Joylynn.

Suddenly she smiled. "I will not complain any more about you, either," she said. "From here on, you are my friend."

"More than that, *Ina*," High Hawk said. "She . . . will . . . be your daughter. Your daughter. She will be the one who will give you grandsons and granddaughters."

Those words seemed to bring a soft light into the older woman's eyes. She broke away from High Hawk and went to Joylynn. She surprised everyone who was watching by hugging her.

"I welcome you into my life," Blanket Woman said, her voice breaking. "I welcome the children you will bring into my life."

Joylynn wasn't sure what to do or say, for what if she disappointed the older woman by not being able to give her grandchildren?

High Hawk's smile was what she needed. She felt a quiet joy within her heart and knew at that moment that somehow she would bear him a son and this woman a grandson.

Suddenly she hugged Blanket Woman. Joylynn

was filled with warmth when the old woman returned the hug.

High Hawk's eyes widened. He was astonished by this sight, but knew now that even this was a part of his dream of paradise.

He smiled and went to the two women he loved, drawing them both into his embrace while his people worked at building their lodges and the children romped and played.

He did not see Andrew and the way he was watching the joy of the people he was supposed to have hunted down and killed.

CHAPTER TWENTY-SIX

Joylynn had helped dig Blanket Woman's cache pot, giving the two women time to bond. Blanket Woman had promised never to cause Joylynn any trouble again, and she believed her. She so badly wanted their future to be bright and warm; she wanted them to be a true family.

High Hawk's scouts had been sent in various directions to look for buffalo and had returned with good news. Plenty of buffalo had been spotted on this new land, where no man had had a chance to kill them off.

Joylynn was riding proudly beside High Hawk as they set off for the hunt. The warriors planned to kill only as many buffalo as were needed to keep the Wolf band in meat for the duration of the winter.

Joylynn was proud to be a part of the hunt, even though she was not going to take part in the actual hunt, but would be an observer.

Yet some of the Pawnee women saw Joylynn's mere presence during the hunt as taboo, fearing that she might bring their husbands, brothers and cousins trouble if she rode with them. Some thought that the mere sight and smell of her would warn the buffalo to flee.

Others thought Joylynn was courageous to do so many things that they had only seen men do. They had been told that Joylynn had been a rider for the Pony Express, which was also a male preserve.

Most of the women saw her as someone strong and courageous enough to be a chief's wife, whose strength and stamina would cause her to bear their chief many strong sons.

"I'm so glad that you are letting me go with you today," Joylynn said, drawing High Hawk's eyes to her. "But I understand why you don't want me to be an actual participant in the hunt, even though I hunted often with my father. He would let out a loud 'whoopee' when I downed an animal to put meat on our supper table."

She swallowed hard. "I miss my father terribly," she said. "Mama, too, but I had more of a relationship with my father than Mama."

"Your *ahte* is looking down from the heavens even now, pride in his eyes that he has had a role in bringing up a strong and wonderful woman like you," High Hawk said. "I am sure your *ina* is looking down at you, as well, with love."

"I always wanted to make them proud," Joylynn

murmured. "And now I want the same for you. I don't want to let you down, ever. You . . . are . . . my world."

"You are my world, my woman, as well as my people's," High Hawk said. He looked quickly to the right when the sound of many horses' hooves frightened quail from their roosting places.

"Quail make a good meal," Joylynn said, having also seen the flight of the birds.

"Today we seek much larger animals, whose meat will last for the duration of the long winter," High Hawk said, again looking ahead for signs of the buffalo that had been sighted by his scouts.

He knew they must be drawing near the herd, for they had traveled half a day now.

"How are you feeling about Andrew?" Joylynn asked. "Do you still believe he is being truthful? Or do you think that all he says and does is a ploy to draw us into trusting him until he is well enough to travel back down the mountain?"

"I want to trust him. Certainly, Two Stars believes that he is sincere. They sit often and talk about their religions and the differences between their Gods," High Hawk said, his long black hair blowing in the wind. "If Andrew is playing a game with my people's religious leader, he will pay dearly in the end for his betrayal. For now, I will trust as Two Stars trusts."

Joylynn scratched at her left arm, where wet clay and herbs had been rubbed into her flesh before leaving for the hunt. High Hawk had told her that the clay and sand served useful purposes on the hunt. Clay reduced the chances of being bitten by insects. The *parakaha*, a fragrant herb, prevented sunburn.

Joylynn was dressed in fringed breeches that had been loaned to her by a young brave of her size. She also wore that brave's fringed shirt, while High Hawk and his warriors wore only breechclouts and moccasins. High Hawk's hair was loose and flowing, while hers was worn in one long braid down her back.

All but Joylynn carried bows and quivers of arrows for the hunt. High Hawk had taught her that gunfire spooked the buffalo, causing them to stampede. High Hawk had told her how he had laughed when he saw the ignorance of white men using guns to hunt them.

Joylynn carried her rifle only for protection, should a buffalo come after her. She would have no choice but to shoot it, only then risking a stampede.

Since they rode in an area that was safe from whites interfering, the Pawnee carried their bows unstrung. Bowstrings made of braided sinew would stretch and weaken if kept continually under the great tension that was necessary during the hunt.

"When there was no need to hurry into a hunt as we are doing today, young boys would join us," High Hawk said. "It is a good time for the young braves. They take their small bows and arrows and shoot at birds that flutter up from the grass. The young braves sometimes even take careful aim at butterflies darting before them."

He chuckled as he continued to describe what he recalled so vividly in his mind's eye. "When I was older, but yet not old enough to join the true hunt, I was among those who would gather to walk in a line abreast and drive out birds, rabbits and other small creatures to be killed. At day's end, enough small game was taken back to the village to fill our mothers' cook pots. The true hunters would come in later with the larger meat for their families."

High Hawk paused and placed a hand above his eyes, slowly scanning the land on all sides of him; his warriors did the same.

Then he lowered his hand as Joylynn edged her steed closer to his. "What else are the buffalo used for besides food?" she asked, truly curious. She wanted to return to the village with as much knowledge as she could.

She had much to learn in order to be the best wife possible for this young Pawnee chief.

"The best hide coverings are made from buffalo, not deer," High Hawk said, glad that his woman wanted to know so much of his people's customs. "Bed coverings, clothing and saddles are also made from buffalo hide. Sinew from the animal is used for stringing our bows. My people's women soften and dress the skins with brains from the buffalo. Mallets are made of the hoofs. Water bags are made from the bladder."

"Buffalo!" Three Bears said as he came up to High Hawk's left side. "They have been sighted around the bend, where the stream turns into a wide river."

"Spread the word," High Hawk said.

In his eyes was an anxiousness and gleam that Joylynn had never seen before. She could not help feeling the same excitement, even though she would not participate in the hunt. Just being with High Hawk at such a moment was enough to cause her heart to race with excitement.

High Hawk turned to her. "Go and stay far behind the warriors, where you can safely observe," he said. "Do not move from that place unless by chance the buffalo are scared into stampeding, or they run toward you."

"I will be alert at all times," Joylynn murmured, resting her hand on her rifle, which was primed and ready as it stood in her gunboot at the right side of her horse. "Good luck."

"Good . . . luck?" High Hawk repeated, arching an eyebrow.

"That is a way white people wish good fortune on their hunters," Joylynn explained.

High Hawk smiled broadly as he reached over and took one of her hands in his. "The hunt today, a wedding tomorrow," he said. "Tomorrow, my woman, you will be my bride."

"Tomorrow," she murmured, then watched him ride away with the others. She followed more slowly until she saw the buffalo herd just as she rounded the bend, where tall trees had until now kept them hidden.

She gasped in astonishment at how many buffalo she saw. A vast herd stood there together, grazing on the tall, green grass that swayed in the breeze.

She drew rein and searched out a less dangerous place. Seeing a slight hill where she could look down upon the hunt in safety, she rode up the slight incline. On the back side were thick trees that would also provide protection.

On two sides, the land stretched out far and wide, and on the other lay the river, with its pristine water reflecting the sun and the clouds floating away in the blue sky.

Just to be certain she would remain safe, she drew her rifle from the gunboot and rested it on her lap, then settled in more comfortably on the saddle. She had brought her binoculars, which hung around her neck.

She lifted them and gazed through the glass, watching the men slowly approaching downwind of the herd. The buffalo still were not aware of the danger drawing near.

Some of the herd grazed peacefully, while those closer to the river pawed the earth with one hoof.

She could hear some of the buffalo bellowing, others snorting.

And then her breath caught in her throat when she saw all of the hunters, with High Hawk in the lead, take their assigned positions as they formed a horseshoe shape with the open end toward the buffalo herd.

Some warriors now advanced on foot and made a line at the ends closest to the herd.

Those with the fastest horses were at a greater distance from the herd. But they waited and watched, and only when several of the buffalo suddenly sat down, resting in the grass and dirt, did the warriors ride at a hard gallop toward them.

The buffalo obviously heard the rumble of the horses' hooves, for Joylynn saw them turn their heads toward the sound. Those buffalo that were standing could see the advancing warriors, yet still stood watching, as though not certain what to do.

Those that were sitting were just starting to rise. Gradually, they all began to move away. But just before they broke into a trot, the Pawnee hunters were among them.

The warriors on foot were shooting their arrows into the animals already, but they could not get closer because of the danger. This part of the hunt had to be conducted by those on horseback.

When the buffalo really began to run, Joylynn watched in awe as High Hawk and the mounted warriors were able to select which buffalo to shoot.

Joylynn knew, from what High Hawk had told her earlier, that they prefered to shoot a female because the meat was more tender and easier to prepare.

Joylynn had also been told that sometimes there was a competition among the hunters. The object was to see how many buffalo one could shoot with a single arrow.

As she peered through her binoculars, she saw that when a buffalo ran, it exposed an area behind the leg where the tough hide was thin. Some men were able to shoot low through this spot. If an arrow was shot with sufficient force, it went completely through and into another animal, killing two buffalo with one arrow.

She was awed by the accuracy of each warrior. Many buffalo were taken down, and before she knew it, the others had run away to be hidden from sight in a thick stand of trees.

She still stayed away from the warriors as they began to prepare the buffalo's skin and meat for the return to their village. It almost made her ill to watch as the butchering began. It was not a delicate or pleasant task. It was messy work, with the summer flies and gnats almost unbearable. They were so bad that some warriors stood by, waving willow branches over the carvers.

But she knew they would much rather butcher the meat under these conditions than during the winter months, as they would have to do if their supply of meat ran out before spring. In the winter, the buffalo meat and skin began to freeze before it could even be processed.

High Hawk had said that the blood would cake and ice on the hunters' hands. In such cases, the hunters would place their hands in the vagina of a downed animal, until they were warm enough to continue with the work.

Joylynn could no longer look through the binoculars. It was too gruesome a sight. She only hoped that when it came time to eat this meat, she wouldn't remember so vividly what she had witnessed today.

"I will be all right," she whispered to herself, sighing heavily as she continued to wait until the meat was loaded on the horses.

After a while, something told her to look in the direction of the hunters again, and when she did, she found High Hawk waving at her.

She quickly saw that all of the meat was packed on the backs of the horses and covered. The horses had been led down by the river, where the men were already running into the water with their breechclouts on, washing off the clay and soil of the day, as well as the blood from the butchering.

She knew that sand would then be rubbed into the skin to further cleanse it.

She gazed at High Hawk again as he rode toward her with his burdened horse. She could see that his body was sparkling and clean beneath the rays of the sun. His wet hair clung to his shoulders and down his back. Obviously, he had already bathed.

Glad that the hunting and butchering was done, and even more anxious to return to the village so that she could prepare for her marriage, Joylynn mounted her steed, rode down the steep incline and met High Hawk.

"It is done," he said. "There will be much food on our table, as well as my mother's and Two Stars's, for I am the one who does the hunting for all of us."

"I'm so glad it's over," Joylynn said, riding beside him as they headed toward home. "I had no idea it . . . it . . . would be this gruesome."

"Now you see why the women, for the most part, do not get involved," High Hawk said. "Some Pawnee do include their women, who come to butcher after the buffalo are killed. Even some children participate. But I feel the women of my village have enough to do without adding to their tasks."

"I'm glad," Joylynn said, laughing softly. "I would hate to think that I would have to dirty my hands with such blood . . . and . . . guts. I'm a strong woman, but not . . . that . . . strong."

"Tomorrow has been brought closer by the time it has taken for the hunt and butchering," High Hawk said with a twinkle in his eyes. "And you know what tomorrow means for us."

"How could I forget?" Joylynn said, holding her head back to feel the sun warm on her face. She closed her eyes in ecstasy at the thought of being with High Hawk again and making love, this time as his wife.

She looked over her shoulder as the warriors rode up behind them. They wore a look of victory at having killed enough buffalo to sustain their people for the long winter months.

She could feel their pride.

It was good to be a part of such a wonderful people as these. She hoped that some months ahead, she would make the number of Pawnee grow as she brought another Pawnee child into the world!

She smiled at High Hawk, feeling confident that nothing would stand in the way of her bringing a son into this world. This time, the child she carried in her womb would be there because of a wonderful moment of lovemaking with her husband, not like before, when the child had been the result of a horrible rape.

This time, she would cherish every moment the child was inside her.

She began thinking of names, trying to choose one that would fit the son of a powerful Pawnee chief.

Then a name came to her that made her heart skip a beat.

Sleeping Wolf!

Yes, she would see if High Hawk would agree on the name Sleeping Wolf for their firstborn son. Wouldn't it please Blanket Woman to know that her own firstborn was being remembered in such a way?

Glad that the thought had come to her, Joylynn smiled softly at High Hawk. She hoped this gesture would further strengthen the bond between her and High Hawk's mother!

CHAPTER TWENTY-SEVEN

"Where are you taking me?" Joylynn asked as she clung to High Hawk's neck while he carried her away from the spot where moments ago they had spoken their wedding vows.

His people still danced and sang to the accompaniment of rattles made of dried gourds filled with seeds, drums and the lovely music from a flute of red cedar.

"To a special place where we will celebrate our first night as man and wife alone," High Hawk said, continuing to run alongside the stream that slowly widened and deepened the farther they got from the village.

"Anywhere is special as long as I am with you," Joylynn said, oh, so happy that finally they had been able to speak the vows that made them as one forever. He could not be any more handsome than he was now in his headdress of fox skins, his white, fringed doeskin outfit, with fur moccasins on his feet.

His long hair flowed down his back, and Joylynn's was loose today as well. As he carried her, her hair swung down across his arms in rhythm with the swaying fringes of her own snow-white doeskin attire. The coral-colored beads adorning her dress flashed beneath the lowering sun.

"You have waited long for this day, so I wanted to be certain it was one that would live in your memory forever," High Hawk said, still running along the stream, which was widening now into a river.

"How could I ever forget this day?" Joylynn murmured. "And your mother was so sweet and kind to me. I shall never forget when she gave me her gift. It is such a beautiful sewing kit that she made especially for me."

"It is the custom of our people that no woman should be married without owning her own sewing kit," High Hawk said. "*Ina* wanted to be the one to give you yours."

"I shall learn to sew, honest I will," Joylynn said, smiling up at him. "If a sewing kit is so important, the new wife using it must not disappoint her husband. High Hawk, I have never seen such beautiful awls, sinew threads dyed so many beautiful colors, and paints, beads and porcupine quills already dyed different colors and ready to be applied to the dresses and moccasins I will learn to make."

"As well as clothes for your husband," High Hawk said, giving her a teasing smile. "It will be a life far different from what you are used to."

"*Ho*, quite different," Joylynn said, nodding. "While I lived with my parents, I ignored my mama's teachings, but instead listened to my father's. I so loved the outdoors. I thought sewing and cooking were tedious."

"But now?" High Hawk said, still trotting alongside the river. "You will not mind caring for a husband, doing all the things women do for them?"

"I cherish every moment now of being able to make you happy," Joylynn said. "Even cooking. Your mother told me today how your favorite dish is prepared. The flesh of a calf is boiled with pomme-blanche roots in a broth made of water and marrow from the bones of cows. Lungs of the buffalo are added after being dried and roasted on coals, along with corn."

"My mother is an excellent teacher, and obviously you are an astute student," High Hawk said. He slowed his pace, then stopped in a curve of the hauntingly beautiful river. He nodded and gazed toward the clear water.

Joylynn followed the path of his eyes, then gasped in awe. "A canoe?" she said. "I have never seen you or any of your people in canoes."

"Last night several of my warriors left the village and made this canoe especially for our wedding day," High Hawk said. "It is not as large as most, but large enough for what we will do with it."

"We're going to go for a ride in this canoe?" Joylynn asked excitedly.

"*Ho*," he said, stepping up to the canoe with her. When Joylynn could get a better look at the canoe, her eyes widened. "Rose petals?" she gasped as she gazed in wonder at the wild bright red rose petals spread along the bottom of the canoe.

Lying on each side of the canoe were two paddles.

"Especially for you," High Hawk said, easing her down into the canoe.

The rose petals were cool and soft against Joylynn's flesh as she ran her fingers through them, and the smell was so heavenly, surely no expensive French perfume could smell more wonderful.

"This is so beautiful," Joylynn murmured as she gazed up into High Hawk's eyes. "Rose petals. And so many. You have made this a day I shall think back on forever and smile."

High Hawk smiled and shoved the canoe into deeper water, then waded out and climbed inside. "My people are not canoe people, but there are times when we have needed them, and we have mastered the art of making them," he said, settling down on his knees behind her. "This canoe is smaller than most, so we must position ourselves on our knees before paddling. Stay where you are and I will kneel behind you. From where you are, your view will be unobstructed. Today we will both see the marvels of this land yet unseen by any other man or woman."

"I . . . have . . . never been in a canoe. I don't know how to paddle one," Joylynn said, suddenly nervous. Thus far she had impressed him by being able to do things that most women could not.

"Watch me for a moment. Lift the paddle and place it in the water," High Hawk said. "Begin pulling it through the water as I am pulling mine. You must get into the same rhythm as I. Do not use the muscles in your arms, but let the rotation of your torso move your paddle through the water."

Joylynn did as he said, smiling when she discovered how effortless it was, especially with him using his paddle in the same rhythm as her own.

"My people mainly travel by horse, but when I am in a canoe, I cannot help thinking that, besides making love, this is what the body is made for," he said softly. "Canoeing is one of the gentlest, least disturbing and most graceful ways of moving through physical space."

Joylynn gazed over her shoulder at him and saw a look of joy on his face. There was something almost rapturous about being out there on the river, only the two of them, moving so easily through the pristine water.

She knew they were experiencing something together that would be with them always . . . a landscape of wildness and purity, so vast and ancient, that the distinction between individual existence and nothingness was almost meaningless.

She turned her eyes away from him and enjoyed the experience to the fullest. On her knees, she focused on the way the paddle made a little swirling whirlpool as it bit into the water, and how it cast off two more little whirlpools when she took it out at the end of the stroke. She found that a slight twist of her wrist turned the blade vertical and made it easier to take it out of the water.

For long stretches, the only sounds were the drops of water falling from the paddle as she brought it forward and bit into the water again, and the little straining sound, like a trickling rivulet, that the bow of the canoe made as it parted the water.

She was stunned to see that the river was filled with fish in pulsating abundance, streaking away from the bow of the canoe as it made its way through the water.

She gazed toward the riverbank and saw a lot of beavers and their lodges, and the sharp spikes of the aspens and jack pines that they had gnawed off.

Elsewhere, three otters were standing up on their hind legs, chattering adorably.

She sighed with pleasure and lifted her paddle up from the water. She had never seen such a lavender-pink sunset as was mirrored on the glassy surface of the river.

And just as she noticed it, she realized that High Hawk had turned the bow of the canoe landward.

She looked ahead and was struck almost speechless when her gaze fell upon a pure white tepee standing a short distance from the riverbank. Outside, a fire was already burning. No doubt High Hawk had instructed someone to start it.

She looked on both sides of the tepee and into the forest of pines and aspens that stood statuesquely behind it and saw no one. Surely whoever had come had traveled by horse and was now headed back for the village.

Ho, she could feel no one's presence except their own. Her heart raced in anticipation of the moments that lay ahead as High Hawk landed the canoe.

She smiled up at him as he came to the side of the canoe and lifted her into his arms.

"My wife, tonight is ours alone," he said, his voice husky. "Come. See what I have prepared for you."

"You?" Joylynn said, clinging to his neck. "You built the tepee? When? And how could you have started the fire when I have been with you so much of the day?"

"The tepee was built by my own hands, but Three Bears came and prepared the rest for his chief and his bride," High Hawk said. He took her inside the tepee, where more red rose petals were strewn over blankets and pelts that had been spread thickly on the earthen floor.

"It is all so beautiful," Joylynn sighed. Her heart pounded when he brushed her lips with his, then laid her gently on the thick bear pelts.

As the sun cast its lavender glow down the smoke hole overhead, and the outdoor fire made of cottonwood logs sent wisps of soft fragrance into the open entrance flap, High Hawk slowly, almost meditatively, removed Joylynn's clothes.

Feeling drugged with passion, she lay there and watched as he removed his own clothes, even tossed aside his headdress of fox skin, until he was kneeling perfectly nude over her, his knees straddling her tiny form.

As they lay on the plush furs with the crackling fire so close outside the entranceway, the clear, liquid fluting of a hermit thrush hidden in the nearby trees pierced the gathering dusk. To that sweet music, High Hawk and Joylynn slowly ran their hands over each other's flesh.

The song of the bird was of the most exquisite purity, embroidered with brilliantly improvised rising and falling arpeggios.

It filled the tepee with its loveliness as High Hawk rolled Joylynn's nipples with his tongue, awakening a raging hunger inside her that she had only known since she had made love that first time with High Hawk.

She gave herself up to the rapture, then sighed with wonder as he kissed her with a lazy warmth that left her weak.

She quivered with passion when she felt his manhood touching and softly probing her hot, moist entrance.

"I love you so," she groaned against his lips, sighing with intense pleasure when he thrust himself deep within her. He began moving slowly inside her, then faster with quick, sure movements that blocked out everything but the rapture that was blossoming in Joylynn's heart.

"As I love you," he whispered against her lips. "Forever and ever, my woman, my wife."

She tried to draw air into her lungs, to respond in kind, but could only tremble as the rhythmic pressure of his heat within her created a euphoria that was almost more than she could bear.

As his steely arms enfolded her, she again felt his hunger in the hard, seeking pressure of his lips. He kissed her as his body continued to move within her.

"Feel how I want you," he whispered against her parted lips as he gazed into her passion-clouded eyes. "I shall always want you as much."

"As . . . I . . . want and . . . need . . . you," Joylynn managed to whisper, although she felt almost mindless now with the building pleasure within her.

She couldn't think any more, could only feel. She gasped when he swirled his tongue across her breasts, sucking her nipples, one at a time, into his mouth, his teeth gently nipping each.

Her fingers bit into his shoulders and she closed

her eyes as the ecstasy spread within her. His hands were all over her body now, touching, moving, dancing.

High Hawk was trying to hold off the inevitable for as long as he could, for he wanted his wife to feel pleasure such as she had never known until tonight.

But it was hard not to let it all go, to feel the utmost of pleasure a man could feel while with the woman he loved. His need was so great, he could hardly fight off the hot, white flames that seemed to be roaring in his ears.

He could not get enough of her soft flesh as his tongue and lips moved over her body, especially her breasts. He again licked one nipple and then the other, yet not missing a stroke within her. He knew she was building now to the highest pleasure a man and woman could give one another.

"I am there," Joylynn cried, clinging to him as the most wondrous of sensations claimed her, sending wild ripples of pleasure throughout her entire being.

She was liquid inside, filled with heat and longing. She arched her back, closed her eyes, dug her fingers into the flesh of his shoulders, then cried out as she felt him delve more deeply inside her with his heat. He was thrusting, ever thrusting, his breathing hard as he held his cheek against one of her breasts, then made one more deep plunge inside her. His body quaked and trembled as he spilled his seed inside her waiting womb, while sharp contractions of pleasure knifed through him.

And then they lay side by side, breathing hard, both aware that night had fallen as the full moon cast its white sheen down through the smoke hole and over them.

"It was so wonderful," Joylynn murmured, clinging to one of his hands. "It was even more enjoyable than the other time."

"Each time, as you become more relaxed with lovemaking, you will experience something more beautiful than the last," High Hawk said, reaching over and brushing some of her damp, fallen locks from her cheeks.

"I shall teach you many ways to love," he said huskily.

"There are more ways than what you have already shown me?" Joylynn asked as she sat up and gazed in wonder down at him.

"Many," he said, chuckling. "But for now, there is something else I have planned tonight that I think will please you."

"Nothing could be better than what we just experienced together," Joylynn murmured, but when she saw him already rising to his feet to go outside, she followed him. She sat down on a blanket that he spread out before the fire.

She watched him go a short distance away, and her eyes widened when she saw him kneel beside a square-shaped depression that had been dug in the ground. It was covered by a buffalo bull hide that he was now lifting from it.

"What is that?" she asked, wrapping the blanket around her shoulders and going to kneel beside him.

She was suddenly aware of a wonderful aroma, and knew that something had been buried there to cook.

"You may have noticed that Three Bears was gone for most of the day, as well as part of the prior night," High Hawk said. "As a gift for our wedding night, he dug this depression in the ground and lined it with leaves, on which he spread out a large number of buffalo ribs. A layer of clay was spread over this, and over it was built a slow-burning fire. After it burned down to glowing ashes, the fire was covered again in order to retain its heat as it slowly cooked the meat below."

"He did all of this for us?" Joylynn said, glad to have such a friend.

"*Ho*, for us," High Hawk said, continuing to remove everything until he reached the steaming ribs. The tantalizing aroma rushed up from the newly uncovered pit.

Joylynn took the blanket from around her shoulders and spread it out beneath the moonlight.

High Hawk removed two meaty ribs, handed one to Joylynn, then sat down beside her with his own.

As the night songs of crickets and frogs filled the

air around them, they ate until they were almost too full to move.

"The rose petals, the canoe, the beautiful tepee, and now this?" Joylynn said, sucking her fingers clean of grease, one by one. "It seems too wonderful to be real."

She scooted closer to High Hawk.

He slid an arm around her waist and drew her next to him. They both gazed contedly into the moon-splashed water.

"This is a version of Eden," she murmured, leaning her head against his shoulder. "How fortunate it is that you have found this wilderness valley for your people that has not, until now, known the hand of man."

"It is a place that I hope is never discovered by whites," High Hawk said.

"Yet there are two white people among your Pawnee," Joylynn said softly. "I am one; Andrew is the other."

"You are Pawnee now, but as for Andrew, I am not yet certain what he is," High Hawk replied. "He is, of course, white, but does he now have the heart of a Pawnee? He has grown so close to my people's shaman. If his friendship is pretense, I—"

Joylynn moved to her knees and knelt before him. She placed a gentle finger to his lips, stopping him from saying any more. She would not allow anything to detract from their private, wonderful moments.

"Not tonight," she said softly. "Tonight is ours, only ours."

He swept her into his arms and carried her back inside the tepee. There, he laid her down on the pelts, then made slow love this time, so that each of them could savor every moment of this magical night.

CHAPTER TWENTY-EIGHT

A month had passed since their night of lovemaking in the beautiful white tepee. The day was cool, the breeze somewhat nippy. High Hawk and Joylynn had just stepped from their lodge.

"Are you certain you feel comfortable letting Andrew leave?" Joylynn asked as she and High Hawk watched the former soldier walking with Two Stars.

"He has proven to be honest in all that he has said and done," High Hawk said, still watching Andrew. "And the heavy snows of winter will begin falling soon. It is best that he leave now, or he will have to remain the winter with us."

"Do you see anything wrong with him staying?" Joylynn asked as they started walking slowly toward Andrew. "He gets along with everyone, and he has such respect for the elderly."

"It is the man's talking leaves that bother me,"

High Hawk said tightly. "The book that he calls his Bible. Too many children are showing interest in it. They gather around him as he reads from it. Our people's God is *Tirawahut*. The children cannot ever forget that."

"I believe he has chosen very carefully what he reads to them," Joylynn murmured. At times she had stood close herself, listening. "What he reads are stories about children and their joy in the world."

"I still see danger in the young man staying here," High Hawk said.

"But isn't there more danger in his leaving?" Joylynn asked. "What if he is made to tell where he's been?"

"He has promised not to tell anyone, and I sense there is much honesty in his words and behavior," High Hawk said. "His trust has been earned. It is time for him to return to his own world and seek his dream of becoming a preacher. He cannot fulfill that dream among my people. I will not allow it."

Andrew had turned and seen them walking toward them, as had Two Stars.

They had both stopped and waited.

"I must do what my heart tells me to do," High Hawk said, pausing a few feet from Andrew and Two Stars. High Hawk and Joylynn hugged Andrew in turn; then High Hawk placed a gentle hand on Andrew's shoulder.

"Young brave, you have earned the right to your

freedom," High Hawk said. "You may go. Several of my warriors will accompany you down the mountain pass. When you are at the bottom of my mountain, you will be allowed to travel alone. You will have a horse and provisions enough to last until you find a white man's town. But there is one thing I ask of you: Refrain from going anywhere near a white man's fort. If you do, and the commander learns that you have been living among red men who ambushed soldiers, they will force you to tell them where our village is. I trust you enough now to know that you will not reveal such information."

He looked at Andrew's fringed outfit. It was made by Indian hands, yet he knew of some white scouts that wore the same, so he did not believe what Andrew wore would be a problem. His cavalry uniform had been burned long ago.

Andrew, seeming stunned by High Hawk's decision, said nothing.

"Today you *will* leave," High Hawk said. "It is important that you leave now in order to get off the mountain and find somewhere that you can call home before the frigid temperatures and snows of winter arrive. As you notice, today's air is cooler than it has been. It is a warning of what is to come."

Andrew's eyes wavered as he looked at High Hawk, then at Joylynn, then at High Hawk again. "But I don't want to leave," he blurted out. "I am at peace here. I'm . . . happy. Can't I stay?"

Two Stars spoke up. "This young brave has found a place among us, and I would feel a sadness inside my heart if he were to leave," he said. "I understand why you are eager for him to depart. It is the Bible, is it not?"

"It is what he teaches from that Bible," High Hawk said tightly.

"It is only a book, nothing more," Two Stars said. "In it are words of his God. I have enjoyed hearing about it and being read to from it. But it has not altered my beliefs. Nor will it alter anyone else's."

"My Bible is precious to me because it was a gift from my mother," Andrew said. "And it is my only possession. That is why I carry it with me at all times. If you allow me to stay, I promise not to preach from it."

Andrew swallowed hard. "Please do not make me leave," he said, his voice breaking. "My mother is gone. I am alone in the world. I feel that I have finally found another true home here. Can't I stay among your people and live as one with them?"

Joylynn was relieved to know that this young man was sincere in every way toward the Pawnee.

She hugged him again, then stepped away from him and gazed into his eyes. "Andy, if you stay here, how can you become a preacher?" she asked. "You surely have the calling, for you know the Bible better than anyone I have ever met."

"I can practice my kindness and caring amid the

Pawnee people," Andrew said. "I do not have to actually preach. It is my love for God that is important. I can spread that love amongst the children as I would if I were a preacher."

Joylynn saw him glance at a pretty young woman of about his age. The girl blushed and lowered her lashes bashfully.

Joylynn smiled and gave Andrew another hug, whispering into his ear that she knew the true reason he wanted to stay. As she stepped away from him, she saw how he blushed and nodded at what she had said.

Seeing that Joylynn seemed so impressed by the young man, and so trusting of him, High Hawk placed a hand on Andrew's shoulder. "I give you my blessing to stay, if that is what you truly wish to do," he said, looking at the pretty young girl. Although it had happened quickly, Rose had most certainly become the object of Andrew's deepest affection.

High Hawk did not resent their obvious feelings for one another. Had he himself not been drawn into loving a white woman as quickly as it seemed that Andrew had grown to love Rose, and she him?

"I also give my blessing on your feelings for one of our Pawnee maidens," he said, surprising not only Andrew, but also Joylynn and Two Stars.

They both stared in disbelief as Andrew flung himself into High Hawk's arms and thanked him over and over again.

High Hawk stepped away from Andrew. He gazed into his eyes. "Now, I would not be all that thankful yet, for Rose has a father and he is the one who must give the final blessing," he said, his eyes twinkling. "And you must pay a bride price for the girl, even if you are now only wishing to court her. What do you have to offer her father?"

Andrew's eyes widened; then he took his Bible from his rear pocket and nodded toward it. "I will give her father my Bible, for that is all I have left, and it is, as you know, very precious to me," he said softly, looking up at High Hawk.

Joylynn's heart seemed to skip several beats when she saw what Andrew wanted to use as his bride price. She, too, looked guardedly at High Hawk, and found it hard to read how this young man's suggestion had struck him.

High Hawk had only moments ago spoken against the Bible, and here the young man was ready to use it to win a Pawnee father's approval.

High Hawk was speechless for a moment. He gazed at the Bible questioningly, then into Andrew's eyes. He knew how this young man felt about his talking leaves; Andrew's willingness to give away his Bible said much about his feelings for Rose.

The more High Hawk thought about the matter, the more he believed Andrew's suggestion would work on his people's behalf. If one of the Pawnee had possession of the Bible, it could not be used to persuade his people to believe what was written on its pages.

"*Ho*, as I see it, the Bible will be gift enough," High Hawk said. "Go now if you wish. Offer it."

"Truly?" Andrew said, swallowing hard.

"If it is your choice to part with your only possession, one that you care so much for, then so be it," High Hawk said. "Go. Do not delay your talk with Rose's father."

Andrew glanced over at Rose, whose eyes were filled with eagerness and love, then gazed into High Hawk's eyes again. "I'm a little afraid," he said. "What if he turns me down? He has no idea how I feel about her. When he learns of my feelings, he might forbid me ever to see Rose again."

"You will never know unless you ask," High Hawk said. But in his heart he was glad about what was happening, for he no longer had to worry about Andrew telling white people things that could harm the Pawnee. When he had made the decision to bring Andrew among his people, it had been a hard one. Yet he now knew that it had been a wise one!

Rose came up to Andrew and shyly gazed into his eyes. "Come. I will go with you," she said softly. "*Ahte* is home now, with *Ina*."

Touched by the young people's obvious affection for each other, Joylynn took High Hawk's hand and stood with her husband and Two Stars. She watched the two go to Rose's tepee. She could see Andrew's hands trembling as he held the Bible while Rose called her father's name outside the entrance flap.

When the flap was thrown aside, Rose's father's large frame filled the opening. His eyes narrowed angrily as he gazed from Andrew to his daughter, and then at the Bible in Andrew's hand.

Andrew gulped hard as he gazed into the dark eyes of Brown Horse, who had yet to say a word.

"Sir, I have come to offer you my Bible as a bride price for your daughter," Andrew finally said, his voice trembling. "It is my most prized possession. I hope that you will accept it, knowing that it is of great value to me, yet I am willing to part with it in order to court your daughter, and then marry her."

Brown Horse stared at the Bible again, then suddenly stepped back from the entrance flap, closing it between himself and the world outside.

Joylynn covered a gasp with her hand. She could see how devastated Andrew was at the brusque way he had been treated, and the refusal of his gift.

His feet seemed frozen to the ground, his eyes still on the closed flap, while Rose clung to his arm, sobbing.

High Hawk was at a loss as to what to do, for he had never seen any of his warriors treat a young man in love so callously.

High Hawk supposed it was because Brown Horse's daughter had brought a white man to his tepee. And, too, he had probably been mortified by the offer of the talking leaves, something that held little value to him.

High Hawk stood his ground as Joylynn rushed over to Andrew and Rose, looking at each with a quiet apology in her eyes, even though it was not she who had wronged these young people.

High Hawk waited for Joylynn to say how she felt, then he himself stepped up to Andrew and Rose, his eyes troubled. Was it possible that this rejection would cause Andrew to have hard feelings, not only for Rose's father, but for the Pawnee people as a whole?

Andrew had been publicly humiliated. He had been denied his right to court and marry the woman he loved, and denied in the worst way possible.

"Young brave, do not despair because Brown Horse has rejected your bride price," High Hawk said as Andrew slid his Bible back inside his rear pocket. "Many bride prices are turned down until the one the father thinks is enough is finally brought to him and accepted. Andrew, a true bride price usually comes in the form of a beautiful horse."

Andrew's eyes brightened, hope suddenly in them again. "I will hunt and find a wild horse and tame it," he said in a rush of words. "I will bring it back for Rose's father. Surely he will not turn it down."

"Your plan is good," High Hawk said. He nodded toward his own corral. "Come with me, young brave. I shall loan you one of my steeds for your hunt. I will give you what is required to capture a proud, wild steed. And there are some in a valley yonder. I have seen them."

"In which direction is this valley?" Andrew asked anxiously. "I will go there."

"I shall point your way to the valley," High Hawk said, pleased to be a part of this scheme that would keep Andrew among his people.

Andrew turned to Rose and took her hands in his. "I shall return soon, and your father will not be able to refuse my second bride price," he said. He hugged Rose as she flung herself into his arms.

"Go and return soon," Rose said, tears spilling from her eyes.

"I shall," Andrew said, then stepped away from her. He walked briskly to High Hawk's corral, where he was given a muscular roan.

"I shall place my best saddle on the horse and give you a rifle in case you are threatened by a mountain lion," High Hawk said.

After Andrew was mounted and ready, with High Hawk's rifle slid inside the gunboot at the side of his horse, Joylynn was filled with a sudden apprehension. The sight of this young man on a horse again, and with a rifle in the gunboot, caused her to fear the outcome of this moment. Was it possible her husband was trusting too much?

She knew why he was going so far to please this

young man. He hoped that by doing so, his trust in Andrew would be rewarded again, that Andrew would return with a beautiful horse on a rope behind the stallion.

Rose hurried to Joylynn's side. She wiped tears from her eyes as she gazed up at Andrew. "Come back soon," she said, stifling a sob behind a hand. Joylynn sensed that even Rose had some doubt of ever seeing Andrew again.

Joylynn stepped closer to High Hawk, tempted to tell him of her fears, but she knew that it was best not to question his judgment, authority, or his trust, certainly not in front of the many people who had come to watch Andrew's departure.

"Rose, I will see you soon!" Andrew said, pride in his eyes.

As he rode away, Joylynn saw Andrew reach back and pat the Bible in his pocket.

That gesture made her almost certain that she would never see Andrew again, not unless he returned with a whole cavalry of men to do what they had been prevented from doing earlier.

She slid a hand into High Hawk's and clung to it, hoping he could not feel the sweaty coldness of her palm, or divine the deep worry inside her heart.

CHAPTER TWENTY-NINE

A growing number of bald eagles, casting massive winged shadows over the icy water of the stream, marked the first days of November. The mammoth birds buzzed the flocks of geese and ducks gliding overhead, on their way south to warmer weather, then circled back.

Having heard the commotion, Joylynn and High Hawk stepped from their tepee just as several eagles settled down onto the limbs of the willow trees. Others stood on the ice, while some were roosting already for the night on outstretched limbs of the fir trees and ponderosa pines in the shadows of the deep, dark canyon beyond.

Just before sunrise they would lift off and wing toward their feeding grounds.

With wing spans as wide as eight feet, the bald eagles were strong and agile fliers.

"The heavier snows will begin any day now,"

High Hawk said as he gazed at the thin layer of snow on the trees and ground that had fallen during the previous night. He slid an arm around Joylynn's waist, drawing her close to his side. "And Andrew has never returned, as he promised. Even now my warriors are searching one last time for him."

"I doubt they will find him," Joylynn said softly. "When you handed him that rifle, I saw a look in his eyes. It was the look of someone who has been given a second chance at life."

"I did not see that look," High Hawk said thoughtfully. "I truly believed him to be a man eager to do what he could to win the woman he loved. But I was wrong. He has been gone for many sunrises now. It does not take that long to find a horse suitable to be offered as a bride price."

"He might have loved her, but not enough," Joylynn said, her voice drawn. "Poor Rose. Her heart is broken."

"And Two Stars," High Hawk said, sighing heavily. "He trusted Andrew more than anybody. He fears that our people will see him as a foolish old man who trusted too much, for he showed even more trust than I."

He lifted the entrance flap and stepped aside so that Joylynn could enter the warmth of their lodge.

"Everyone loves Two Stars so much, and all know of his goodness. No one will hold it against him that he put such trust in someone who spent many hours with him, speaking of *Tirawahut*," Joy-lynn said. "Andrew did truly seem interested."

"There have been no signs of Andrew any-where," High Hawk said, bending to one knee and lifting a log onto their lodge fire.

Then he sat down beside Joylynn and gently placed a blanket around her shoulders. "We will have at least the winter months before he can re-turn with armed soldiers to try to kill off my peo-ple," High Hawk said sadly, his gaze following the flames wrapping themselves around the new log. "That will give us time to prepare for the fight. We will be the victorious ones, not the white eyes. My warriors will be perched in prominent places where they can see everything below. Their vigilant eyes will not miss one movement. Andrew will surely be with the soldiers, leading them to bring death upon the Pawnee. He will be the first to die."

That thought sent a chill up Joylynn's spine. Al-though she now believed the young man was a trai-tor, his death would bring heartache to more than one Pawnee.

Rose and Two Stars.

Unless the long months of winter inactivity led them to think about how Andrew had tricked them with his dishonest ways. Perhaps by spring they both would be bitter enough over the betrayal to see that his death was warranted.

"My husband, I have news today that will help

ease the anger in your heart," Joylynn said, reaching for one of his hands. She brought it over and laid it on her stomach.

She didn't even have to speak the words. He knew.

"You are with child," he said, his eyes filled with pride.

"*Ho*, I am with child," Joylynn replied, smiling into his eyes. "When the flowers are blooming along the mountain passes and by the river where we spent our first night as man and wife, I will bear you a son."

"It will not disappoint me if the child is, instead, a girl," High Hawk said, slowly sliding his hand over the doeskin dress, knowing that beneath it, inside his wife's womb, was a child that he would always cherish. "If the child is a girl, I hope she is in your image, for I have never seen anyone as beautiful as you."

"Even if she is ugly, you would love her," Joylynn said, giggling. "Because she will be yours and mine, our firstborn."

High Hawk moved to his knees facing Joylynn.

He slowly removed her dress, revealing her well-rounded breasts and a flat belly that would soon be growing into a round ball.

He ran his hand over her stomach, then leaned an ear low, scarcely breathing as he listened.

"It is too soon to hear anything within," Joylynn said, laughing softly at how excited he was. "But one day you will even be able to feel its movements inside me."

He gently laid her down on the soft blankets and pelts beside the fire, then began kissing her body, starting at the nape of her neck.

Joylynn's heart pounded as the touch of his lips and tongue brought rapture to her. She closed her eyes and enjoyed each kiss.

When he flicked his tongue over one of her nipples, she sighed with pleasure.

And when he slowly kissed his way downward, across the flatness of her belly, her skin tingled with aliveness.

She raised her fingers to his hair and wove them through his long, thick tresses, then gasped with a new sort of pleasure when he flicked his tongue between her legs, where she had only recently discovered there was so much feeling and life.

As he kissed and licked that strange little nub of flesh, feelings that Joylynn had never felt before leapt into her heart.

Although she felt this might be wrong somehow, the pleasure she was feeling caused her to accept what he was doing, not question it.

The more his tongue and lips caressed her there, the deeper the feelings of pleasure went inside her.

Moaning as a blaze of desire fired her insides, she slid her hands away from his hair and slowly tossed her head back and forth.

She was responding to every nuance of this new way of making love. She even spread her legs wider apart so that he could have better access. The sensual throbbing increased.

Suddenly a bolt of heat spread through her and she realized that she had just experienced the same culmination she always felt when he was inside her, loving her in the usual way.

This time, her whole body was rocked with sensation and she knew that he had just taught her a new way of making love, and she had yielded, heart and soul, to it.

Still trembling, still feeling sensations where his tongue and lips had been, Joylynn opened her eyes and gazed questioningly at him.

"What you just did . . ." she began, but did not know what else to say about what had happened.

"Was it beautiful for you?" he asked, searching her eyes.

"So much so, I am still shaken by it," Joylynn said softly.

He removed his own clothes and stretched out beside her on his back. When he reached for one of her hands, placing it on his erection, Joylynn's breath was stolen away. Although he had made love to her with that part of his body, she had never actually . . . touched it.

Now she was, and she was very aware of the heat of his flesh there, and its tightness.

She started to ask him what he wanted her to do,

but she didn't have to. He had wrapped his hand around hers and was showing her how to move her hand on him.

She saw his eyes take on a strange sort of deep darkness as she continued to move her hand on him. His own hand now fell aside to give her full access to his heat.

She could hear his breathing becoming faster, and he closed his eyes in ecstasy.

"You are making love to me now as I just made love to you," he said huskily. Then he stiffened his legs as he felt the pleasure building within him, a pleasure that she was creating by the skill of her hands, even though she was new at this.

"Am I doing everything right?" Joylynn whispered, not stopping her strokes.

When he opened his eyes, and she saw how drugged they seemed to be, when he smiled and nodded, she knew that he was feeling the same pleasure he had given her.

He closed his eyes again, but this time thrusting his hips. His moans and groans told Joylynn just how much pleasure she was giving him.

She gasped when she saw his body quiver and quake, and something smooth and milky white came from his manhood, spilling endlessly, it seemed, into the palm of her hand.

And then his body subsided into a strange stillness, and Joylynn watched what had been such a large size slowly shrink in her hands.

Hearing her silence, and knowing that she would be filled with questions, he opened his eyes and reached for his manhood, sliding it away from her hand.

Before saying anything, he reached for a soft doeskin cloth and wiped her hand free of his sperm, then tossed it aside, sat up and drew her into his embrace.

"We will make love again in this way, but the most pleasure comes from our bodies being joined," he said softly. But before he could say or do anything else, a voice spoke from beyond the closed entrance flap. It was Three Bears requesting admittance.

"Three Bears and the others have returned from their last search for Andrew," High Hawk said.

He quickly dressed, as did Joylynn. Then they went to the entrance flap.

Outside, Three Bears's face told it all. There was no smile, only annoyance.

"Again we found no sign of Andrew," Three Bears said tightly. "He is probably even now sitting among people of his own kind, warm, comfortably full with white man's food, and already planning to come with the soldiers up to our new home in the mountain."

"I now believe that is so, too," High Hawk said glumly. "But I had to make this one last search for him. Since you saw no signs of my steed, nor the rifle I lent the young brave, which you would have found if he had been killed by a cougar or bear, I now believe that he has returned to his own world. I only hope that he is not laughing about the foolishness of this Pawnee chief."

"Please don't think that," Joylynn said, gently taking one of his hands in hers. "You encouraged him to go and hunt for a horse out of the goodness of your heart. No one with such a good heart should be faulted for it."

High Hawk smiled softly at her, always amazed at her ability to take away the feelings that he knew were harmful to him.

Three Bears gazed skyward, and then looked again into his chief's eyes. "We came home when we saw the thickening clouds," he said. "I sense they will bring much snow."

"*Ho*, much snow," High Hawk said, nodding. He clasped his hand on his warrior's broad shoulder, where a thick bear robe lay. "Thank you for searching this one last time. Go and thank the other warriors for me. Also tell them there will be no more searches for the young man who broke the heart of one of our maidens and the trust of their chief."

Joylynn looked past Three Bears and saw Rose standing just outside her lodge, tears streaming from her eyes. Rose, too, knew that this was the last time anyone would search for the young man who had betrayed not only her chief and blessed shaman, but also . . . her love.

Joylynn wanted to go and embrace her and say

things that might make what Andrew had done to her more bearable, but she knew that Rose had a mother who would do this for her. Even now the older woman stepped from the lodge and embraced Rose.

Three Bears nodded, then turned and went back to the others in the search party. High Hawk and Joylynn watched him spread the word of their chief's wishes; then the two of them went back inside their lodge.

Silently Joylynn sat down beside the fire and began cutting up vegetables that she had taken from the cache pit she shared with Blanket Woman. She now knew the art of preparing all the foods that her husband enjoyed eating. She was also cooking for Blanket Woman today, who was not feeling well.

Although there had been many strained moments between them in the past, Joylynn hoped that Blanket Woman did not have an ailment that would take her from this world.

"I will go and check on *Ina,*" High Hawk said, throwing a heavy blanket around his shoulders.

"Tell her that I am preparing food she will enjoy, for it is food she taught me how to cook," Joylynn said, smiling at High Hawk as he stopped and looked back at her.

She felt so blessed that he had grown to trust her before he allowed himself to love her.

There was complete trust between the two of

them, and she could hardly wait to hold their baby in her arms, then offer it to him.

Ah, what a wonderful moment that would be!

As he walked from the tepee, she tried not to think of anything negative at this moment. They had just shared such wonderful lovemaking and had talked of their child so happily.

That darn Andrew! He might spoil everything!

And then there was always the haunting fear that Mole might somehow discover where she and the Pawnee were. If so, she knew to expect the worst.

"Andrew or Mole," she whispered.

If either of them showed up on this mountain with the cavalry, everything could change in a heartbeat.

She shivered at the thought.

CHAPTER THIRTY

April, the Sunflower-Planting Moon

Joylynn, big and pregnant, too large to help the women prepare the land for planting, stood just outside the entranceway of her tepee, her eyes on the sky.

The previous autumn, the waterfowl had flown south to the Old Woman Who Never Dies, carrying gifts to ensure a good harvest for another year.

Since the Old Woman Who Never Dies caused the plants to grow, and sent the goose to signify corn, the duck to stand for beans, and the swan to represent the gourd, the arrival of the waterfowl was a good signal that she gave her blessing and the planting season could begin.

Joylynn's hands rested on the great swell of her belly; her doeskin dress was much too tight now.

But knowing that the child would come at any

time now, she had not sewn a larger dress for herself. She did not want to waste good doeskin. If she could bear the weight of the child, she could bear the tightness of the dress for a few more sunrises.

Her feet were swollen, but she would not allow such a simple thing as that to stop her from getting where she wanted to go. Joylynn walked to the edge of the village and gazed toward the valley, where the crops would be planted near the river bottom. Many women were there this early morn.

In preparation for the time of the birds' arrival, the women had hung large amounts of dried meat and other offerings on drying racks that had been set up in the valley.

Joylynn was told that, usually, when the women were preparing an old plot for planting, they would rake it and carry the dead grass and stalks beyond the fields.

But this was a new field, and they were cutting the brush and spreading it out on the ground; the standing trees had been ringed, ready to be felled.

The women would lay the trunks and branches of these fallen trees on the ground to be burned over the field in order to make the soil soft and pliable.

The women were very excited and filled with hope over what had happened yesterday. They had seen geese winging their way from the south, then noticed one group circle a moment over their offerings on the drying racks, only eyeing them, and then settling on the opposite shore of the river.

Elated, not caring that the birds had ignored their offerings, the women had counted again and again the number of birds.

To their great joy, there had been exactly eleven.

They had shared this joy with Joylynn, running to her and telling her that the number eleven was a sign that the corn crop would be very good.

However, it was April, too early to plant corn, but just the right time to set sunflower seeds in the borders around the corn and vegetable patches.

To the Pawnee, April was known as the Sunflower-Planting Moon. The sunflowers added color to their gardens, protected the other crops and provided meal and oil for eating.

Sunflowers were the first to be planted and the last to be harvested.

Hearing a distant sound of thunder, Joylynn glanced at the sky. She saw no signs of clouds, which meant that the storm was far away and probably would not interrupt the women's work.

Joylynn had been told that the first thunder heard in the new year was the sign of the reawakening of the earth and the beginning of the natural cycle of growth.

She had been taught by Blanket Woman that *Tirawahut* talked to the people in the thunder, and they were glad to see the lightning flashes and hear the low rumblings of his voice. This was the time of quiet prayer within the lodges and of renewal of certain Sacred Bundles whose powers helped sustain life.

That first thunder's roar had come six sunrises ago, bringing with it the fresh, clean smell of rain and hope.

Restless, with most of the women away from the village at work in the fields, Joylynn felt somewhat useless today. She knew that she was much too large to be of any help in the valley. She knew that she should not be thinking of doing any hard labor at all. Thus far, she had had no trouble carrying High Hawk's child safely within her womb. She did not want to do anything that would harm it now.

She looked over her shoulder at the children at play and at the elderly men sitting around the huge outdoor fire, puffing on their long-stemmed pipes and talking. Then she glanced at the huge council house. Her husband was there with his warriors, except for those who were on guard, watching for the approach of anyone who might be an enemy.

It seemed that she was the only one who did not have something to do. Her lodge was neat and clean, her day's meal was cooking in a pot over the flames of her lodge fire, and her fingers were pricked from too much sewing.

So what else was there to do but take a walk and pluck some fresh spring flowers, to bring their beautiful scent into her lodge?

Smiling, her decision made, she went back to her

tepee and grabbed a small wicker basket, then walked slowly from the village.

She walked onward until she entered a valley where she could not see the women preparing the fields, or the tepees in the village.

It was only her, the wind, the sun and an occasional soaring bald eagle. She saw a dark line of trees not far away to her left, and then the tall wall of rock that led into the canyon beyond.

On those canyon walls were many eagles' nests, far from where the Pawnee sentries were watching for enemies.

"I am not here to bother you or your hatchlings," Joylynn said to one of the eagles, which had swooped low to eye her curiously. "I am here only for flowers. Will you guide me to the loveliest? I shall forever be grateful, for my feet are beginning to throb and I do not want to go home without flowers in my basket."

To Joylynn's astonishment, the eagle soared away, then swept low again, its eyes on Joylynn. It had shown her a wide stretch of wild daisies just over the rise, where the eagle was still hovering.

And beyond that, she saw a huge variety of wildflowers of all colors. The scent wafting toward her was something akin to heaven.

"Thank you," Joylynn said to the bird as she walked in a wide circle amid the flowers. The eagle rose higher into the sky, and then was gone as quickly as it had arrived.

But Joylynn was too busy to notice that the eagle was gone, for she was bending and plucking pretty flowers and laying them in her basket.

She followed the field of flowers up to where the stand of trees began, their dark shadows suddenly looming over Joylynn. She shuddered at the mysteriousness of the trees and the silence and shadows surrounding them.

Remembering just how alone she was, Joylynn started to turn to go back home, but stopped when someone stepped from the trees, a rifle aimed directly at her stomach.

To her horror, she realized it was Mole. The man she loathed with every fiber of her being had come again, to threaten not only her child, but herself!

She could hardly believe this was happening. But her eyes told her that it was Mole, standing there leering at her, a half-smoked cigarillo hanging limply from the corner of his mouth.

Although this man was heavily whiskered with a gray beard, she knew that it was he. She would never forget those pale blue, empty eyes. And through the whiskers she could see his ugly moles, like dark eyes, staring back at her.

"Gotcha," Mole said, taking the cigarillo from his mouth with his free hand. He flipped it over his shoulder, where it fell upon a thick stand of dead leaves and lay smoldering.

"How did you know where I was, and how on earth did you survive the attack?" Joylynn said, her voice trembling. "I know I shot you. I just know it wasn't anyone else, yet . . . yet . . ."

"The same as you, I've got nine lives," Mole said, laughing wickedly. "I left you for dead that day I raped you. How in tarnation did you walk away from that strangling alive?"

"I'll never tell, but how is it that you are alive? I did hit you with my bullet, didn't I?" Joylynn asked.

"Naw, don't believe so," Mole said, idly shrugging. "Must've been your imagination."

"How . . . did . . . you find me?" Joylynn asked, shivering when he took one long look at her belly. She had placed both hands on it now, her fingers splayed wide in an effort to protect her child from his filthy eyes, and especially . . . him.

"How did you find the Indian stronghold?" she quickly added, drawing his eyes up again.

"I ran across a lad just before the snows came to these mountain ranges," Mole said, chuckling beneath his breath. "I got the truth outta him, all of it. That's when I knew you were still alive, and who you were living with. But it would've been too chancy to travel up the mountainside at that time, with snows threatening."

A part of Joylynn went cold inside, for she knew who that "lad" must have been.

Andrew!

Oh, surely he *had* been on his way to escape from the life he had found among the Pawnee, for if he had reached the bottom of the mountain, he had not gone to find himself a horse to bring back for a bride price.

He had taken advantage of High Hawk's goodness by not only taking the horse that High Hawk had loaned him, but also the rifle.

"How did you know that the young man told you the truth?" Joylynn asked, trying to put the bitterness she now felt for Andrew from her mind. She was almost sure he had died shortly after giving Mole the information he sought.

"It didn't take much sense to realize where this lad had been when I saw how he was dressed," Mole said. "He had on Indian attire, so I figured that he'd been with Indians and would know where their stronghold was. He even wore moccasins."

"Did . . . you . . . kill him?" Joylynn asked, still caring enough for Andrew, after all, to ask. She would never forget how the children had loved him, as well as Two Stars and Rose.

"Naw, but I'm sure he wished he was dead after I got through convincing him to part with the answers I needed," Mole said, laughing throatily.

Hearing that Andrew had not willingly handed over such information was a little good news for Joylynn. Perhaps Andrew did care for the Pawnee, especially the woman he had professed to love.

Perhaps he had merely wandered farther than he had thought on the day he was hunting wild horses. And perhaps he was still alive, and could one day tell the truth about himself.

"What are your plans for me now that you found me alone?" Joylynn blurted out. "As you can see, I . . . I . . . am heavy with child."

"Yep, I see that well enough with my eyes," Mole mocked. "And I also see the way you're dressed. You're an Injun squaw who's going to give birth to a savage Injun brat. I'll get my jollies killing both you and the child at the same time."

He visibly shuddered. "This time I don't have no intentions of raping you," he said. "You don't do much for my sexual appetite, so big and all."

Suddenly Joylynn saw her life flashing before her eyes. Everything she had gone through to find a life that meant something to her was going to be taken away. And she knew that Mole would be certain she was dead this time. But surely he wouldn't fire that rifle! It would bring the entire village of Pawnee warriors, as well as the sentries.

The sentries. How on earth had he gotten past them?

Then she knew. He had come from the back of the mountain where the Pawnee sentries thought they were safe from attack.

Just as Mole took a step closer, his rifle raised, obviously ready to bring the butt end of it down across her head, Joylynn took a shaky step away from him. She screamed when she saw an arrow fly between her and Mole, quickly becoming imbedded in his belly. His firearm went off when he dropped it.

His eyes wild and wide, he grabbed at the arrow, then looked past her and saw High Hawk running up to Joylynn and taking her protectively in his arms.

"Thank the Lord," Joylynn cried, clinging to him. "Oh, thank *you*, High Hawk. Thank you, darling, for saving me from . . . from . . . a terrible death at the hands of that . . . that . . . creature."

"This white man surely had a death wish, or why would he have come to this mountain alone?" High Hawk said just as Mole fell to his knees, his hands still gripping the part of the arrow that stuck from his belly.

"I . . . ain't . . . alone," Mole said. Then a strange sort of gurgling sound came from deep within him, and he fell straight onto the arrow so that the other half protruded from his back.

Mole's final words, that he wasn't alone, sent a warning through both High Hawk and Joylynn.

High Hawk grabbed Joylynn up into his arms, struggling with her heavy weight, then started running toward their village. He stopped abruptly when he heard a voice behind them.

They both recognized the voice.

It . . . was . . . Andrew's!

Both Joylynn and High Hawk wondered if Andrew was aiming a firearm at them.

High Hawk was almost too afraid to turn and see. He couldn't bear to see the confirmation of Andrew's betrayal.

High Hawk turned slowly around and found Andrew standing there, gaunt, pale, and with a rifle lowered at his side.

"I lied to Mole," Andrew said, his voice drawn. "I told him I'd not wanted to play the role of Indian, but that I wanted you all dead just like Mole did."

"But still you brought him up the back of the mountain where you knew that I felt it was not necessary to establish sentries," High Hawk said, slowly lowering Joylynn to her feet.

If Andrew fired upon him, at least Joylynn would be spared, momentarily.

High Hawk knew that it would take too much time to grab an arrow and place it on his bowstring. If only he had kept an arrow at the ready! Would he pay for his error in judgment by losing his beloved wife and unborn child, and then his own life?

"It was the only way I could survive long enough to tell you what had really happened to me when I didn't return with a horse as I had promised," Andrew said hoarsely. "I had only one way to survive this terrible man's wrath, and that was by pretending I would help him, that all along I'd planned to bring the cavalry back and kill you and your people."

Andrew laughed softly. "Dumb as an ox, Mole believed me," he said. "I knew that there would be no way he could kill any Pawnee, because I wouldn't let him. Mole put his trust in the wrong man."

Suddenly there was a loud squeal behind High Hawk and Joylynn.

Rose came running past them.

The gunfire had brought everyone to see what had happened.

Rose had seen Andrew standing there, his firearm lowered at his side, and Mole dead on the ground.

She had known it was safe to run to the man she loved!

Andrew dropped his rifle and took Rose tenderly into his arms. "Rose, Rose, I almost died finding my way back to you," he said, clinging to her and sobbing. "While searching for a horse for my bride price, I went too far. I . . . I . . . got lost. As I was trying to find my way back to the stronghold, I ran into that horrible man named Mole. He almost beat me to death in order to get answers from me."

"But you are all right now?" Rose asked, leaning away from him, touching his gaunt face with a hand. "You are so thin. But . . . you . . . are alive!"

Again she flung herself into his arms, clinging.

"Yes, I'm alive," Andrew said, a sob catching in his throat. "I survived and stayed in Mole's hideout until the weather improved enough to travel up the mountain again. I was with that man for the duration of the winter. He made me hunt for food. He tied me up at night when we slept. And then the weather finally changed for the better and the snows began melting from the mountainside. I started out with Mole up the mountain and I had thought I'd led him to where the sentries would spy us and would recognize me and kill him. But again I was disoriented. I had no idea I was bringing him up the back side, not the front, where the sentries always were."

"You took such chances," Rose cried. "If you had found the right way to the village and the sentries had seen you, they would have taken you for an enemy alongside Mole. They would not have stopped to ask questions. They . . . they . . . would have shot both you and the evil man, side by side."

"I'd have chanced anything to find my way back to where I belonged . . . to you," Andrew said thickly. "I'd allowed Mole to get this close, while all along knowing that I would kill him before he had a chance to harm your Pawnee people. I . . . I . . . felt that it was safer to travel with Mole on my way back to the stronghold than to travel alone, since I don't have the same knowledge of how to survive in the wild. I took advantage of Mole's knowledge of the mountain and how to survive the cold, by pretending to be his partner in crime."

"Yet he still tied you up at night?" Rose said, leaning away from him to search his eyes.

Andrew nodded. "I was his captive the whole time, his pawn. I . . . I . . . feel like such a fool."

"Yet he is dead and you are alive," Rose said, smiling at him. "I do not think you a fool, but very, very brave. You survived these past months while living on the edge of death with that . . . that . . . monster."

"But, Andy, where were you when Mole stepped from the trees, his rifle aimed at my belly?" Joylynn asked.

"I'm sorry if I didn't plan carefully enough," he said, gulping hard. "I would have died if he'd managed to kill you before I caught up with him. You see, he saw you alone before I did. He ran away from me after spotting you. I had just gotten close enough to shoot him when High Hawk's arrow did the deed for me."

He looked slowly from Rose to High Hawk to Joylynn, and then back at High Hawk. "You do believe me, don't you?" he asked guardedly. "You do believe me when I say that I was not in cahoots with Mole, that I never knew him before he took me prisoner, not even when he was a part of the cavalry I was with that day when . . . when . . . he and I were the lone survivors. You've got to believe me when I tell you that I used him in order to find my way back here alive."

Rose heard the silence all around her.

She stepped away from Andrew and went pale as she looked around at everyone. The onlookers were moving slowly forward, making a tight circle around their chief, his woman, and Rose and Andrew.

"I would not lie about this," Andrew cried. He looked pleadingly at Rose, then fell to his knees before her. "I love you, Rose. I did all of this because of you."

He looked over his shoulder into the shadows of the trees, then gazed into Rose's eyes again as she placed soft hands on his cheeks.

"In there, amid the trees, you will find the steed that I brought back for the bride price," he said, his voice breaking. "There are three horses, Rose, in the shadows of those trees. The horse that High Hawk loaned me, Mole's, and the one I tamed for you and brought with me to offer your father. Rose, the steed is as white as the snows that fell on the mountain this winter. You will surely be glad to ride alongside me on that steed through the wildflowers, chasing butterflies and watching eagles soar. Won't you, Rose? Won't you?"

Three Bears stepped away from the others and went into the forest.

He came out again with three horses, their reins tied together.

Among them was the steed that High Hawk had loaned Andrew, a roan, and then a lovely white mustang that had surely been found among those that High Hawk had seen upon their first arrival in this new land of the Pawnee.

"He tells the truth," Three Bears said, standing with the horses behind him.

"I knew it," Rose cried, falling to her knees before Andrew and hugging him. "I knew you loved

333

me. I knew there was a good reason why you had not returned. Oh, my Andrew, how horrible that you had to live with that evil man the whole winter through when you and I could have shared a warm tepee as man and wife."

"We will share everything forever, my darling, now that I have found you again," Andrew said, drawing her into his embrace and softly kissing her.

Everyone watched, then silently turned and walked back toward their village, while High Hawk and Joylynn stayed behind with Andrew and Rose.

"Andrew, come now with us," High Hawk said, laying a hand on the young man's shoulders. "I believe you and Rose have a lot to tell one another. I will take my wife home. We will leave this evil man lying here, food for wild animals and the hatchlings in the eagles' nests."

"Thank you for believing me," Andrew said, standing, then flinging himself into High Hawk's arms.

Joylynn noticed that he still had his Bible. It was torn and frayed at the edges, but it was still being carried in his rear pocket.

When she got back to her tepee with High Hawk, Joylynn sat down beside the lodge fire as High Hawk added wood to it.

"Did you believe all of Andrew's story?" she blurted out.

He didn't reply, only gave her a look that she could not decipher.

CHAPTER THIRTY-ONE

A soft breeze blew through the waterfall, sending a spray over Joylynn and High Hawk as she knelt down beside a fresh grave in the Wolf band's new burial grounds. High Hawk stood tall over her, holding their two-year-old son in his arms.

Joylynn spread beautiful autumn flowers over the grave, said a silent prayer, then rose up and stood beside High Hawk. "I miss her so much," she murmured. "Your *ina* and I had become so close. It was as though she were my own mother."

"She grew to love you as much," High Hawk said, a deep sadness in his eyes. "But she just could not go on. I believe her body began to fail her when my *ahte* was murdered. I believe she only managed to hold on this long because of her grandson. She dearly loved holding him and playing with him."

Joylynn turned and gazed at her son, who was

the exact image of his father, with long black hair, midnight-dark eyes and lovely smooth copper skin.

Their three-month-old baby daughter, Moonbeam, who remained at their tepee with Rose watching her, had much of Joylynn's looks except for her hair. It was as black as her father's and brother's, which made her grass-green eyes stand out, beautiful and entrancing.

"I'm so glad that we named our firstborn after your brother," Joylynn murmured. "That brought such joy to your mother's heart. I had thought that she was doing much better, because she was so happy. But her heart was just too tired to go on."

"*Ho*, when you suggested our son be named in the memory of my brother Sleeping Wolf, my *ina's* eyes lit up as I had never seen them before," High Hawk said, his voice breaking. "She marveled over our son's straight back and handsomeness the very moment she saw him, and when you suggested the name, it was a wonder to behold how my *ina* rejoiced. You are a good woman, my wife. Through and through."

"As you are such a good man," Joylynn said, sliding an arm through his.

In the morning sunlight, her husband looked so handsome and noble. He wore his fringed buckskin attire, with the lone eagle feather hanging from a loop of his hair at the side of his head.

It seemed that as he aged, he grew even more handsome.

She knew now that even when he was old and gray, he would still be someone who would take her breath away.

He had proven himself to be just as wonderful a father as he was a husband. He treated his children with such gentle care and love.

She remembered her own father's love and saw the same caring in her husband.

She had been twice blessed, with two men to love her and care for her so much.

At times like this, she so missed her father and his smiling eyes and gentle hands.

But now was not the time to think about sadness, for the spring had arrived with its blessings. The crops had been planted and were now tiny sprouts shooting up through the rich black earth.

The eagles had given birth to new hatchlings that were just now learning how to perch on the edge of their nests, soon to join their parents in the sky.

Joylynn turned and gazed at the waterfall, seeing many rainbows in it as the water splashed down. It reminded her of another waterfall, another grave. Sleeping Wolf lay there, eagles his companions, just as the eagles at this waterfall would always be Blanket Woman's.

How had her husband described it? *Ho*, his brother would always be flying with the eagles. So now would his mother. She could just see Blanket Woman and Sleeping Wolf meeting in the heavens, joined again, this time forever.

She gazed down at the blanket around her shoulders. It was one that Blanket Woman had made for Joylynn just before she died. It proved how Blanket Woman had been given her name, for Joylynn had never seen such a beautiful blanket. It was made of fine blue cloth, heavily and tastefully adorned with silk ribbons of various colors. It had a band of embroidered work made from beautiful tiny beads, a foot wide, running around the bottom.

Back at her tepee, her daughter lay on a blanket that was also made by Blanket Woman's old but deft fingers. It was the same as Joylynn's but much tinier so that it could be wrapped comfortably around Moonbeam when Joylynn took her from her cradle to nurse her.

"We should get back to the village," Joylynn said, stepping away from High Hawk. "Rose is large in her pregnancy now and might be tiring from caring for Moonbeam this long. Her child should come any day now."

"Andy has proven to be such an honest, caring man, whose every breath seems to be taken for his beautiful Pawnee wife," High Hawk said, placing Sleeping Wolf on the ground, so that he could run and play on their way back to the village.

When a butterfly landed on his son's hand, High Hawk smiled at the wonder in Sleeping Wolf's eyes.

He knelt down beside his son. "That is a butterfly," he said. "Is it not beautiful?"

"Butterfly," Sleeping Wolf said, repeating after his father. "Beautiful."

"That is right," High Hawk said, patting his son on his bare shoulder. "You are learning to speak quite well now, my son."

The butterfly suddenly took wing. "Sleeping Wolf, watch the butterfly as it flutters away," High Hawk said. "It will go to a flower now and sip nectar from it so that it will have energy enough to fly on to another and another."

Sleeping Wolf giggled and ran after the butterfly as High Hawk stepped closer to Joylynn and slid an arm around her waist. "*Tirawahut* has been good to us," he said. "The white eyes have not yet discovered our stronghold. Our people feel safe now and no longer fear that each day may bring doom to them. It is a good time for us all."

"And I adore the new name that you have chosen for me," Joylynn murmured. "Pretty Moon, after that first night we met one another. Oh, was not the moon so brilliantly bright and large that night?"

"My wife, it led me to you," High Hawk said. Then his eyes widened when he saw someone running toward them, shouting excitedly.

"It is Three Bears," High Hawk said, raising an eyebrow. "I wonder what brings such excitement into his voice?"

"His wife," Joylynn said, her eyes widening. "She

has surely given birth. She has gone far past the time when she should have had her child."

Panting hard, Three Bears stopped when he reached them. "Two babies at almost the same time have been born into our Wolf band of Pawnee," he said when he finally caught his breath. "My wife gave birth to a son, and Andy's wife gave birth to a daughter!"

"Both?" Joylynn exclaimed.

Then she reached a hand to Three Bears's arm. "Are they all doing well?" she asked, then took a step away from him. "Rose was caring for Moonbeam. Who is there with Moonbeam now?"

"She is in good hands, for Yellow Blossom came to care for her," Three Bears said, smiling. "And, *ho*, all is well. The newborn children are healthy, and the mothers and fathers are well, happy and proud."

"As we are happy and proud for you, my friend," High Hawk said, placing a hand on his best friend's shoulder. "Today our people have much to rejoice over. Let us return to the village and celebrate together."

Three Bears flung himself into High Hawk's arms and hugged him fiercely, then stepped away from him, gave Joylynn an affectionate hug and ran on ahead of them toward the village.

"As I was saying . . . all is well," High Hawk said, smiling at Joylynn. "All is very well."

She returned the smile, so content she felt she might burst from happiness. She would not ever linger on the sadness of her past, only the goodness of today, and the future, which she would always share with the man she adored . . . her Pawnee chieftain husband, High Hawk!

Dear Reader,

I hope you enjoyed *Savage Tempest*. The next book in my *Savage* series, which I am writing exclusively for Leisure Books, is *Savage Quest*, about the proud Blackfoot Indians. The book is filled with much romance and authentic history about the Blackfoot.

Those of you who are collecting my Indian romance novels and want to hear more about the series and my entire backlist of Indian books can send for my latest newsletter, autographed bookmark, and fan club information by writing to:

Cassie Edwards
6709 North Country Club Road
Mattoon, IL 61938

For an assured response, please include a stamped, self-addressed, legal-sized envelope with your letter. And you can visit my Web site at www.cassieedwards.com.

Thank you for your support of my Indian series. I love researching and writing about our nation's beloved Native Americans, our country's true first people.

Always,
Cassie Edwards